I0700871

READERS ARE SAYING...

"The Vineyard Mistletoe Christmas is a clean, second change, family-centric, heartwarming romance. No one should have to live a the run from an abuser. Jane and her son Noah have finally returned to the island and her family.

When Jane discovers her ex is expanding his business on the island, she considers fleeing again. I love this series, all the sisters and the fact that are returning to the island.

You can have extra strength when you have family supporting you. Jane realizes that she needs to stand and fight for her freedom from Devon.

I love the drama and mysterious happenings - both current and past. Overall, this well-plotted book solves Jane's issues and moves us closer to discovering what happened to the Stafford sisters' parents.

There is a lot to keep your interest and I did not get much accomplished until I got to the end of this exciting tale!" ~Bernadette, C.

★★★★★

"I could not put the book down I am so anxious for the rest of the series. I am anxious for the answers to all the questions!" ~ Amazon Reader

★★★★★

"This was a story of struggle, growth, and learning to love yourself. Jane, our FMC, went through a lot in her life that broke down her self esteem. She had to learn to find her inner strength and hold onto it. Thats hard when you've experienced abuse.

She was stronger than she believed and proved it in the way she lived and protected her son. I found her to be remarkable in the ways she utilized her trauma to help others.

Then there is Ward, our MMC. He was strong, protective, and humbled by Jane's sweet and tender heart. He didn't want to let her and her son down.

He was a great gentle man that saw Jane and reminded her who she was. He was wonderful. This story had abuse, so watch that if you have triggers, family and friends, a mystery that turns out to be more than was thought to be, and second chances. The story line was great!" ~Sheri, BookBub Reader

THE VINEYARD MISTLETOE CHRISTMAS

MELODY ARCHER

WANT MORE SWEET AND CLEAN ROMANCE?

Eliza and Daniel Stevenson's Love Story is *waiting for you!* Simply, click the link below to grab your copy of this FREE Sweet and Clean Romance :)

Go here: www.memorablefictionbooks.com/pages/ free-book

This Christmas Beach Romance Mystery, is dedicated to our daughter-in-love, Amanda. She arrived from Brazil one cold and snowy Christmas Eve a few years ago to finally live together with our oldest son Qualan, her husband.
Much like Jane, the heroine in this story, our Amanda is a brave, hard-working woman with a compassionate heart full of love, inspiring all who have the privilege of knowing her.

CHAPTER ONE

ane

Jane Stafford jerked as loud beeps startled her.

Glancing down, she reached for the pager attached to her belt. It was her neighbor and good friend Isabella's phone number.

Jane's heart accelerated.

Swallowing quickly, she shoved down the panic. Fear formed knots in her belly.

There wasn't any good reason for her neighbor to call on a Friday afternoon.

It had been seven years since she had taken her small son and escaped her ex-husband. But still, it seemed strange to see her legally changed name on the screen.

Pearl Mallery.

Jane had changed her son's last name too.

She hadn't wanted to make the change, but it needed to be done to keep them both safe.

Jane decided she would call Isabella back in a few minutes, after she nailed down the rest of the details for this event.

Time was of the essence.

As a forty-year-old wedding planner and single mom, Jane couldn't afford to lose this job. So, she pushed herself to pretend happiness while planning a happy day for yet another future bride and groom.

Her job was beyond discouraging.

It was soul-crushing.

With each wedding Jane planned, it was becoming more and more difficult to endure the painful reminders of her own past mistakes.

She needed this job.

She needed the money to support her son, Noah.

She couldn't afford to fail.

Working hard to be perfect was something that was all too familiar for Jane. She'd been doing it since she was a young girl.

A childhood trauma had forced her to make a difficult choice:

No longer would anybody see her existence as a mistake. No longer would anybody see her as a burden to her parents or anyone else. No longer would anybody see her as unworthy of acceptance and love.

Young Jane had resolved to be as perfect as she could be. Even at the cost of not having the chance to be who she truly was.

She wanted to belong. She wanted to be safe. She wanted to be loved.

Jane longed for the kind of true love her parents had for one another.

Unexpectedly, a vivid image of her parents' wedding anniversary party from her childhood returned.

The reminder of her parents' love for each other had been forever embedded into her mind as a cherished memory.

It had been Christmas Eve and their grandparents and close friends on the island were together in the large great room at Gramps and Grams' beach cottage.

For weeks, Jane had been so excited as she and her grandmother planned her parents' surprise anniversary party.

It had been Christmas Eve and the party had gone very well. Family and friends were excited to celebrate the twenty married years of John and Anne Stafford.

It was a big moment that all the people close to them enjoyed.

Jane's father and mother began to renew their vows to each other. Her parents stood near the Christmas tree. The large room full of guests was filled with all sorts of beautiful Christmas decorations.

Then came the best part.

Her father and mother's eyes had shone with all the love they had for each other as they looked deeply into one another's eyes.

At that moment, her father kissed her mother under the mistletoe.

Vividly she remembered her heart swelling with a sense of love during that moment so long ago.

All her life, she yearned to have a love so strong and tender, for herself.

As a sensitive eight-year-old girl, Jane had been so caught up in feeling the emotions of love between her parents.

At the most important moment of her parents' celebration, Jane's hands dropped the engraved crystal plaque that her grandparents had custom made for their vow renewal.

To make matters worse, her mother's younger brother, Uncle Tony, yelled at her in front of all their family and friends. *Why do you always ruin things? Can't you do anything right?*

That awful, humiliating experience with Uncle Tony ignited in Jane a resolve to do everything in her power to become perfect.

With fixed purpose, Jane began her new decision by helping her parents as best she could.

Everyday she dressed herself in order to please others. She cleaned her room until it shone.

By the time she was a teenager, many of her weaknesses had been fixed, so that, to other people, she would appear almost perfect.

But all that effort wasn't good enough.

When the first man she ever loved suddenly left college and abandoned her one Christmas, Jane knew she wasn't good enough.

Her heart was broken.

In one fell swoop, she lost everything.

In her despair, she lost the one man she truly loved, she quit college, and she stopped believing in her dream.

Soon after, she started as a waitress in a run-down diner. It was there she met the man she married.

That decision turned out to be her biggest mistake yet.

Jane rubbed the faded scar on her cheek as memories returned to haunt her.

She'd been forced to escape with her young son.

She ran, and ran, and ran. Moving to seven different cities in the past seven years had made her dog-tired.

Jane couldn't help but be reminded how different her life might have been, if she hadn't quit everything when Ward abandoned her in college.

However, when Ward broke up with her at Christmas, after her first semester of college, she was so heartbroken.

In one fell swoop, she had decided to quit everything.

Despair had filled her every waking moment.

She began waitressing.

Day after day she barely made it through the day, working on autopilot. Her heart had been broken into a million pieces by the man to whom she had given her heart.

Then, one day in the coffee shop, she met a man who thought she was beautiful.

He used all the right words to win her, so one day she married him.

This man was now her ex-husband.

The day she married Devon was her biggest mistake and the worst day of her life.

Jane's mind burned with memories that haunted her to this day. Seven years ago, on Christmas Eve, Jane overheard Devon talking to a woman, whom he referred to as his wife. He talked with her about their daughter.

She confronted her ex about it.

Devon admitted that the day he married Jane, he had hired a friend to pose as a fake member of the clergy. Her ex said the marriage license documents they signed were fake.

In fact, their entire marriage was all fake.

He was still married to his first wife.

When Jane asked why he lied to her, Devon flew at her in anger, hurting her over and over again.

Her son tried to save her, but her ex harmed their Noah.

That was the last straw.

In the middle of the night, Jane risked it all to escape Devon's tight control over them.

The day Jane and Noah were finally free of Devon was the best day of their lives.

Still, after all these years, her ex's cruel insults circled around and around her brain, filling her head with insecurities and doubts.

You're nothing but a dumb blonde. You're weak and pathetic. Even your beautiful face is starting to fade to nothing. I don't know what I ever saw in you. You aren't good enough to be my wife. Looking back, what I should have done is left you to slowly die as a waitress in that dirty diner years ago.

Alongside those vivid memories, bile surged up her throat.

Quickly, she swallowed as the soft sounds of women's voices floated in the air around her, interrupting her dark thoughts.

The bride-to-be and her mother had arrived.

Jane waved in their direction and then looked around, surveying the beach area where the nuptials would take place in a couple months.

She hoped the wedding date that the bride and groom chose in December would be a warm day.

Looking up, she spotted dark clouds hovering in the normally blue sky. It taunted her and forewarned about a coming storm.

Her thoughts shifted and an uneasiness knifed through her body, mirroring the stormy clouds.

With a quick glance around, Jane adjusted the large sunhat she wore over her black wig and sunglasses.

Jane had become quite good at hiding her true identity over the past few years.

Sadly, living with a fake identity had been necessary.

People in this city knew her as *Pearl Mallery*, the wedding planner.

Jane longed to go back to using her real name. But that was impossible.

Her ex-husband would find out about her every move.

For Jane, the safety of her son was the best reason in the world to hide away.

Her mother's heart wouldn't allow her to do anything less.

She was willing to do whatever it took to protect herself and her son, Noah.

For now, the two of them were safe.

But at any hint of danger, they would be forced to quickly move again.

Her eyes scanned the area again, pulling the wide brim of her hat downwards with a shaky hand.

As she didn't see anyone suspicious, she released a wobbly sigh of relief.

She was tired of living in fear.

She was tired of sleepless nights.

She was tired of living on the run.

Tamping down the negative thought spiral, Jane turned to focus on the project at hand.

Grabbing her camera, she took a few photos of the sandy beach area. She would look through them later to help her plan the best places for the wedding accessories.

Finally, the bride and her mother reached her.

After a conversation about their desired Christmas accessories and their insistence that this be a romantic holiday wedding, the two women left.

Watching them leave, Jane couldn't help but be surprised that the twenty-something bride insisted on a Christmas Eve wedding.

It was risky to plan a wedding outside — especially with the cooler December weather.

As if to prove her point, a rumbling began in the dark sky above.

Jane shivered.

This wedding day was to be held on her most dreaded holiday.

Jane hated Christmas more than any other holiday.

For most people it was a joyful and hopeful time.

For her, it was a painful reminder of suffering and loss.

Her first love left her on Christmas Eve.

Then, a few years later, Jane and her son endured the

cruelty of her ex-husband. The most narcissistic man she'd ever known.

The same man who was supposed to love and protect her and her son, turned out to be their worst abuser.

Shaking her head, she did her best to shake off the terrible memories.

Jane forced a smile on her lips.

She should be happy they could live in this beautiful city near the beach. Noah was safe and she had many clients who wanted her services. What more could she want?

Still, worries flooded her mind.

Without warning, the loud beeping from her pager filled the air.

"That's my pager," Jane whispered to Kara, her assistant.

Panic welled up from somewhere deep inside.

Looking down, she reached for the pager attached to the belt at her waist. She noticed the name and phone number highlighted there.

Her neighbor and friend Isabella was trying again to get in touch.

Jane's heart accelerated.

There wasn't any good reason for her neighbor to call on a Friday afternoon.

Forcing herself to breathe slowly and deeply, she tried to quell the panic.

Isabella wouldn't call unless it was urgent.

She needed to leave… now.

"Kara, I need to go. If you could finish up the last few

details for the Crenshaw wedding, that would be helpful." Jane spoke in low tones to her assistant.

"Of course. I'll call you later."

Jane barely heard her assistant's voice over the loud beating of her heart.

Anxiety flooded her.

Questions plagued her.

Why was Isabella calling? Did something happen to her son?

Jane ran towards her car as the panic increased.

"Isabella, I got your message. What's up?" Jane dialed her neighbor's phone number as soon as she sunk down into the front seat of her car.

As she locked the doors, she could hear her neighbor's strained voice on the other end of the line. "There's something important I need to tell you, Pearl. Hurry home."

From her friend's anxious tone of voice, Jane sensed something had gone terribly wrong.

"Is my son alright?"

"I'm sure he's fine. Just pick him up from school and hurry back here, okay?" The urgency in Isabella's voice didn't help to calm Jane.

"Alright. I'll pick up Noah from school. Then we're on our way home." She hung up the pre-paid phone and stuffed it inside her purse.

Jane's mind raced with worry as she steered the small, used car through the busy city streets.

Thirty minutes later, Jane parked in front of the

school. Hurrying inside, she looked at her watch and realized Noah would just be finishing his last class for the day.

She didn't have long to wait before she spotted her son walking towards his school locker.

His blue eyes widened when he spotted her. "Hey, Mom. You're early today." Noah placed a couple of books in his backpack and slipped it over his shoulders.

Jane slipped an arm around her twelve-year-old son, giving him a quick hug. "I am early. But I couldn't wait to see you."

That was true enough. Ever since the phone call with Isabella, she had all but raced to see her son again.

It wasn't too far-fetched to believe that her ex-husband would somehow find Noah.

Jane was convinced he would take her son away from her.

It was her worst fear.

Together they walked quickly to the car. They got inside, and Jane began to drive.

As they meandered through the streets that led to their neighborhood, she asked Noah, "How was school today?"

Noah sighed. "It was okay. Same old, same old. How was your day, Mom? Did you go to the women's shelter today like you planned?"

"I had a good day. But, sadly, I didn't get to the women's shelter. My appointment with the bride and her mother took longer than expected." She couldn't help feeling disappointed that she missed talking to some of the women she had been helping to heal from abuse. "But maybe I'll go tomorrow. Yes, that's what I'll do. I'll stop by in the morning."

Jane smiled warmly as she was reminded of the place where she spent time helping a few hours a week.

The women who showed up for help were escaping verbal, physical, or financial abuse from their boyfriends or husbands.

Each woman arrived at the shelter with bruises or some type of trauma.

Many of them came with children by their side.

They were in a similar position to where Jane was years ago.

"I'm glad you help other moms and kids who are in trouble. Just like we used to be, right, Mom?" her son said softly.

Jane glanced at him. "That's right, Noah. And I'm glad to help someone else."

She was grateful her only child had a compassionate heart. He wanted to help others.

Noah looked out the car window as they passed an old house. A boy his age and his dad were playing ball in the front yard.

"Mom, where do you think Dad is now?"

Jane's heartbeat accelerated as she slowed to a stop at a traffic light. "I imagine your dad is still at his house in Las Vegas."

"I guess." Her son's dejected tone made her sad.

"I'm sorry, son. I know you miss having a dad. But your birth dad isn't safe for you to be around." Jane sighed.

Noah turned his head and after a few moments whispered, "I know, Mom. I still have nightmares from that Christmas when I was five years old. He hit you over and over and when I ran from my bedroom to try to help you, Dad slapped me so hard that I flew across the floor."

Jane parked the car one street over from the run-down apartment where they lived.

Turning to her son, she gently slipped her hand in his and squeezed.

"Oh, Noah. I do remember that day," she whispered, sad at all the scars he carried at such a young age. Reaching one hand up, she gently cupped his cheek. "I'm so sorry that happened to you, son. No child should ever have to live through that."

Noah's shoulders slumped. A crease forced between his brows whenever he talked about his dad.

Her son turned to look at her, a hint of moisture in his large blue eyes. "Mom, I'm alright. I'm just glad we left when we did."

"Me too, Noah. But I should have left your father sooner, before he had a chance to hurt you." Jane's eyes misted and memories washed over her. "I was too weak, too timid, and too afraid. And I'll always be sorry for that. But that's no excuse."

Her son grabbed her hand. "Mom, it's okay. I was afraid too."

Jane waited. She knew her son well enough to know that he needed time to share his deepest feelings.

His dark brown eyebrows scrunched together. "I guess, I just miss…"

Her son swallowed and shook his head.

Jane swallowed, understanding all too well. "I understand, son. You miss having a dad that loved you — you miss what you never had."

"Yeah." Noah shrugged.

With a gentle hand, Jane brushed the stray blond wisps of hair that hung over his eyes. "I'm so sorry, Noah. If I could change the past to a happier one, I would."

"I know you would, Mom. It's alright."

Regret clung to her belly like a painful sore that never healed.

What had she been thinking?

Her most important job had been to protect her son and she failed.

She had waited until the situation between her and her ex-husband had gotten out of control before she found the courage to escape with her small son.

Why had she waited to leave that horrible man? What was wrong with her?

Jane swallowed back bile as memories circled round and round in her head.

Insecurity, rejection, and fear clawed at her soul, tightening their grip ever further.

For as long as Jane could remember, she suffered terrible insecurity, fear of rejection, and abandonment. Feelings of unworthiness and never being good enough always went in tandem with those other thoughts.

Her parents had loved her, but with their sudden deaths in the boating accident when she was nine years old, her heart had filled with abandonment and loss.

There were other events from her childhood that only added to those painful memories.

A knot formed in her belly as she remembered.

Unexpectedly, she was pulled out of those dark thoughts by the rumbling sounds of her son's belly.

Grateful for the interruption, Jane grinned. "Sounds like we need to get some food for you. Let's get going."

Together they walked to the next street over, to the dilapidated apartment building which they had made their temporary home.

They hurried up the steps of the paint-chipped building. She looked both ways to see if anyone was watching or following them before going inside.

They hurried up two flights of stairs to the third floor.

As soon as they reached her neighbor's door, she knocked.

"I need to stop by to talk with Isabella, Noah," Jane whispered.

Her son's eyes lit up. "Can I come too? I want to play the new video game with Rafael."

"Sure." Jane smiled. She was glad Noah had a friend nearby to spend time with.

She knocked on her neighbor's door.

Isabella opened the door wide and gestured for them to come inside.

"Come in, both of you."

Noah hurried to where Rafael sat playing a video game.

Jane followed Isabella to the kitchen table.

They had become good friends when Jane first moved to the apartment a little over a year ago.

Jane was grateful to have a friend.

Assured that Noah would be busy for a while, Jane whispered to Isabella, "You called my pager. What's going on?"

Her friend spoke in a low whisper, "I have some news. You're not going to like it."

"I thought as much." A sense of foreboding swept over Jane. The hairs on the back of her neck stood on end.

Isabella went on to explain. "Do you remember when you asked my sister Maria to keep her eyes open for the man in the photo?"

Jane swallowed, nodding slowly. "I remember."

Knots coiled tightly in her belly, anticipating the worst.

"Well, it turns out, that man in the photo showed up this morning at the coffee shop. Maria said he looked like the man in your photo, except his blond hair was thinner and his belly larger." Isabella's dark eyes searched hers.

Her neighbor held out the photo her sister had taken this morning at the coffee shop. "This man is Noah's dad, no?"

Jane sucked in a breath as she stared at the photo. The man wore a 1940s dark grey Fedora hat with a wide black band that circled the middle.

Despite the disguise of the hat, Jane recognized the thick black eyebrows, the beady dark brown eyes, and the thin lips firmly pressed together.

Jane nodded. She should have guessed that her friend would be able to put the puzzle pieces together with her story. "Yes. It's him."

Her voice shook as she explained, "That man is my ex-husband. But he's not safe. I need to keep him from finding my son. Years ago, he abused us both. I've been desperate to get away from him ever since."

A shudder ripped through her at the thought of her former husband finding Noah.

In her worst nightmare, Noah's father would kidnap him and begin to abuse him like before.

"You better sit down. You're as white as a sheet." Isabella gently gripped Jane's hand and led her to a chair at the kitchen table.

She swallowed back the bile that forced its way upwards. "I can't believe he's here. It can only mean one thing. He's found us again."

Jane brought shaky fingers to her throat as a shudder ripped through her.

"What are you going to do?" Isabella reached across the table and held her other hand.

Jane closed her eyes for a moment, trying to think past the fear that flooded her mind. A shaky whisper was all she could manage, "I don't know."

Her friend was quiet for a moment before she said, "Perhaps you should call one of your sisters. Go back to the island for a visit. They will help you."

Jane remembered the last phone call she had with her best friend Kenna Macleod.

They had grown up on the island and throughout the years continued to call or send each other letters and cards.

In their last phone call, Kenna had asked Jane if she would consider moving back to the island. She was convinced her son Cameron and Noah could become good friends.

Most of all, Kenna reminded Jane that the two of them

would be able to go shopping and get together for coffee. To truly be there for each other again.

The thought of going back to the island to be close to her best friend appealed to Jane.

So did the idea of being close to her sisters.

But she didn't know how that would be possible.

Jane turned to Isabella. "Maybe I should call my sister. I've only been back to the island a few times. But there are some secrets I haven't told my friend or my sisters about my life. They might be shocked if they knew the real me."

"Well, maybe it's time you told them. I think you might be surprised how sharing secrets with those you love can bring healing and give you the support you need," Isabella whispered. "But make your decision fast, because I don't think you'll want to wait for Noah's dad to find your son."

Jane swallowed back emotion and nodded.

Turning, she stared at her innocent son.

Noah was the most precious gift she'd ever been given.

Jane was not about to allow that violent man who had terrorized them back into their lives.

"Isabella, you're right," Jane spoke in a raw voice. "I need to act fast. There's no way I'm letting that man get within one mile of Noah. I'll call my sister tonight."

A chill ran up her spine. Her thoughts spun in circles.

Jane needed to move herself and her son out of this city.

She needed to act fast.

ane

JANE PACED the small living area in her apartment as she dialed her friend Kenna's phone number.

Her overwrought nerves caused her hand to shake as she held the phone against her ear.

Fear flooded her body from the news Isabella had given her.

She desperately needed to talk to someone she could trust.

"Hello, Jane?" Kenna's calm voice on the other end of the phone line was soothing to Jane's troubled heart.

"Yes, it's me, Kenna. Is this a good time to talk?" Jane asked, wanting to respect her friend's time.

"Of course, Jane." Her friend hurried to explain, "I always have time for you. How's it going?"

Jane sighed. "I thought all was well — until today."

"Oh?" She could tell from the inflection in Kenna's voice that she was wondering what had happened. "Did something go wrong today? Is Noah doing alright?"

"Yes, my son is well. In fact, Noah's visiting one of his good friends across the hallway from my apartment. My neighbor invited Noah to stay overnight with her son. The two of them wanted to finish playing a new video game." Jane couldn't help the smile that turned up the corners of her lips as she thought about her son.

"I'm glad your son is alright." Kenna sounded puzzled. "So if you're not calling about your son, tell me what went wrong today? I must say, your voice sounds a little stressed."

Jane swallowed, trying to think of how to tell her friend what was going on.

"I am stressed." She forced a calmness she didn't feel. "Okay, here goes. When I got home from work, I stopped by my neighbor's apartment. Isabella informed me that Devon, my ex-husband, was seen at the coffee shop down the street."

Jane bit her lip as she remembered the photo that Isabella had of her ex-husband.

"My neighbor's sister works at that coffee shop. Months ago I'd sent her a photo of Devon. I asked her to let me know if he showed up at the coffee shop where she works. As it turns out, he made an appearance this morning."

"Uh, oh. That's not good." Worry and concern clouded Kenna's voice. "So what are you going to do?"

Jane sighed. "I'm not sure. I mean, could it be a coincidence that my ex-husband just happened to show up at a nearby coffee shop?"

"Jane, I think you know the answer to that."

She sighed. "I know. But I want to know how he could've found my location. I mean I've been using my other name, Pearl Mallery, ever since Noah and I moved here."

"Well, I don't doubt Devon has his ways. After all, your ex-husband did inherit his late father's business and the truck load of money that came with it," Kenna reminded her. "I wouldn't put it past him to use his money and influence in order to find you."

Jane began to pace her apartment as anxious thoughts flooded her mind.

Once more, she was grateful her son had decided to stay overnight at her neighbor's apartment. A mother's protective instinct rose up with the fierceness of a mother bear protecting her cub.

She was determined to do everything in her power to protect Noah from learning about his father's actions.

"I suppose that's true." Jane looked outside her window, noticing the red glow of the setting sun. She looked along the opposite street, her eyes darting back and forth to see if she saw anyone who looked like her ex-husband. "Sadly, Devon always was determined to control me and Noah."

"So what are you going to do?"

Jane ran a hand through her hair.

What was she going to do?

Anxious thoughts crowded her mind. "I don't know."

Kenna said, "I think you and your son should return to the island. There are so many very good reasons for you to come back, Jane."

Jane picked lint off her shirt, nerves getting the better of her. "That's strange you should say that. I just called my sister Lizzie and she said the same thing. In fact, she invited Noah and I to stay at the Inn with her and Jonathan until we can get things sorted out."

"See? I'm not the only one who is telling you it's time to come back home." Her friend chuckled.

"But I'm not sure if that's a good idea." Jane didn't really want to return to her childhood home. There were too many painful memories of growing up there.

"You said there are reasons for me to return. What do you mean by that?"

Kenna released a sigh. "If you move back, you'll live close to your sisters. They are the only family you've got left. And don't forget, if you were nearby, you could help your sisters find out what happened to your parents in that boating accident." Her friend paused.

"Of course, you and I would finally be able to see each other anytime." Kenna chuckled. "But let's set that aside. I believe the most important reason for you to return is so you can finally be at peace. You've spent the last few years on the run and hiding. I really think it's time for you to move away from your painful past so you can embrace the freedom to be who you are, Jane."

Anxious thoughts caused a tightening of the knot in her belly.

"I just don't think I can do that. Not with my ex-husband still determined to find me and my son."

Kenna said, "I understand that. But have you thought that by moving back to the island, it might be your best chance to have a fresh start? You would be safer than you've ever been if you returned to the Sweet Beach Cove community. Many people love you around here. I really believe folks here would support and help to protect you."

A longing so swift and intense flooded Jane that it nearly took her breath away.

She desperately wanted to finally be free of the constrictions that had been around her life ever since she took her son and ran away from her abusive ex-husband.

Was it possible for her to finally be free of the chains that kept her in hiding for all these years?

Just as quickly as that thought came, she rejected the idea. "I really can't see that happening, Kenna."

"Well, I believe it is possible. But let's save that talk for another day, Jane." Kenna spoke softly, "I think perhaps there's another reason that's stopping you from returning to the island."

"Like what?" Jane was curious what her friend was going on about.

Kenna sighed. "Ward Hampton. You loved that man years ago and wanted to marry him. Did you know he's retired from his job at the news station in Boston and has moved back to the island?"

Jane expelled a breath. "My sister mentioned Ward moved back to the island to help take care of his father in his senior years."

"That doesn't surprise me. Ward is a good man," her friend added.

A warm glow filled her as she listened to Kenna's words. She thought of all the good memories she had of Ward.

But, immediately following that thought, memories of the sharp pain of his rejection caused her to catch her breath.

She couldn't forget how he suddenly decided to transfer to a different college. To leave her alone.

"I'll admit, I'm scared to allow myself to get close to Ward again," Jane whispered. "If I let myself fall in love with that man again, I'm afraid my heart wouldn't be able to handle it if he abandoned me a second time."

Kenna sighed, then spoke softly, "I'm so sorry Ward hurt you, Jane. But maybe he's changed since your college days."

"Maybe. But I just don't think I can open my heart again." Jane rubbed the back of her neck as worry and fear warred inside her.

Kenna was quiet for a long moment. "Well, my friend, I think at the very least, you should give Ward the chance to explain what happened. I think you owe it to yourself and to him."

Jane sighed. "It's all water under the bridge."

"No, my friend, if you're still bringing it up years later, the wound is still festering."

Sometimes Kenna's ability to be a truth-teller was frustrating in the extreme.

Yet, if she were honest, her words were exactly what she needed to hear.

"I suppose you're right." Jane sighed. "I'll consider having that talk with Ward."

"Good." Her friend chuckled. "And one other thing. Jane, even though you have many reasons for not wanting to return to the island, I still think you should consider it. You have friends and family here who love you. Moving here might be just what you need to heal."

ONE HOUR LATER, Jane was still thinking about her friend's words as she drove to the women's shelter.

Was it possible for her to finally find healing on the island where she had experienced so much pain and loss?

Maybe.

But she couldn't help feeling like that was an impossible hope.

She parked her car and began walking towards the back door of the women's shelter.

Loud, rolling thunder rumbled in the stormy night sky, echoing the disturbing tempest in her own emotions.

Using her staff-controlled key, she opened the door and stepped inside the large building. She was grateful to be able to volunteer and help the women who came here from abusive homes.

Jane spotted Martha, a staff member, talking with a young blonde-haired woman who looked agitated and distressed.

There were other women walking into the common area, some with crying children, doing their best to calm them.

Martha saw her, and motioned for Jane to join her.

"Jane, I was wondering if you could talk with Eden?" Martha asked. "She's new to the shelter. I need to help Janice in the kitchen."

After Martha walked away, she started to speak with the distraught woman,

"Of course, Eden, I'm Jane. I'm happy to get to know you." Jane glanced at the two empty chairs near the front entrance. "Why don't we sit down over here and we can talk."

The woman followed her to the chairs and sank down. Stray tears continued to make a trail down her red cheeks.

"Why don't you tell me the reason you came here tonight, Eden," Jane spoke in a soft voice, hoping to calm her fears.

She couldn't help but notice that the woman's fingers shook as she gripped a white handkerchief.

"Seven years ago I married my husband. We were happy and in love. I worked as a secretary and helped to put him through his college courses until Ray finished his degree as an accountant." Eden went on to explain.

"We decided together we would try to have children after he finished his degree. Then just a few months later we agreed on the subject again, just before Ray finished his schooling."

A sob escaped and, with one hand, the woman dabbed the tears that streamed down her cheeks.

Jane reached over and gently held her other hand, in an effort to reassure her that someone cared.

Eden continued telling her story. "To my surprise, I learned I was pregnant this past week. I told Ray tonight when he came home. I thought he would be excited that we were finally expecting the baby we dreamed of together. Instead, Ray got very angry with me."

The woman shook her head. "Not only did he get angry, but Ray told me he was leaving me. My husband said he wasn't ready to be a father. Then Ray admitted he was having an affair.

"When I asked why he was doing this to me, he told me he didn't love me anymore. Then he said I needed to move out because he decided to sell the house. I reminded him that I had been the one paying the mortgage for the past five years to put him through college. That's when Ray yelled at me. He said he needed the money. Then my husband threatened me. He said there would be trouble if I didn't agree to sell the house."

Jane's eyes widened as she listened to Eden's story.

A sob escaped Eden's lips. "I can't believe my husband would do this to me. I can't believe this is happening."

Sobs shook her shoulders and Jane reached over and wrapped the woman in a hug.

"I'm so sorry this happened to you, Eden. You definitely didn't deserve to be treated this way." Jane leaned back after the woman's tears lessened. She looked down and noticed red and purple bruises on her arm and on one cheek.

"Did your husband hit you, Eden?" Jane asked softly, already knowing the answer.

Eden swallowed and nodded slowly. "Yes. I'm more shocked by that, than I am about anything else he's done. In all the years we were married, he only hit me twice. But he was always sorry and said he wouldn't do it again. Now

I realize Ray wasn't telling the truth. I shouldn't have trusted my husband."

Jane embraced her a little while longer, letting Eden lean on her for comfort and support.

Finally, the woman sat back in her chair, and shook her head.

Turning to look at Jane, she said, "Now, what do I do? I'm pregnant and alone. And I have no home."

Jane squeezed her hands. "Eden, you made the right decision to come to the women's shelter. You can stay here where you'll be safe. Stay until you feel like you can move on."

"Thanks for that. I'm scared and alone. I feel weak and vulnerable. Even more so now that I'm pregnant." A crease of worry formed between her brows.

"I understand a little of how you're feeling, Eden," Jane whispered. "I was in your shoes seven years ago, when I took our small son and ran away from my abusive husband."

Eden looked over at Jane with a new awareness. "I didn't realize that. But you got away from him and were able to find your way?"

Jane nodded. "I got the help I needed at a women's shelter too. So I want you to know you'll be safe and cared for here."

"Thanks, Jane. I'm grateful I was able to find this place tonight." She yawned.

"Eden, you look tired. Let me help you find a room." Jane went to talk with Martha who told her the room number.

She walked the distressed woman to her room.

Eden reached for her and Jane embraced her in a gentle hug. "You'll be safe here now. Just rest. Don't worry about anything tonight. Instead, try to sleep."

Eden nodded. "Thanks for your help."

"Anytime." Jane said her goodbyes and retraced her steps back to the kitchen. After helping to clean up the main rooms, Jane left the women's shelter.

The rain softened to a light drizzle as she began to drive home.

Jane was about six blocks from home when she noticed the same car following her that she'd seen when she first left the women's shelter.

Turning down a side street, she thought she would try to lose whoever this person was.

But the vehicle stayed on her tail.

Jane needed to get home, so she raced to her apartment and parked the car.

Grabbing her purse, she ran towards her building.

Just as she opened the door to her apartment, she spotted the same car now parked across the street.

The man behind the wheel wore a 1940s Fedora hat, just like her ex-husband always wore.

His dark eyes narrowed as they bore into hers.

Fear swept over her.

She shivered.

With hurried movements, she opened the door and went inside.

Jane ran up the flight of stairs to her apartment.

Her heart raced.

Her breath nearly stopped.

Her body went into a cold sweat.

Over and over again her thoughts went around in circles like a hamster wheel.

He knows where my son and I live. Now I have no choice. I must do everything in my power to protect Noah.

I must take my son and leave.

&

FINALLY, he had found her.

After seven years of playing this cat and mouse game, he'd finally found Jane Stafford — his ex-wife.

Except she didn't use her real name anymore.

Jane must have thought she was clever changing her name to Pearl Mallery.

But he had discovered her hiding place anyway.

Thanks to his beautiful fiancé Brandi.

His fiancé had been searching the Net for a well known wedding planner, when she discovered a list of the best wedding planners in the nation.

It turned out that the name Pearl Mallory from San Diego was on that list.

When Brandi showed him the woman's photo, he instantly recognized his ex-wife.

Even with the fake black hair and black rimmed glasses, he would never forget the face of the woman who escaped him.

Years ago, she had managed to get away with their son in the middle of the night.

Jane had stolen his only son, Noah.

Devon was resolute.

He must get his boy back.

It was time for a reckoning.

At long last, his ex-wife would be forced to come face-to-face with the fact that she had deceived him. With how she had made him angry.

Anybody who made him angry lived to regret it.

When he was a little boy, his stepmother had done the same thing. But when he was old enough, he had made sure his stepmother regretted ever deceiving him.

Jane would regret her choices too. He'd see to it.

Devon watched her hurry into the run-down apartment.

He watched and waited.

His son, Noah, was somewhere in that building.

Soon enough, Noah would be beside him again.

Devon turned and pulled out the photos in his wallet.

A photo of Jane and Noah from that Christmas just before they ran away from him.

A sudden streak of anger flooded him.

He ripped the photo so that half of his ex-wife's face was cut off.

There. That looked just right, now.

Now it was just Noah in the picture.

Soon, they would be together, father and son, just like they were always meant to be.

Now that he had found his ex-wife and son, he was determined that he would never lose track of them again.

Whatever it took, wherever they went, he would find Noah.

This time, he would never let his son go.

CHAPTER THREE

ane

JANE HURRIED OFF THE PLANE, her son following close on her heels.

As was her habit, she pulled the wide brim of her sunhat down, so that much of her face was hidden.

Turning, she watched as Noah adjusted his red baseball hat so the brim shadowed his eyes.

She had called Lizzie last night. Jane was relieved when her sister offered for them to stay at her place.

Lizzie had always been willing to welcome family into the large beach cottage she had inherited from their late grandmother.

Jane couldn't help but feel blessed to have such a kind sister.

"Look, Noah, your aunt Lizzie is over there waiting for us," Jane whispered to her son as they walked. As soon as they received their luggage they made their way to Lizzie.

"Jane, it's so good to see you. You too, Noah." Lizzie briefly hugged them and then gestured for them to follow. "My car is waiting. When we get to the Inn, you have rooms waiting in the family wing, so you'll be able to relax there."

A longing flooded her to finally be able to rest.

Maybe she could do that now that she had returned to the island.

Yet, as she looked out the window, fear coiled like a snake in her belly.

Memories haunted her of what had happened here.

Today, she returned to the island where she spent her childhood. This island was the place where she had lost the family she loved.

Rejection and loss had been part of her life for years. And even more so after she married and later escaped her ex-husband.

As Lizzie drove the car, Jane looked out the window. Familiar places like her late grandmother's community church, her old high school, and her best friend Kenna's street came into view.

Familiar places stirred pleasant memories of the love of family, steadfast hope, and the joy of friendships.

Like the friendship Jane had with her best friend, Kenna Macleod.

Soon they would be able to see each other again, face to face.

A wave of warm nostalgia flooded Jane.

The car turned a corner and Grams' old beach cottage came into view.

Jane fingered the small pendant — the pearl necklace that graced her neck.

A gift from her beloved grandmother.

This particular necklace had lesser monetary value than any of the other heirloom jewelry Jane had inherited from her late grandmother.

Yet, it was this pearl necklace that was the most meaningful. She loved it most of all.

As she fingered the shiny white pearl at the end of the gold chain, Jane was reminded of her beloved Grams' wisdom and her gentle advice.

It was right after her parents' deaths that her grandmother held Jane in her arms and gave her the pearl necklace.

Grams had whispered in her ear: *Remember, Jane dear, whenever you get scared, think of this small pearl. Remember, a pearl is the only gem produced by a living organism. The pearl goes through an ordeal — because the pearl layer protects the oyster until it's out of harm's way. But after all the trouble it goes through, a beautiful stone is formed.*

The pearl emerges from the conflict, victorious and beautiful. Perhaps that's one of the reasons the Good Book writes that a woman is said to be more precious than jewels and her value is far above rubies or pearls.

That's who you are, Jane.

My darling granddaughter, you have just emerged from a fiery trial with the deaths of your mom and dad. You are like this pearl — emerging even more beautiful and stronger from all the hardships you've suffered.

I want you to always remember to hold onto faith, no matter what conflicts or trials you suffer in life. I'm giving you this pearl necklace to help you remember that. Much like the precious stone of the pearl, you are valuable, beautiful, and precious. During difficult times, hold onto faith, hope, and love. Promise me you'll do your best to remember."

"I promise, Grams," Nine-year-old Jane had whispered with a wobbly voice, thick with emotion.

As Jane fingered the shimmering pearl, her beloved Grandmother's words once again flooded her heart.

But, however she might try, just thinking of Grams' words did not fill her heart with peace, like she hoped they would.

Her face grew flushed and she shivered, trying to calm the fear rising in her heart.

As they walked up to the door of her sister's inn, Jane renewed the promise to her grandmother. *It's so very hard not to focus on fear right now, Grams. But I promise to do my best to remember to hold onto faith, hope and love like you taught me.*

Turning to Lizzie, Jane whispered in a shaky voice, "Thanks again, Lizzie, for giving Noah and me a place to stay."

"Jane, you are family. There will always be room for you and Noah. *Always.*" At Lizzie's reassuring words, Jane blinked back tears that pricked the back of her eyes.

"You're so kind to us, Lizzie. I don't deserve it. But I am very grateful all the same," Jane whispered as they walked the pathway towards the front door.

Lizzie slipped an arm around her shoulders, pulling Jane into a quick hug.

Opening the front door, her sister whispered, "Go and get settled in your rooms and then we'll have some tea together in the den. My son Jake will be up to check on Noah soon."

Jane smiled through the shimmer of tears. "Thanks, Lizzie. I'll be back for tea in a little while."

As she walked towards her bedroom, she removed her sunhat and sunglasses. She was grateful that her son's room was next to hers.

"Noah, your cousin Jake will be stopping by your room soon. He wants to spend some time with you. I'll be downstairs enjoying tea with your Aunt Lizzie, alright?" Jane smiled at her son.

"Sure, Mom. I like cousin Jake. I'm glad I'll get to see him." Noah's eyes brightened at hearing his cousin's name.

Jane fingered the clothes Noah was taking out of his suitcase. She opened the dresser drawer and started to help him organize his new room.

Noah began to refold his jeans, placing them on the bed.

She looked over and noticed the discolored skin on his left wrist.

"Noah, I can see your eczema is worse today, Noah. Is it because you're feeling stressed?" Jane couldn't help but remember the first day she'd noticed her son's discolored and itchy skin.

It was the day after they escaped from her ex. Noah had only been five years old, but his little body had been showing signs of stress.

Ever since that day, Noah had gone to several doctors.

He'd been placed on medication that helped soothe irritated skin.

"Yeah." Her son nodded. Reaching into his duffel bag, Noah took out the canister that held his meds.

Grabbing his water bottle, he swallowed one of the pink, oval-shaped pills the doctor had given him.

"Talk to me, Noah. Is it the move that has you worried?" She needed to hear from her son what he was feeling.

"I think it's because we left suddenly." Her son turned to her. "Mom, what happened? Why did we need to move away again?"

Emotion caught in Jane's throat at Noah's question. Perhaps it was time she was finally honest with him. Her son was now old enough to understand.

"The night I returned home late from the women's shelter, someone followed me home. It was your dad."

Jane watched Noah's eyes widen in fear at the news.

"He parked across the street from our apartment. When I spotted him, he looked very angry. I have to tell you, I'm worried and scared for your safety, as well as mine. That's the reason we moved so suddenly." Jane sighed heavily.

Noah sat down on the bed. Jane sat beside him and turned to look into his bright blue eyes.

Her son nodded quietly. "I thought it might be something like that." Noah toyed with the red handkerchief that Grams had given him. His fingers traced the letters of his name his late great-grandmother embroidered with white thread onto the cotton.

Noah whispered in a shaky voice. "Mom, do you think

we'll ever stop running from Dad? Why can't the two of us stay in one place? I want us to have a real home. Maybe we could have a home here on the island. I want to be able to make lifelong friends and to stop being afraid. Maybe if we had a real home, I could even get my own dog."

Noah's blue eyes, so similar to her own, looked over at her filled with unshed tears.

Suddenly, it struck her forcibly how very difficult this life of running had been on her young son.

"I'm so sorry, Noah. The way we've lived, running away and moving from city to city, has become a way of life for me. I was trying to protect you — but I don't believe I was fully aware of how terrible these past few years have been for you." Jane reached over and squeezed her son's hand.

"I just want us to finally have a peaceful life as a family, Mom." Her son's blue eyes looked over at her with such longing that it took her breath away.

Jane shivered as so many emotions swept over her.

Anger at herself for allowing her ex-husband's abuse to dictate her life for so long.

Fear of the unknown — would she ever be freed from the lasting effects of her abuser?

However, the biggest emotion she felt in this moment was regret. She had allowed fear and intimidation from her ex-husband's past abuse to rule her and ruin her and her son's lives for far too long.

It was time for a change.

Noah, you're right." Unshed tears misted her eyes. "We need to finally have a peaceful life as a family. It's time for us to have a real home of our own. I promise to do my very best to try and make that happen for the two of us. Alright?"

Jane squeezed his hand again as if it were her lifeline.

Her son sighed in relief. "Thanks, Mom. I know you will."

Noah reached over and slipped his arms around her neck.

Jane's heart melted.

Her mother's heart filled to overflowing as she held her son in her arms.

Love for her son spilled out all over again.

And she vowed in her heart to keep her promise.

NOAH'S WORDS continued to roll around in Jane's mind as she hurried down the stairs towards the den.

How would she be able to find herself and Noah a home to live on the island?

Worry lines squeezed between her brows.

Would there be a way to keep Noah safe from his father?

Jane said a quick prayer for help before she turned the doorknob and walked into the den.

This room had been her grandfather's favorite room in the house.

She looked around the room and saw the recently renovated fireplace and the fresh paint on the walls.

Jane gasped at the sight.

"Oh my goodness, Lizzie. The den looks brand new. It's beautifully redone." Jane smiled, looking around at the freshly painted walls and the new knotted pine wood floor.

Last year, a woman who worked for Lizzie had been hired by Vera Cantrell to deliberately set fire to this room, leaving it charred and in ruins.

Vera Cantrell was now serving time in jail for her crime.

But, since that terrible fire, Lizzie and Jonathan had done their best to restore the den.

Lizzie stood to her feet as Jane entered. Alex and Charlie followed and soon Jane was engulfed in a flurry of hugs.

"Jane, I'm glad you like the new look. I was grateful to have Jonathan's help. His experience restoring old houses made the repairs after the fire easier. He insisted we restore this room to its former glory." Lizzie sighed, smiling happily as she looked around.

"Well, I believe both Grams and Gramps would have been very pleased with the final result." Jane smiled approvingly.

"Thanks, Jane. I'm glad you think so," Lizzie commented. "But enough about me. Come and sit down, Jane, tell us what's going on with you."

All four sisters sat in the comfy sofas near the fireplace.

Lizzie poured a cup of tea for each of them.

"But first, you must explain to us why you're wearing that black wig, dearest Jane. I can't wait to hear that story," Charlie interrupted. She'd always been the curious sister and Jane knew she wouldn't rest until she had heard all the details.

"Oh that's right. Sorry, I forgot." Jane swallowed. She was so used to wearing the wig that she barely noticed anymore.

With a shaky hand, she reached up and pulled off the wig. Her blonde hair was tied in a low ponytail at the nape of her neck.

Without the wig, she felt exposed.

Jane's heartbeat accelerated as she thought about her ex once again. "Well, it's a long story. I believe it's something I haven't shared. But I suppose it's time I did."

"I agree, Jane. It's past time." Charlie nodded, taking a sip of tea.

Lizzie handed her a hot drink.

Jane's fingers gripped the handle and shakily set it down on the coffee table.

Swallowing back anxiety she began to tell her story. "It all started when I married Devon Hollingsworth."

Charlie rolled her eyes. "Isn't he the man who you married years ago?"

Jane nodded, swallowing quickly. "That's true. What I didn't tell you, is that the big blow-up between Devon and I happened on Christmas Eve years ago. That's when I discovered he'd been lying to me."

Releasing a shaky breath, Jane explained, "I had just come out of the shower, when I overheard Devon talking on the phone. He was talking with some woman he called his sweetheart and was asking if his daughter received her Christmas present."

She finished telling her tale, "So I called him out on it. I told him I overheard his phone conversation. Devon told me that we were never really married. He was actually married to the woman he had just spoken with on the phone."

Charlie sucked in a breath. "What kind of deranged man would do something like that? In other words, your marriage to Devon was all fake?"

"Yes, it's true. I was so naive." Jane shook her head.

Alex said softly, "I think it probably had more to do with the fact that you had recently been jilted by Ward and were desperate for love. This guy must have said a lot of pretty words to make you believe him."

"Something like that." Jane shuddered at how gullible she'd been. Why had she believed Devon and his compliments when they were dating? She had been so naively innocent and trusting. Then she made an even bigger mistake. She'd gone and married him.

"What happened next?" Charlie leaned forward, her elbows on her knees, listening to every word.

Jane said softly, "Sadly, that's when things went from bad to worse."

Alex asked with low angry tones, "What exactly did Devon do to you, Jane?"

Fear rushed through her, as she felt all the emotions as if it all happened yesterday. "He slapped me and threw me against the wall. I hit my head hard. Our wedding photo crashed from the wall to the floor, the glass shattering into tiny pieces. Then, as usual, he called me many demeaning and insulting names. He hit me again, bruising my arms and face."

Jane shuddered at the memory. "When I cried out in pain, Noah came running into the room. He tried to stop his father. My son, who was only five at the time, tried to protect me. But Devon walloped my son hard. His small body flew across the room. For me, that was the last straw. I knew I must leave quickly to protect my son."

Looking over at her sisters, she continued, "That night, when Devon lay sleeping, I escaped with Noah — leaving my fake husband for good."

Alex's cheeks stained red, her words laced with anger, "That horrible, horrible man. By all rights, he should be behind bars."

Jane offered a sad smile. "I agree. But, sadly, that hasn't happened yet. I'm grateful to you all — my sisters — for defending me. It means the world to me that you're all on my side."

"Of course we're on your side, Jane. We're family. Family sticks up for each other and supports each other through good and bad times," Lizzie commented. "However, I can't believe that man isn't locked up for how he treated you and Noah."

Jane shook her head. "That's because I never told the police. When it happened, I panicked. I couldn't think of anything except protecting my little boy. All my thoughts were focused on how badly Devon had hurt my son. Noah was my world. So I simply ran away. That first time, we ended up at a women's shelter in Seattle. That's also where I miscarried the baby I was expecting at that time."

"Oh, Jane, I'm so sorry." Lizzie, as well as her other sisters, offered heartfelt compassion for her pain.

A tear slipped out of the corner of one eye. "Thank you for saying that. That was a difficult time, although maybe it was for the best that I didn't have another child by that cruel man." Jane shuddered.

"Since then, I've always longed for another baby, but I'm older now. It's probably already too late." Quickly she wiped away the last stray tears. "After that, we stayed for a few more weeks at the women's shelter. I continued to pray every day that Devon wouldn't be able to find us. The sad truth is, I've been running ever since."

"That explains it. So that's the reason you wear the black wig." Charlie guessed. "You don't want Devon to find you and Noah."

Jane nodded. "Yes. That's the reason I came here this weekend."

"What aren't you telling us, Jane?" Alex leaned closer, her eyes focused on hers.

Jane sighed heavily and whispered in low strained tones, "I didn't tell my son, but a neighbor of mine saw Devon at one of his favorite coffee shops in San Diego. I just know he's searching for Noah and me. It seemed like he was just waiting for Noah and I to make an appearance."

"Wouldn't it be easy enough for Devon to find you?" Alex asked. "All he would need to do is look up your name on the internet. He could find out where you were."

"Well, that's the other secret I need to tell you all. Right after I escaped from my ex-husband all those years ago, I legally changed my first and last name. Most people call me by my new name, Pearl Mallery," Jane explained. "I did what I believed I needed to do to protect my son. I changed Noah's last name as well. So even if Devon looked up my name on the internet he wouldn't find us."

"That was clever," Alex replied.

"It was necessary." Jane shivered as more memories of that terrible night returned.

Jane continued telling the rest of her story, "More recently, I had help to sneak out of San Diego. When my neighbor mentioned her sister saw my ex-husband in that coffee shop, she offered to drive my son and me to the airport."

"So that's how you made your escape." Charlie sighed. "I didn't realize you legally changed your name, Jane. Do you want us to call you Pearl now?"

"No. With family and close friends, I'm still Jane," she replied.

Charlie released a breath. "Good, that's a relief. I've always liked your name."

"Thanks, Charlie." Jane smiled softly. "I do too, to be honest. More than anything, someday I would like to change my name back to my real name again. But since Devon is still searching for us, I'm not sure that will be possible."

"Well, I'm glad you and Noah made it safely to the island. Do you think that man knows where you went?" Charlie asked.

Jane shook her head. "No. In all the times we moved in the past, I never once returned to Martha's Vineyard. But still, Devon does know I grew up on the island, so who knows?"

"We'll need to keep a look out for him. Everyone of us." Charlie sighed and looked over at Lizzie and Alex.

Jane set her tea cup down on the coffee table. "Thanks for your help. Sisters, I must tell you that I'm so very tired of running. I'm weary of moving from place to place all the time. I long to finally have a home of our own for Noah and me."

She rubbed the sides of her head with her fingers, blinking back tears.

In a shaky voice, Jane whispered, "But I'm scared it is hopeless. I'll never be able to settle in a safe community and make real friends. I've always needed to move to a different location for fear of my ex finding me and my son. For years, it's been a dream of mine for both Noah and me to finally find a home of our own. But I'm afraid that's just an impossible dream."

Lizzie came over and gave Jane a hug. "Heavens, Jane. No wonder you are weary of it all." When her sister stepped back she said, "But don't give up. Maybe someday, having a forever home for you and Noah will be possible."

Her sister's comfort and encouraging words were just what Jane needed to hear.

Alex looked over at Jane, a question in her eyes. "I'm just thinking out loud here, but have you considered moving back to the island for good? We would be here to look out for both you and Noah."

Jane looked over at her sister, blue eyes widening in surprise.

"I guess — I mean, I just thought, what's the use? Devon would likely find me and Noah eventually. But that's not the only reason. The rental prices for houses on the island I'm sure are far higher than I can afford." Jane shrugged, feeling the heavy weight of hopelessness once more.

"But, Jane. What about those heirloom jewels you inherited from Grams?" Alex pointed out. "Some of those gems are rubies and diamonds. You could sell them. They're quite valuable."

Jane nodded. "I left them in a safety deposit box in Boston. I put them there after I received my inheritance and never touched them again."

"I'm glad the jewels are safe. But perhaps now would be a good time to get them appraised. Even if you don't want to sell them, at the very least you would have a good idea of their value," Charlie suggested, taking a sip of her tea.

Jane thought about it and nodded. "I suppose you're right. If nothing else, an appraisal would be a good idea. I mean, in all honesty, the jewels might not be worth very much because they are very old."

"However, you may be pleasantly surprised," Lizzie insisted.

"Maybe." Jane appreciated Lizzie's optimism, but in her heart she didn't hold much hope.

Still, she was grateful her beloved late grandmother had wanted to give her all her old jewels as her inheritance.

Grams knew Jane had always admired her heirloom jewels, even as a little girl. She had often play-acted like she was the hostess of a big wonderful party and would pretend she was wearing her grandmother's beautiful jewelry.

Jane had never wanted to sell those heirloom jewels. But they weren't doing any good sitting in that safety deposit box either.

She knew her grandmother would have wanted her to enjoy them in whatever way would help her the most.

"Well, I'm glad you'll have the appraisal done, Jane," Lizzie added. "I think I might start looking around the island for a place to live. You never know what might show up."

"Thanks, Lizzie. I guess that would be alright. I just don't have much hope that there will be any homes that I can afford." Jane bit her lip.

"Oh ye of little faith." Lizzie chided with a twinkle in her eyes. "Let's do a little digging before we give up completely."

Jane smiled. "I'm sorry, you're right, of course."

She sighed heavily, feeling weighed down with what seemed like an impossible dream. It was time to change the subject.

"Tell me more about what's happening with you all."

For the next little while, Alex, Lizzie, and Charlie each talked about their lives.

"I can see that it's almost time for dinner." Lizzie looked at her wrist watch. "Let's go to the dining room. I think Charlie and Jane will be pleasantly surprised by tonight's guests."

Lizzie smiled warmly and they all followed their oldest sister to the dining room.

***

JANE'S EYES widened as she saw who was seated at the dining room table.

Ward Hampton.

He was seated next to Jake at the dinner table.

Jane sucked in a quick breath.

He was the last person she wanted to see.

Her sister Charlie also seemed surprised to see Zach Whetstone seated at their table.

"Looks to me like our oldest sister is matchmaking again," Charlie whispered in Jane's ear.

Jane nodded. "Yeah. I'm not sure how I feel about that."

That was a lie.

Jane did know how she felt about it.

She didn't like it at all.

The last time she saw Ward, they had a polite conversation about their work, but it didn't really go further than that.

If Jane were honest, she could admit to a mixture of emotions every time she saw Ward.

Feelings of betrayal still stung, at the way he'd suddenly left mid-semester to transfer to a different college years ago.

Anger still burned inside her at how Ward had dated her, only to drop her like a hot potato in the end.

That was only one of the early lessons that had sparked her distrust in men. How could she have so innocently trusted Ward?

One thing was for sure: she had definitely loved that man more than he had ever loved her.

She had learned her lesson — the hard way.

What puzzled Jane the most was why the very popular news anchor — the handsome Ward Hampton — still remained single after all these years.

Charlie seated herself next to Zach and that left only one empty chair at the table between Ward and her niece Annie.

Jane sat down, squeezing her hands tightly on her lap under the table. She didn't want anyone to know how nervous she was.

Ward turned to her and in a low whisper said, "It's good to see you again, Jane."

A blush stained her cheeks at his words. With a quick glance in his direction, Jane nodded and whispered, "I'm surprised you came for one of Lizzie's dinners."

"Well, since I retired from broadcasting a few months ago and moved back to the island, I have more time for other things like visiting people and accepting dinner invitations." Ward tossed her a rogue smile.

The same smile that had attracted her to him years ago, was now just as attractive.

However, Jane's heart wasn't as trusting as it once was.

Terrible experiences with men had left her battered and bruised.

"I hope your new retired lifestyle is enjoyable for you, Ward." Jane offered a small smile, still unsure of what to say to him.

Ward grinned. "It's already shaping up to be a quiet and enjoyable adventure."

Jane raised one eyebrow, curiosity flooding her as to what it would be like to have a quiet adventure.

But before she could question the man beside her, her brother-in-law interrupted.

"Let's say a blessing before we enjoy this delicious chicken dinner." Jonathan offered a quick prayer of thanks from his place at the head of the table.

Jane looked over at Lizzie, whose adoring gaze was on her husband by her side.

Soon, Lizzie was speaking, "Thank you for coming, everyone. I'm thrilled that my sisters Alex, Charlie, and Jane joined us for dinner. Jane and her son, Noah, will be staying with us for a little while. We couldn't be happier."

"Thanks, Lizzie and Jonathan, for having us as your guests." Jane winked at her son and turned back to her sister.

Jonathan nodded. "We're always happy to have my wife's family stay with us."

Lizzie added, "Jane, you are very welcome. We're thrilled to have the two of you stay with us." She smiled warmly before she started to pass the food dishes around the table.

Jane sighed, looking around the table at her son. Noah was seated beside his favorite cousin, Jake. The two were grinning and having so much fun talking, that they were missing the rest of the conversation around the table.

But at long last her son was finally able to relax and enjoy himself. And for that she was very grateful.

"Jane has some exciting news," Charlie suddenly commented.

Wide-eyed, Jane turned to her sister.

What was your younger sister about to share?

"Jane has decided to find an appraiser for the inheritance she received from our late grandmother. It'll be exciting to finally discover how much those heirloom jewels are worth."

Her sister's enthusiasm about the jewels was contagious.

"Yes, I am looking forward to it. However, I first need

to find a trustworthy gemologist who will agree to do the appraisal."

Ward turned towards Jane. "I happen to have a friend in Boston who appraises gems for a living. Maybe we could go together to the city. I could introduce you, if you'd like?"

Jane couldn't help but tense at his question.

At first, she wanted to say no, but the practical side of her won out. She needed to find out what those old jewels were worth.

Jane stammered a reply, "I—I suppose. Er, I mean to say, yes, that would be helpful, Ward."

"Good. We can plan for next week then. I'll call him tonight and get a time set up for us to meet with him."

She shifted nervously in her chair, unused to someone else taking charge of things in her life.

It was typical of Ward Hampton to take charge of the details of her life.

Years ago, when they dated in college, it had been his way to take the lead in their relationship and in decision making.

Back then, she had been happy for him to take charge. He was very quick to take command and make decisions.

Today, however, frustration sizzled in her belly.

Painful memories of when Ward had suddenly stopped college and left her alone years ago stabbed at her heart once more.

She swallowed back bile quickly.

Years ago, she loved him so much.

When Ward left her, he'd broken her heart into tiny pieces.

Jane adjusted the napkin beside her plate with a shaky hand.

The sad part was – even though she still harbored anger towards this man — her traitorous heart loved him still.

Her belly fisted into a tight ball of nervous energy.

She reached for her cup of tea hoping to settle her stomach.

Unexpectedly, Ward leaned towards her. "I'm looking forward to our trip to Boston together. I've missed hearing your soft laugh. I've missed seeing your beautiful face. I've missed feeling your gentle presence. I'll be counting the hours until I can spend time with you again, Jane."

Sucking in a quick breath, Jane nearly choked on her tea.

Heat rose from her neck to her cheeks.

She turned and stole a glance at the man beside her.

After all these years, Ward was not only incredibly handsome, but he still had a way with words that could make her heart melt… every time.

How would she be able to keep him at a distance, when her traitorous heart only wanted to spend more time with him?

CHAPTER FOUR

ward

WARD HELD the door open to Colin Rathburger's office.

His friend worked here as an appraiser of gems.

He'd first met Colin years ago, when he had attended a benefit gala during his years as a news anchorman. Then, later on, he had asked Colin to do an appraisal on his mother's emerald necklace and bracelet.

He trusted Colin.

When Jane had agreed to come to Boston with him to meet his friend, he was pleasantly surprised.

"I'm excited to hear what Colin has to say about your grandmother's jewels."

She peered up at him, a warmth in her big blue eyes.

His heart beat faster just being near Jane.

This was the woman whom he had loved since their school years together on the island.

As they reached his friend's office, he stopped and leaned over to whisper, "It'll be fine."

Her cheeks blossomed pink, adding to her beauty.

"Thanks. I'm just nervous." Jane swallowed. "I've been on pins and needles ever since the gems were delivered to Mr. Rathburger's office."

Ward grinned. "Well, we're about to learn the result."

Jane's fingers tightened on her clutch purse.

Ward knocked on the door and an assistant led them inside. "Mr. Rathburger is expecting you."

Jane inhaled a deep breath and walked towards the slender, slightly gray-haired man.

"Good to see you again, Ward. I hope all is going well for you now that you've retired from broadcasting." Colin tossed a quizzical glance at his old friend.

"It's going well. It's nice to be back on the island where life is slower paced," Ward said.

Colin commented, "I suppose that's true. Everything seems to move a bit faster here in the city. I envy your quiet lifestyle." His friend hesitated before adding, "I must tell you, I believe everyone will miss seeing your handsome face on the nightly news. You've become a trusted face on television, on which many people rely."

A subtle heat rose from his neck to his cheeks.

He couldn't help but feel somewhat embarrassed when anybody talked about his success as a news anchorman.

Ward chuckled softly, his deep voice soft as he replied, "Colin, I'm not sure there are too many people who miss me, but I appreciate your kind words all the same."

"Welcome." Colin turned to look at the woman next to him. "It's good to see you again, Jane. Are you ready to hear the results of the appraisal of your heirloom jewelry?"

"I am." Jane's voice shook slightly.

The gemologist led both of them into his office. "Jane, I got the idea from our conversation earlier that you thought perhaps the gems you inherited would be too old to be of any value."

Jane nodded. "I think I just assumed, because these were old heirloom jewels, they wouldn't be worth anything."

Colin shook his head and a smile began to appear. "Go ahead and have a seat."

With one hand, he waved to the two soft office chairs located in front of his desk.

Ward sat beside Jane and they looked at his friend.

Colin stepped behind his desk and, sitting down, picked up the documents.

Looking over at Jane, his smile widened. "Jane, I believe you will be pleasantly surprised."

She raised one eyebrow in disbelief. She looked over at Ward's friend. "I'm glad. So tell me. What have you discovered?"

Colin grinned, put on his reading glasses, and looked down at the document he held in his hands.

"First, I must tell you, as I studied and appraised these gems, I was surprised. As you know, this set of jewels included red diamond necklaces and white diamond necklaces."

The gem expert continued to explain, "They all had

matching diamond earrings and bracelets. There were also ruby earrings with matching ruby necklaces and two emerald necklaces with matching bracelets. All of the gems are very high quality, in spite of their age." Colin grinned.

Ward turned to her. "Jane, that sounds like good news."

Jane squeezed her hands together, twiddling her fingers together. Was she nervous?

With a hesitant voice she asked softly, "So my grand-mother's jewels are worth something after all?"

Colin grinned. "Yes. In fact, you'll be pleased to learn the results of my appraisal. These are some of the highest quality gemstones I've ever seen. I would place their value at several million dollars."

He handed her the report with the exact figures.

Jane gasped out loud.

"Thanks for looking at my grandmother's jewels, Colin. This has been eye-opening." Jane stood to her feet.

"You're welcome." Colin reached over to shake her hand. "My assistant will give you the appraisal documents on your way out."

Together they walked out of his friend's office.

They stopped quickly when Colin's assistant handed Jane an envelope with a copy of the appraisal.

He placed a gentle hand on the small of her back as they walked out of the building.

As Ward drove their rental car to the airport, Jane was quiet. It seemed like she was deep in thought.

"Are you surprised by the result, Jane?" Ward asked as he turned the car towards the road that led to the airport.

"Very surprised." Jane turned to him as he parked the

car. "It's strange to think that now I might actually have some options."

Ward grinned. "Yes, you certainly do. We'll need to find some interested buyers. However, I don't think that will be a problem. I think there are enough wealthy folks looking for high quality jewelry."

"Maybe," Jane replied. "I'll admit, I have been hesitant to think of selling these jewels. The gems were an inheritance from my beloved grandmother. Many times at important dinners at the beach cottage I remember seeing her wearing the jewels. To me, these heirloom jewels have sentimental value."

"I understand. It can be hard to let go of items that hold a lot of meaning for us." Ward paused for a moment. "However, if you do decide to sell them, you'll have options. If you want to put the jewels on the market, what do you think you would do with your newfound wealth?"

Ward helped her out of the car and they walked towards the airport terminal.

It wasn't until they sat in the waiting area, waiting for their plane back to the island, that Jane spoke again, "I'm not sure, Ward. Ever since I left my ex, for years I've dreamed of living in a community where my son and I truly belong."

Ward began, " Of course. You want to have a home for you and your son."

He was puzzled by the pained expression and the crease that formed between her brows.

"Something is troubling you, Jane. What is it?" He leaned closer and whispered in her ear.

He couldn't help the hope that grew inside him. Would she trust him enough to share her personal life with him?

"I thought it might be nice to find a place to rent on the island for now. To be near family. I told my sister Lizzie I'd be willing to look around, but I'm afraid to get my hopes up."

"Afraid? That's not the Jane I used to know." Ward turned towards her, a teasing light in his dark eyes.

Jane swallowed. Her lips trembled a little. "I've changed, Ward. I'm more scared now than I've ever been. It's true. I believe it's because there were some awful situations and terrible people I've faced in the past few years — some of which I still must deal with every day — that have made me afraid."

"I—I'm sorry Jane. I didn't know," Ward stammered uncomfortably. Compassion welled up from deep inside him.

He couldn't help but wonder what was so terrible that it caused Jane to be fearful and to be afraid to hope for a better life.

Ward thought about the two of them.

It was his deepest desire that Jane would grow to love him again.

However, the two of them had only recently started to get reacquainted. The truth was that there were still misunderstandings between them that needed to be resolved.

Would they ever be able to establish a friendship and have trust between them again?

He longed to do everything in his power to earn her trust.

Ward could only hope Jane would be willing to give him a chance.

❦

JANE'S NERVES throbbed and she shifted uneasily.

Was he shocked by her story?

Perhaps she should explain.

"It's alright, Ward. I understand. But I do want to let you know I'm not as young or as carefree as I was when we were in college. Life's been difficult." Jane sighed heavily.

Her fingers twisted together on her lap, a sure sign she was nervous.

Silence between them stretched for a long time, before Ward leaned close, speaking softly, "I'm sorry life hasn't treated you kindly, Jane."

He leaned closer, his breath tickling her ear.

Heat rose from her neck to her cheeks at his words.

He whispered again, "If you'll allow me, I'd like to be the one to bring back the carefree side of you that life stole from you, Jane."

Emotions of hope and longing tumbled over in her mind, like a tumbleweed blown down the road by a high wind.

It was hard to believe the same man whom she had dated years ago wanted to see her happy.

Fear and hope warred on the inside.

She had already been abandoned by him a long time ago — the day he suddenly left her to transfer to a different college.

Knots formed in her belly.

She was convinced her heart would not survive being broken again.

"Ward, I don't think that's a good idea. Don't you remember what happened between the two of us in college?" Jane stammered her response, nervously wiping sweaty hands on her pant legs.

Ward sighed. "I do remember. But I didn't tell you the full story back then of the reason I needed to leave you and transfer to a different college. Give me a chance to explain what happened, Jane, before you refuse."

His words struck a deep chord inside her.

Kenna had told her the same thing.

Jane's conscience pricked at her. It wasn't fair to refuse him so quickly.

The right thing to do would be to set aside her fears and at least give him a chance to tell his side of the story.

She swallowed and nodded. "Alright, that's fair. Let me know where you want to meet. And I'll listen to what you have to say."

Ward reached over and squeezed her hand. "Thank you, Jane. I promise, you won't regret it."

She wasn't sure about that.

Anxiety swirled inside her belly.

Would her heart be able to handle spending more time with the man who had been her first love?

Could she protect her heart from falling for him again?

JANE STEPPED inside the *BeansWithBooks* coffee shop, happy to meet with her friend.

There was so much she wanted to talk about with Kenna.

That included the topic of Ward Hampton.

He had texted her an hour ago, asking if, sometime in the next week, she could meet him on the beach to talk and enjoy the sunset.

Jane shifted uneasily on her feet as she stood in the lineup to order her coffee.

A moment later, the man in front of her finished with his order and turned towards her. Jane looked up, surprised to see the tall figure of Ryan Hart.

The blue police uniform and gun belt he wore made him easily recognizable.

"Well, if it isn't the elusive Jane Stafford." Ryan's blue eyes shimmered with delight and he leaned close. "For a minute, I thought I was dreaming. But I'd recognize your incredible blue eyes anywhere."

Heat stained her cheeks at his compliment.

But she couldn't help but wonder about his comment of her being elusive. He had tried to date her in high school. They had gone to some football games and he had taken her to the senior prom, but she had never fallen for him. At least, not as hard as she'd fallen for Ward.

Jane's eyes widened and she stammered, "Th—thanks. How have you been, Ryan?"

"I'm good. Much better now that I've seen you." Ryan winked at her.

"You haven't changed much." Jane hesitated before she

went on. "Lizzie told me that you and Tiffany got divorced. Sorry to hear that."

Ryan ran a hand through his wavy hair and looked out the window for a few minutes before answering, "Yeah, well, I guess what we had together just wasn't meant to be. And you, Jane?"

"I'm single. But I have a son who keeps me on my toes." Jane smiled as she thought of Noah.

"A son. That's good, Jane." Ryan sighed. "Have you come back to stay in our island community?"

Jane nodded. "Yes. It's looking more and more that way."

"Good." He took a sip of his coffee deep in thought. "Maybe we could have some fun together?"

Jane chuckled. Ryan Hart had always been a man eager to try new adventures. In high school he had always been the one to lead his friends into new and sometimes unexplored places.

"I must ask, what sort of fun do you have in mind?" She wasn't about to risk her life for a little bit of fun.

Ryan leaned close. "Spend a few hours with me on my boat this Saturday. I'll help you get reacquainted with the waterways that surround the island. What do you say, Jane?"

After hearing what he had in mind, she agreed. "That sounds safe enough. Sure."

She gave him her phone number.

"Alright. I'll call you." Ryan leaned downwards and whispered, "I look forward to it."

Jane watched him walk away, wondering if she'd lost

her marbles to agree to a few hours of boating with Ryan Hart.

As she ordered her coffee, her thoughts were chaotic and confused.

"Jane, come join me at the window table." Kenna managed to sneak up beside her.

Relief flooded her when she saw her friend's smiling face.

A grin turned up the corners of Jane's lips and she followed.

She greeted her friend with a big hug.

"Kenna, it's been a really long time since I've seen you in person." Jane sighed, looking her over. "The last few years have been good to you, my friend. You look the same as you did in high school."

Her friend chuckled, shaking her head. "Jane, I appreciate your ability to lie with a straight face."

A giggle burst from deep inside.

She had always admired the way her friend spoke what was on her mind.

Many times, Jane had wished she could be more like Kenna.

The two of them had always been so different.

Where Jane was hesitant, and insecure, and often felt a need to hide who she really was, Kenna was straight forward, authentic, and not shy about getting to the truth of the matter.

She appreciated her friend all the more today.

"I've missed you, Kenna." Jane sat across the table and took a sip of coffee.

"Tell me what's been going on in your life and with your family." Jane lifted her coffee cup and took a sip, looking over the rim at her friend.

"Funny, I was about to ask you the same thing." Her friend grinned. "I'll tell you a little about me. But first, I couldn't help but notice Ryan Hart was talking to you. What did he want?"

Kenna stirred her mug of chai tea with a teaspoon, studying her intently.

"Oh, you know Ryan. He's always flirting and trying to have some fun."

A crease of worry formed between her friend's brows. "You aren't interested in him, are you?"

"In Ryan Hart? No. He's not my type. But he did ask me to go boating with him on Saturday. Without thinking, I agreed. I'm sure it's just a harmless few hours on the water, Kenna." Jane grimaced.

"Maybe. Just watch yourself with him, Jane," Kenna whispered in low tones. "I don't trust that man."

"I'm sure you're right, Kenna. And I promise to be careful." Jane sipped her coffee. "Now tell me what's going on with you?"

Her friend grinned. "I'm always happy to talk about my family. My husband, Callum, has been busy teaching at the local high school. He enjoys it. Our oldest son, Cameron, has his dad for his math teacher this year."

Kenna smiled, "Our son tells me he gets more attention now that his friends have his dad for their teacher. I think he enjoys the attention." She chuckled. "Our daughter, Fiona, is happy to be in her last year of elementary school. She wants to be with the big school kids." Her friend chuckled, shaking her head.

"It sounds like your family is doing well. Are you still working as a nurse at the hospital?" Jane asked.

Her friend nodded. "Yes. But I'm not full-time at the hospital any longer. I cut back my hours so I could have more time with Callum and the children. And I also wanted more time to bake. In the past year, more and more people in our community keep asking me for my cakes, muffins, and cookies, so I've decided to start a little business on the side."

Jane commented, "That's wonderful, Kenna. I remember you always made delicious desserts. I think that's great you're taking the time to do more of what you love."

Kenna nodded. "Thanks. I feel good about it. But enough about me. Tell me about what's going on with you, Jane."

Jane hesitated. Would her friend understand all the strange and terrible things that had happened in her life?

Her friend's green eyes studied her. "If I recall, you used to haul your camera with you everywhere. You took photos of us and of your family. I thought you started college with a plan to get a degree in photography, didn't you?"

Jane nodded, toying with the napkin next to her mug. "I did start those photography classes. But my life ended so messed up. I quit college."

"I'm sorry, Jane. I remember you telling me that you and Ward broke up. Was that when you met Devon?" Kenna asked.

Tears pricked the back of her eyelids. "Yeah. That was the most foolish decision I ever made."

"I remember you told me how that man had a temper and did everything he could to control and abuse you and your son."

At Kenna's look of compassion, Jane decided she would share more secrets. There weren't many people she told secrets to, but her friend was someone she trusted.

"It's true. When he would leave on business trips, he forced me to call him three times a day with a live video to prove I was at home. Things got much worse after Noah was born."

Fear laced Jane's words as she remembered. "Devon told me I couldn't invite any people into our home. He was afraid they would give germs to the baby or they would try to steal our son."

"I'm so sorry, Jane." Her friend sighed.

Jane shook her head slowly. "I regret to say that I continued to stay with that man because of fear. He had threatened me many times that if I left he would find me and kill me."

She shuddered at the memories. "But the day came when he pushed me too far. Devon was home for Christmas and I had just finished taking a shower, when I came out of the room and overheard him talking on the phone. He called the woman 'sweetheart' and asked if their daughter liked the present he gave her for Christmas."

"I remember when you called me and you told me what happened. It was just after you arrived at a women's shelter." Kenna's eyes widened in concern.

Jane nodded. "And because I questioned him about the other woman, Noah and I ended up with bruises."

"Oh, Jane, that's horrible," her friend whispered.

"Yes, it was. That crushing blow was the catalyst for change. It was later that night — in the middle of the night — that I took Noah and we escaped."

"Good for you, Jane. Nobody should have to be put through that kind of abusive relationship." Kenna's tone of voice was unrelentingly firm.

Jane swallowed. "I don't know why it took my ex-husband hurting my son for me to have enough courage to leave him. Why did I wait? Most likely fear. I guess I'm not fearless and brave like you are, Kenna."

Her friend reached across the table and gently squeezed her hand.

"But you are, Jane. It took real courage to take your small son and escape that cruel man. You did it."

"Yeah, I guess I did. But I've been on the run ever since I left him seven years ago. We've moved five different times whenever it seemed like Devon was getting too close to finding where we were." Jane blinked back tears. "I'm so tired of running."

"Is that why you came back to the island — to put down roots, Jane?" Kenna asked.

Her friend had always known her so well.

Jane nodded. "I would like to put down roots. I want to find a permanent home where my son and I can live. I long to live without worry or fear haunting my every waking moment. But I think that's an impossible dream."

"Not true, Jane. I believe you could do that here where you grew up," Kenna added. "You are well liked here on the island. And I hope you know I'll do whatever I can to help you and your son."

"Thanks, Kenna. That means the world to me." Jane nodded and finished drinking the rest of her coffee.

"But I am curious about one thing?" her friend asked.

Jane looked over with one eyebrow raised. "What's that?"

"Have you seen Ward Hampton since you've been back?"

Heat stained her neck and moved up to her cheeks at Kenna's question.

"He came to Lizzie's place for dinner. And then when I mentioned I was looking for an appraiser for the heirloom jewels from Grams, Ward said he had a friend who appraised gems." Jane shook her head. "Next thing I knew, I was in Boston together with Ward. I talked with his friend about Grams' jewels."

"Is there still a spark between the two of you?" At her friend's probing question, Jane shifted uncomfortably.

"I— I am attracted to him even after all these years. But that terrifies me." Jane fiddled with her spoon, her nerves getting the better of her.

Kenna asked, "You're afraid of Ward?"

"No, I'm scared of getting into another cruel and abusive relationship with a man." Jane's voice trembled with her honest answer.

Kenna nodded. "I can understand that. But Ward Hampton is a gentle and kind man. I don't believe he would ever hurt you on purpose."

Jane smiled. "That's what Ward told me recently when we went to Boston together. In fact, he asked if I would give him time to explain what happened years ago, when he suddenly left me in college."

"There you go. He's trying to do the right thing. So are you going to give him the chance to tell his side of the story?"

Jane nodded. "I will. I think it's only fair. But, right now, I'm still very wary of him or any other man. It will take quite a lot for me to trust a man enough to jump into a relationship again."

"With all you've suffered, I can't say I'm surprised," Kenna began, staring at her in silence.

Jane could tell when her friend had more to say. "What are you thinking?"

Kenna sighed heavily. "I remember the friendship you had with Ward during our high school years. He was someone you trusted. Later on, when I visited you in college and saw you two together, you seemed so happy. You used to tell me Ward was kind, compassionate, and a lot of fun. Is that not true any longer?"

Jane shook her head. "I still believe Ward is a good man, but my trust in him was broken. I was so hurt and betrayed when he suddenly left me without a word years ago. I doubt the story he'll tell me will change my mind."

"If he's eager to tell you, then it's possible he had a good reason for leaving so quickly," Kenna added.

"Maybe. But still, he could have told me," Jane insisted.

"That's true," Kenna agreed. "It will be good when Ward finally shares with you his story."

Jane swallowed quickly and nodded.

Fear and uncertainty were at war inside Jane's mind,

against the longing she had to be loved by the one man whom her heart had never forgotten.

The thought of her upcoming talk with Ward made her want to run away from him as fast as possible.

Yet a big part of her heart was desperate to hear his explanation for the way he'd abandoned her.

There was one thing she knew for sure: *it would take a lot for Ward to earn her trust again.*

CHAPTER FIVE

ane

"I'M happy you joined me today, Jane." Ryan turned to her with a grin.

They had just left the dock and were headed out to the Vineyard Sound, just off the shores of the island.

"I'm glad. It's a lovely day to be on the water." Jane sighed, looking over at Ryan who was setting their course using the computerized helm.

"What do you think of my new yacht?" Ryan turned to her with a grin. As long as she had known him, he'd always been seeking some new thrill.

"It's very elegant. And it definitely has all the bells and whistles," she commented.

Ryan's yacht was the very definition of luxury. She

couldn't help but be curious how he could afford this type of luxury on a police officer's salary.

"I bought it recently. My dad and a few others owed me money. When they finally paid up, I decided to buy this boat." Ryan grinned, looking like the teenage boy she remembered.

He grabbed her hand. "Here, let's walk around so you can get a better view of the island from the water. The navigation system is set. We're close enough on this upper deck that I can quickly get to the helm if we need to change course."

They walked onto the upper deck where there were comfortable loungers and chairs.

Ryan pointed to the landscape, "See over there? That is your sister Lizzie's blue beach cottage and to the right of it is the piece of waterfront land that your grandparents owned. That property ends at the cove. Bobby's parents rented that house over by the cove from your grandparents."

He glanced over the area, "You can see the Peterson land right beside it. My grandparents owned that place before they sold it to the Petersons. My brother, Dylan, and I used to go to Bobby's place for trail biking and boating. We spent a lot of time there as kids."

Jane remembered Ryan's twin brother, Dylan. Dylan was the guy who threatened her sister Alex last year and nearly got himself killed in the process.

"I'm glad you have good memories of that area along the waterfront. By the way, how is Dylan doing?" Jane asked Ryan.

Ryan shrugged. "He's still in the psychiatric hospital.

The doctors are concerned about him. In my opinion, Dylan went on a downward spiral because he was desperate for our grandmother Florrie's approval."

"And you don't want your grandmother's approval?" Jane couldn't help but ask.

Ryan turned to her. "No. Besides, I think my brother went about it the wrong way. If I really wanted something, I would simply figure out a way to take it without anyone's approval."

Jane wasn't surprised to hear that sentiment from Ryan. He'd always been more decisive and forceful than his twin brother.

Suddenly, Ryan's phone rang. After a few quick responses, he hung up.

"We need to take the boat to the cove. I have a delivery to pick up for my mom's store." Ryan hurried to the helm.

Soon the boat sped towards the Cove.

Ryan slowed the boat as he moved the boat alongside the long dock that stretched out from the beach.

There were two men on the beach that Jane didn't recognize. And two smaller motorboats were also alongside the dock.

"I can help carry the boxes." Jane started to follow Ryan out onto the dock.

"No, Jane." Ryan spoke sharply as he turned to her. "Just stay on the boat. I promise we can handle it. I'll be back soon."

Jane walked back onto the boat, rubbing her arms. She couldn't help but feel like she just had been given a warning of some kind.

She hurried to the upper deck and watched the men as they loaded the boxes onto Ryan's boat.

He'd said the crates and smaller boxes were filled with items for his mom, Linda Hart's, retail store. Maybe they were Christmas items since the holiday was right around the corner.

One of the men dropped one of the boxes and the top of the box opened up.

Jane stared down at it as the man reached in and pulled the item around, trying to reposition it.

It looked like a wooden cradle.

The cradle had an uncanny resemblance to the baby cradles her ex sold in his retail stores around the country.

Sucking in a quick breath, she placed a shaky hand over her mouth.

Were these wooden cradles from Devon's inventory?

If his products were being sent to Linda Hart's store, did that mean that Devon wasn't far behind?

Was her ex-husband following her to the island?

Panic squeezed the air out of her lungs.

Being with Ryan Hart on his boat, and picking up these boxes, gave her a bad feeling.

Jane couldn't help but think that anything that involved her ex-husband was not going to be on the level.

JANE TOSSED and turned all night.

By morning, she was quite tired as she joined her sisters at the Sweet Beach Cove community church.

After the service, Noah went with his cousins Waylon and Dutton and walked back to Lizzie's place for lunch.

Grams' old pastor greeted each of them after the service.

"So nice of you to join us this morning, Jane. Your late grandmother would have loved to see her granddaughters together." Pastor Tim's eyes crinkled and his smile lines increased.

"I think so too. And, by the way, I enjoyed your message today. Grams would always encourage me from that chapter in Proverbs about a woman who is intelligent, capable, and virtuous, as a reminder that her value is far above rubies or pearls. Your words were an encouraging reminder today," Jane said as she fingered the pearl necklace that hung around her neck.

Memories of her beloved grandmother's reminders to hold onto faith, hope, and love lingered, even after Grams was long gone.

"I'm glad to hear that, Jane. Your grandmother was a wise woman. She is sorely missed in this community." The old pastor's voice rumbled with heartfelt emotion.

"Thanks, Pastor Tim. My sisters and I miss her," Jane added. After a few more pleasantries, she walked back to the beach cottage with Lizzie, Alex, and Charlie.

As they sat down on the deck, the cool breeze twirled their hair. The cousins were having lunch inside with their dads, watching a movie together.

The sisters enjoyed time together as they sat around the rustic wood table that graced the outside deck at Lizzie's place.

Each one sipped their sweet iced tea, making small talk, after finishing a delicious lunch.

Jane looked around the table at each sister, relishing the time she could spend with each of them.

She was grateful for these moments.

Lizzie turned to each of her sisters with a mischievous sparkle in her eyes. Reaching down into her tote bag, she pulled out a worn, leather journal.

"Now that we've finished lunch and all of us sisters are together, I thought we could read a little from Grams' journal," Lizzie began with a grin. "Remember, she wanted us to try to search into the mystery behind our parents' deaths. At the start of this journal, Grams wrote that she didn't think their boating accident was truly an accident."

An uneasiness settled over Jane at her sister's reminder.

"Hopefully, Grams will say something that will help us solve this mystery," Charlie added.

Alex grimaced.

"She will. Today I thought we would read an earlier journal entry from Grams. Looks like this is from when our dad was a teenager," Lizzie announced as she opened up the old leather book and began to read out loud.

Yesterday, William and I and our two teenagers, John and Eleanor, went to celebrate the conclusion of the five week long Striped Bass and Bluefish Derby competition.

During the competition, we watched our friend Dave Elkhart and others we knew fishing, along with other islanders. They were searching for bluefish, bonito, and fast albacore in the blue waters beyond the island.

On that final day, when the winner was announced, I was

pleased to hear that Dave Elkhart won the new boat as the grand prize.

While William talked with Dave, I stopped to say hello to Florrie Cantrell-Jones.

It was a difficult conversation because I've always had the impression Florrie doesn't like me much. However, I've always tried to be kind to her.

"How have you been, Florrie?" I asked her about it because it had only been a year and a half since her husband passed away.

"I'm doing well. I've always been tough as nails, Elizabeth, you know that. Nothing can keep me down for long," Florrie told me in that familiar tone of voice that didn't allow room for surrender.

"I'm glad to hear that," I replied, turning my head as John and his friends headed my way. "Looks like my son needs something."

My son, John, was with his three friends, Ted Cantrell, Bobby Sutton, and Jerry Hart.

Ida Cantrell's daughter Nellie and Florrie's daughter Clemmie joined them.

"I was never sure if those boys would remain friends after what happened last year. Matty's sudden death in that diving accident really shook those boys," Florrie commented.

"Yes, it did. John still wakes up with nightmares about the day Matty died. I think our son feels responsible, because they were searching for treasure and diving in the waters where his late grandfather's ship is located."

"It'll take some time, but I'm sure John will heal." Florrie's comment was somewhat flippant.

"I hope so," I replied.

"Well, I need to get going. I promised Ida I would meet her."

"Of course. I'll see you later, Florrie." I waved her off and began to walk.

As I walked away, I passed Clementine and Nettie as they talked with my son and his friends.

I overheard Nellie say something that surprised me. She whispered to Clementine, "I heard Jerry tell my brother, Ted, that he believes he was cursed from everything that happened on the day Matty died. Jerry said he doesn't think the stain on his hands from that day will ever come out as long as he lives. I wonder what Jerry means?"

I almost stopped in my tracks after hearing Nellie's words.

Nellie's mother, Ida Cantrell, always said her daughter was slow of speech and slow to understand things.

But, when I heard those words, it seemed to me like Nellie understood well enough what Jerry was saying.

I was shocked by what I overheard.

Now, all these questions are rolling around in my head. What stain does Jerry believe he carries when it comes to Matty's death? Why does he believe he's cursed?

I can't help but worry about what happened that day, when John and his four friends went diving for treasure.

Looks like I'll need to have a talk with our son. I wonder if he knows more about what happened on the day Matty died than he's letting on.

Lizzie closed the old leather journal and turned to look at her sisters and murmured, "Grams' journal entry this time was a real surprise."

Charlie nodded. "I'll say. What Grams overheard about Jerry Hart is shocking. Do you think Jerry had a part to play in Matty's death years ago?"

"I don't know. But I do think Sheriff Jerry Hart has

been keeping some kind of secret for a long time." Alex explained, "When Dylan Hart had me locked up in the carriage house, he let me know that his brother, Ryan Hart, was hiding some big secrets that would get Ryan fired from the police force if anyone found out. Dylan also said that Ryan was protecting his father, and in turn, his dad, Sheriff Hart, was protecting him."

Charlie let out a low whistle and raised one eyebrow. "Sounds to me like we need to do some digging to find out what those secrets are."

"I agree," Jane spoke softly. "We need answers."

Jane thought for a moment and realized this was a good time to tell her sisters about what happened yesterday.

"Since we are discussing Dylan and Ryan Hart, I should let you all know what happened yesterday. I went boating for a few hours with Ryan."

"You did what?" Alex's eyes grew wide. "Jane, I can't believe you did that. Don't you remember that his twin brother, Dylan Hart, tried to kill me? I'm scared something might happen to you."

Charlie chimed in. "I'm worried too. I seem to remember Ryan had a thing for you back in high school, Jane. He was always attracted to you. I hope he treated you well."

Jane nodded. "Ryan was kind to me. He took me on his new luxury yacht on the waterway around the island."

"How can he afford a new yacht on a police officer's salary?" Lizzie's eyes sparked in surprise.

"I was curious about that as well. All Ryan said was his

dad and other people owed him money which helped him buy the boat."

Lizzie shook her head. "They must have owed him a lot of money. Most yachts are worth millions of dollars."

"That's true. But there's more." Jane glanced over at each of her sisters before she explained, "Just before we returned to dock, Ryan got a call. Someone told him a shipment for his mom's store had arrived. Ryan was eager to pick it up. So he steered the boat towards the Cove. When we arrived, two men were waiting at the makeshift dock on the Cove, with a lot of boxes they loaded onto Ryan's yacht."

"I wonder what was in those boxes?" Charlie's question had all the sisters nodding their heads. "Did you see anything?"

"One of the men dropped a box, and I saw a wooden cradle. For a moment, the cradle almost looked similar to the design my ex-husband has in his Christmas retail stores. But I could have been mistaken." Jane sighed.

"Wait. You said Ryan was delivering those boxes to his mom's store in Sweet Beach Cove?" Alex asked.

"Yes. That's what he said." Jane tensed.

Alex placed two fingers on her chin, deep in thought. "Maybe your ex-husband is doing business and selling his products at Linda Hart's store. Maybe Devon is trying to expand into different markets. Which is all good."

She shook her head. "But I get this feeling there is more going on. I can't put my finger on it."

"Hopefully, we'll be able to figure it out soon," Lizzie replied. "Meanwhile, there are other questions we need to ask to uncover the mystery of what happened to our parents. For instance, what details have we missed that occurred from the night our parents died?"

Alex nodded. "I've asked myself that a thousand times."

Her oldest sister studied her thoughtfully. "Jane, I think it's time for you to talk with someone who has connections in the police department. We need to find the missing pieces to these questions."

Her brows formed a crease. She couldn't help but be puzzled by Lizzie's comment. "Who do you suggest I talk to?"

Lizzie replied, "Ward Hampton, of course. He has been good friends with Police Officer Neville Shelton for years. And he will have access to files in the police department."

Jane sucked in a quick breath. "You want me to talk to Ward about this?"

Stunned, she couldn't believe what her sister was asking her to do.

Talking with her old boyfriend was the last thing Jane wanted.

"I do," Lizzie said. "I know it's difficult being back on the island and seeing or talking with the man you once loved, Jane, but I think it's important. If Ward could find a way to talk with Officer Shelton and encourage him to talk with Ryan or perhaps find files on Ryan Hart's or Sheriff Harts' activities, it could be a big break in the case for us."

The weight of responsibility sat heavy on Jane's shoulders.

She didn't like the thought of asking Ward for any sort of favors. They simply weren't that good of friends anymore.

"I don't know if I can ask Ward for this favor, Lizzie. Things are not the same between us anymore. We barely know each other." Jane's heart constricted at the disappointed look in her oldest sister's eyes.

Lizzie's look of disappointment was nearly her undoing.

"Are you sure it's only Ward you're thinking of, Jane?" Her sister Alex had always been another truth-teller in her life. "Maybe you're afraid by digging deeper into the mystery surrounding our parents' deaths that you and Noah will come out of hiding and be seen by more folks."

Jane swallowed quickly. "It's true. I am afraid."

"If that's true, I think it's time to ask yourself a difficult question. Do you want to stay hidden away for the rest of your life, or are you ready to fight for what you want?" Alex asked.

Jane sucked in a breath. "My friend Kenna said something similar the other day. And my son has been asking if we could plant roots and begin to make friends. Moving from place to place has been very difficult for him."

"I'm not surprised," Alex said softly. "So maybe it's time you begin to embrace your true identity. Maybe it's time to win this fight against the conflict, control, and abuse that's been chasing at your heels for the past seven years. If you won't do it for yourself, Jane, do it for your son."

Jane swallowed the bile that rose in her throat.

With shaky fingers, she gripped her pearl necklace.

Grams' words returned with force: *You are like this pearl — emerging even more beautiful and stronger from all the hardships you've suffered. I want you to always remember to hold onto faith no matter what conflicts or trials you suffer in life.*

She realized it was time to take a step forward in faith.

"You're right, Alex. I will do it for my son," Jane whispered. "I'll have that talk with Ward and ask if he'll talk with Officer Shelton."

❧

ALL SEVEN SISTERS continued to talk for the next few hours until it was almost time for them to go their separate ways.

Jane's thoughts were jagged and painful as she thought of all the changes she and Noah had unexpectedly been forced to make.

It still felt weird to Jane that she had found shelter at Lizzie's home with her son. She never expected to come here.

What's more — she never expected to stay.

However, her phone call yesterday to Isabella only underlined how critical it was for them to remain at her sister's place.

The conversation with her friend and neighbor circled around and around in her mind.

Isabella had said her ex-husband continued to show up every day and watch the building where they lived.

She said it would be safer for her and Noah if they planned never to return to the apartment.

At her friend's words, the swirling in Jane's mind stopped.

Her emotions had flip-flopped from paralysis into full-fledged panic at Isabella's words of warning.

Distressing thoughts of her ex-husband and what that meant for her and Noah's safety continued to circle around in her brain.

Today, as she remembered that conversation with her neighbor, her situation struck her with a new intensity.

Her former husband was back. Worse, he was stalking every move she made and that of her son.

Her past was coming back to haunt her — just like she had known it would.

As Jane digested the consequences of this new dilemma in her life, questions swirled in her mind: *Why had Devon forced his way into her and Noah's lives again? What did he want? Was his plan to take her son away from her? How far was he willing to go to get what he wanted?*

Shivers flooded her body as fear filled her once again.

"Are you cold, Jane?" Lizzie asked. Her sister reached behind her chair and picked up her brown cardigan sweater. "Here, you can put this on. It'll help keep you warm."

Jane slipped the sweater over her shoulders.

"Thanks, Lizzie."

Charlie turned to Jane. "So, tell us. Do you have any updates on what's happening with you and Noah? Are you going back to San Diego soon?"

Jane ran shaky fingers through her hair in a nervous gesture. "I do have an update. I talked with my neighbor back home and it looks like Devon is still watching the apartment for signs of me or my son. So it doesn't look like we'll be returning any time soon."

"Oh, Jane. I'm sorry." Charlie sighed. "Do you know what you'll be doing then?"

Jane smiled a little. "Lizzie has graciously offered for Noah and I to stay in her house until I can plan my next steps."

Lizzie nodded. "And I'm happy to help, Jane. Stay as long as you need. You're family."

"Thanks, Lizzie. That means the world to me and Noah right now." Jane felt so out of control of her life at the moment.

Fear continued to rampage her thoughts.

She desperately needed hope.

With one hand, she fingered the pearl that hung from the end of her gold chain necklace. Her hand cocooned the pearly white jewel.

Hold onto faith, my dear.

Grams' words whispered from the past.

Jane forced herself to breathe deeply.

"That's great that you'll be staying on the island for a while, Jane. Have you had a chance to get the heirloom jewels appraised?" Alex had always been the sister who didn't like to wait for anything. She was a woman who took action. In many ways, Jane thought Alexandra was the bravest of all her sisters.

Jane wanted to be brave too. But too many fears and insecurities bombarded her mind everyday.

Would she ever be able to get past the trauma she'd experienced in her life, and heal, so she could have courage too?

Jane thought about Alex's question and stammered her answer, "Ward went with me to Boston to visit his friend, who is a gemologist. After inspecting the gems, Mr. Rathburger's appraisal valued Grams' heirloom jewels to be worth so much more than I expected. It's given me hope."

She told her sisters the amount given for the appraisal of the gems.

"Oh, Jane, well, that's wonderful news." Alex's smile widened. "Are you thinking of selling them?"

Jane shrugged. "That's a good question. When I first received the heirloom jewel collection, I thought I would never sell them. However, after being forced to move and live in many different cities for the past few years, I've longed for a home of our own."

Charlie spoke excitedly, "So will you look for a home here in Martha's Vineyard so you can be close to family?"

"Well, I first need to find a buyer for the jewels. But, if I can find someone who is interested in buying them, then I would like to see what homes are available on the island," Jane replied.

She grinned at Charlie's enthusiasm.

Her younger sister had always been so happy when all the sisters got together. She had always inspired a sense of family.

"I know a couple who is wealthy and loves old heirloom collections. I'll talk to them, perhaps they'll be interested in Grams' jewels," Alex said. "If you're interested in selling them, there's no time to waste."

Jane smiled. "Thanks, Alex. I do have the jewels listed for sale on a popular website in Boston for rare collector items. Now we just wait and see."

Katie finally spoke up. "Jane, I'm glad you're thinking

of moving back to the island. I've been thinking about following in your footsteps. You inspire me."

Torrie added her two cents. "I wonder if there are houses in Sweet Beach Cove that Jane would like? We should do some research."

Jane chuckled. "I love you all for your eagerness to help me."

Lizzie looked at Jane. "If you are willing, I'd like to take you to a new house that will be for sale soon. It's the Peterson property. It's a couple miles up the beach. We could walk there."

Jane nodded. "Sure, we could go and take a look."

A FEW MINUTES LATER, all seven sisters began to walk along the beach.

Lizzie and Jane walked together deep in conversation. "I talked with Mrs. Peterson earlier this week. She's the one that told me that they are moving out at the end of the month."

Her oldest sister explained, "She and her husband are getting older and their children don't want the place. They have a small house somewhere else, so they've decided to sell this property. But they are willing to rent the house."

Jane digested this news. "That does sound like a good opportunity."

They walked for a few more minutes until Lizzie turned to walk between some bushes towards a piece of property.

"Follow me. We'll be there soon." Lizzie walked ahead of her and Jane followed close behind.

Soon, Lizzie stopped. Turning to Jane, she said, "Look over there. That's the Peterson place. It's a good sized house on a few acres along the waterfront, Jane. And it comes with a guest house as well."

"I must admit the property looks perfect," Jane whispered.

The house was sprawling and large. It looked like one of those older homes that had been around for decades.

A family home that could be passed down to generations.

"It's such a nice spot and it's along the waterfront too. I wonder if what they are asking for rent will be out of my price range?" Jane turned to Lizzie.

"There's only one way to find out." Lizzie started to walk and headed towards the front door.

"Wait—" Jane tried to stop her sister, but it was too late.

Lizzie knocked on the front door and immediately the door opened to a white-haired lady with glasses.

"Lizzie. How nice to see you." Mrs. Peterson smiled brightly. "And your sisters are here too. Your grandmother would often show me pictures of you girls when we would have our visits. It's so nice of you to stop by. I'm glad you're all here."

Lizzie smiled. "Thanks, Mrs. Peterson. I remember Grams thought of you as a good friend as well."

"She was a good friend. I miss her." The older woman's gray eyes misted. "But I can see little bits of her in all of you, her lovely granddaughters."

A warmth spread over Jane. She hoped that there were little pieces inside of her from her beloved grandmother.

The older woman gestured for them to follow, "Come inside, girls. I'll make a spot of tea for us."

They followed Mrs. Peterson into a beautiful, sprawling home. It was a house with an open view between the kitchen and the living room.

"One of the reasons we stopped by is we wanted to talk to you about your house. When we talked at the grocery store earlier this week, you mentioned that you and your husband had been thinking of selling this place." Lizzie reminded her.

"Yes, yes, of course. And you told me your sister Jane might be interested in looking at our property," the older lady replied.

Lizzie nodded.

Jane said, "I am interested in your house. I want to ask if you're thinking of renting the house?"

"Jane, yes, we were thinking of exactly that. We plan to move to our smaller house in town. We're getting older and it's starting to be more and more difficult to climb the stairs and to clean the place. I'd be happy to show you around the house if you'd like?" The older lady glanced between the girls until her gaze finally landed back on Jane's.

"That would be wonderful, thanks," Jane replied.

"Follow me." The older lady took them upstairs to see the six bedrooms and two washrooms located on the upper floor.

Downstairs were four bedrooms and two washrooms. There was also a large pantry and a large office space.

They finished walking through the house and as they walked to the door, Jane said, "Your home is beautiful, Mrs. Peterson. You have a lot of room here. Lizzie mentioned you also have a guest cottage?"

"Oh my, yes. It's a wonderful three bedroom guest cottage. And, of course, we have eight acres of land. We've enjoyed many family parties and weddings here. There's lots of room."

Jane's heart gave a leap at the older lady's words. It was a house that had known the comfort and laughter of family.

That was the dream that was held the deepest in Jane's heart.

Her thoughts swirled as she looked around at the large main area of the rambling house.

A place for family. A place for generations to live. A place of new beginnings.

She could admit, this property was like that of her dreams.

Words rushed past her lips before fear had a chance to stop her. "It looks like a wonderful family home. What would you be asking for rent?"

The older lady named a figure that seemed reasonable. "I'll get back to you later this week and let you know," Jane replied and soon all the sisters started walking back.

Lizzie beamed. "So, Jane, what did you think? It's a nice spot isn't it?"

"It really is a wonderful home. It's really perfect for Noah and me." Jane paused. "But, before I decide, I first need to see if Grams' jewels will sell for their appraised value."

"Of course, I understand. But I'm pleased to hear you liked the property, Jane," Lizzie added with a big smile.

She loved the Peterson's large home.

It would be the perfect home for her and her son.

In her dreams, she thought of buying the place for her and Noah to have as their forever home.

But Jane couldn't get her hopes up.

What if Grams' jewels didn't sell? Then she wouldn't have the money to live on the island.

She had to think of all the possibilities.

With the many difficulties she'd suffered over the past few years, she wouldn't be surprised if there were more hurdles she needed to overcome.

Would Jane's dream of living in their home for her and her son become a reality — or would it become another impossible dream?

W ard

A WEEK LATER, Ward turned off the video camera and grinned at the gray-haired man seated across from him.

The backyard boasted of lush green poplar trees, perfect for the man with whom he had just interviewed.

His dad.

Ward was convinced his followers on YouTube would love it.

"Thanks for agreeing to talk to me about life on the island when you were a boy, Dad." Ward looked over at his father, who sat comfortably on his soft garden chair in the backyard.

"Son, I'm happy to do it." His dad's voice cracked a little.

George Hampton's age was creeping up on him. He

had just turned eighty-three a week ago. "I hope folks who watch your videos enjoy hearing my stories from the past."

Ward grinned. His dad had always been eager to please. He had a gentle way about him.

Every day Ward was grateful George and Ethel Hampton had adopted him when he was ten years old.

The day they chose him as their son was the best day in his life. There were times when the painful memories of what life was like before he was adopted crept into his thoughts.

However, he did his best to stop dwelling on the bad memories that haunted him. That was the last thing he wanted to focus on today.

Ward was thankful to have been embraced into their family.

He owed almost everything to their love and care for him over the years.

Ward replied, "I'm sure listeners will enjoy it, Dad. I've had several comments over the past few months from folks who want to hear about what life was like on the island years ago. Many people who listen to my videos long to remember the good ol' days and hear from someone who lived back during that time."

Ward packed up his video accessories and turned to his dad. "I just wish I would have had a chance to talk with Mom on video before she died."

"Your mother would have loved that, Ward. She would have thought what you are doing now is wonderful. Your mom always believed in you, son. The way you are bringing joy and inspiration to folks through your videos about island life would have made her happy. She loved this place too." His dad's smile widened. "I still miss your mother."

Ward sighed heavily. "I know you do, Dad. I miss her too."

His dad stood to his feet, his legs a little shaky. Ward walked over to give him support. The older man leaned on him and they began to walk towards the main house.

"Son, I'm grateful you chose to come back to the island to stay. Now that you moved into your old room, I feel happier than I have in years. It's a comfort to know you're nearby." His dad's heart had become even more tender in the past few years.

Ward knew most people would have thought it strange that he moved back to the island, only to move into the same house as his dad.

But they weren't there when he received the phone call last year that his dad had slipped and fallen. The many trips to the hospital afterwards convinced him to retire and come back to his childhood home to help his father.

Ward offered his arm to help his dad inside the house and to his favorite armchair.

"Dad, I'm thankful to be back and living close to you too." Ward gave his dad a familiar fist bump. "Now you just rest. I'll be gone for the evening. I'm meeting someone so I need to get going. Can I get you something to eat or drink before I go?"

"Maybe a glass of water. Thanks, son. Then I think I'll watch my favorite TV show. I ate dinner earlier, so now I'm ready to relax." His dad winked.

Ward grinned. His dad enjoyed sitting in his easy chair

in the evenings. He hurried to fill a glass with water and then placed it on the side table near his dad.

His father's eyes were already beginning to close, so Ward quietly left.

Running upstairs to his bedroom, he quickly changed into comfortable shorts and a t-shirt.

Then, he hurried to the beach where he was to meet Jane Stafford.

His muscles tensed as he thought of talking with Jane.

Would he have the courage to tell her the truth of what happened years ago?

§

THE EVENING WAS STILL WARM, despite the arrival of fall.

As Ward approached the beach, he spotted Jane.

Her beautiful blonde hair hung below her shoulders in thick waves.

She turned towards him.

His breath caught at the sight of her.

Her blue eyes widened and a slow smile formed. Her full lips curved up at the edges, making him feel like he was the only man in the world.

"You came," Jane sighed, her lips quivered slightly, causing him to question if she was nervous too.

For Ward, he was far more nervous.

Anxious knots had formed in his belly since he woke up this morning, as he awaited the serious talk he had promised Jane tonight.

Too many fears tried to stop him from being honest

with her about what happened all those years ago in college.

Would she reject him outright the moment he shared the truth? Would she abandon him and never speak to him again?

As his gaze swept over her, Ward realized deep down he still loved her after all these years. It was the reason fear gripped his soul and wouldn't let go.

Ward swallowed, forcing himself to speak. "I'm sorry for being a little late." His voice cracked with emotion and heat filled his cheeks. "I just needed to help my dad get settled at the house before I met you here. Thanks for waiting for me, Jane."

Jane's eyes widened and slowly she nodded. "That's alright. I didn't realize you were helping your dad, Ward. Of course, now that you're living on the island, that makes sense. It's good that you are close enough to be there for him. Is your father well?"

"As well as can be expected. He just turned eighty-three last week. He's still smart as a whip, but I can tell his body isn't quite as strong as it once was. I'm grateful that I can spend time with him."

Jane smiled. "You're blessed that one of your parents is still alive. I did hear that your mom passed away a few years ago. I'm sorry for your loss."

"Thanks, Jane. It was difficult to lose my mother. She was always my number one cheerleader. But the doctor said her heart just couldn't take it anymore." Ward sighed, running shaky fingers through his hair.

As he thought about his parents, he couldn't help but be reminded of Jane's loss.

"Your parents also passed away when you were still a child, Jane. I'm sorry you went through that difficult time." Ward could relate to the emptiness she must be feeling.

Jane's large blue eyes held a shimmer of tears. Blinking quickly, she looked down for a moment at her feet.

It was a long moment before her eyes sought Ward's again.

"It was a very painful time for me and my six sisters. It's very difficult when you're just a child to be abandoned by your parents — the same people who have been your world."

"It is difficult. I'm so sorry for your loss, Jane." Ward could understand that.

"Thanks, Ward," she said simply and turned to look across the blue water where the orange glow of the sunset touched the ocean.

Perhaps that was the reason his heart had connected with Jane's all those years ago when he had first arrived at Sweet Beach Cove's Elementary School.

Back then he'd noticed Jane right away.

The sadness in her eyes had tugged at his own heart.

When he finally learned that she'd lost both parents, he began to try to get to know her. Throughout the years he had continued to talk with her and, by the time they reached high school, they were good friends.

However, it wasn't until college that they finally began to date.

Regret clung to him like splattered mud.

He had ruined his relationship with Jane the day he left college unexpectedly.

Side-by-side they walked slowly along the beach.

Ward's thoughts spiraled into a tailspin. *Would this woman – whom he still loved after all these years – be willing to forgive him for how he'd hurt her?*

Restless, he couldn't wait any longer.

He needed to tell her the truth of what happened.

"Losing people who are important to you is heart wrenching. Talking about loss reminds me of the reason I left college — and you — without warning, years ago." His voice was raw and full of meaning.

Jane stopped. Turning towards him, her eyes were focused and intense. "Why did you do it, Ward?"

Turning to face her fully, he swallowed, feeling the pulsing nervous tick in his jawline.

Fear tried to stop him from telling the truth.

But he refused to give in to anxious thoughts.

Jane needed him to finally be honest after all these years.

No matter how difficult it was to tell the truth and face her possible rejection, he would tell her the part of his life that he'd been scared to share before now.

"Because I was worried about my past catching up to me." The words rushed out, his voice raw. "I have hardly told anyone about my background, but I wanted to tell you. The truth is, I should've told you a long time ago. I'm sorry I didn't."

Jane slowly nodded. Her blue eyes flickered with worry.

Did she imagine the worst about him?

Shoving down the fear that coiled in his belly, Ward began to share what happened.

It was his last hope to mend the rift between them.

"I lost my birth parents when I was a child. My mom and dad were both addicted to drugs. My mom faced abuse at the hands of my father and, in the end, out of his mind, my dad beat my mother within an inch of her life. She ended up dying in the hospital."

A gasp escaped Jane's lips. "How horrible. I'm so sorry, Ward."

He ran shaky fingers through his hair, nervousness getting the better of him.

Determined, he continued, "After that, my home life got worse. My dad was arrested and put in jail after the beating that killed my mother. I was thrust into a foster home at seven years old and was placed in different homes until I was ten years old. That was when George and Ethel Hampton adopted me and brought me to live in their home."

When Ward turned to look over at Jane, he was surprised to see moisture glistening in her large violet blue eyes.

"I didn't realize you suffered so much heartache in your childhood." She hesitated before she began, "I'm so sorry you were forced to endure so much abuse, Ward. It must have been terrible."

He nodded. "It was. At the time, that way of life was all I knew. The day George and Ethel Hampton discovered me in that foster home, my whole world changed."

She smiled gently. "I can imagine the relief you must have felt."

He nodded slowly and swallowed back emotion. Looking down, he scuffed his shoe on the sand, not speaking for a moment.

After a slight pause, Jane broke the silence between them. "But I'm confused. I don't quite understand how your childhood is connected to the reason you left college years ago. Can you tell me more?"

"Sure." Ward rubbed the back of his neck, asking himself how to begin. "When I was about two months into my year at college, I was doing well and was at the top of most other students in my class."

He explained, "However, Ben Traveers, one of my classmates, didn't like that or felt threatened or something. Anyway, he began to mock me in front of his friends, until one day he forced a confrontation and blackmailed me."

Jane's eyes widened. "What sort of blackmail?"

Pain stabbed at his heart as he remembered. "Ben told me that he had done some digging into my past. He'd found a newspaper article from when I was a child that spoke in detail of my birth mom and dad's drug addiction.

Ward's eyes held pain as he remembered, "Ben told me the article told details of my birth dad's conviction on the beating death of my birth mom and after that I was placed into foster care."

He breathed in a shaky breath, reliving the trauma of his past. "Ben Traveers' father owned one of the largest broadcasting news stations in the country. Ben made it clear that if I didn't leave college, he would spread my childhood story far and wide. His biggest threat was that I wouldn't be able to get a job in broadcasting at most news stations across the nation."

"So that's why you transferred suddenly to a different

college." Jane sighed softly as she digested this information.

Wade nodded. "Yeah. I didn't want my terrible past to ruin any chances I had of landing a career in broadcasting."

Jane shook her head. "I can't believe one of your classmates at college would stoop so low. Blackmail is one of the worst types of threats anyone can make. Telling tall tales about someone else to force them to do what you want is an act of desperation."

He could only nod in agreement.

From somewhere deep inside, new hope blossomed.

The way she defended him was an encouraging sign.

She hadn't run away from him yet, even after he shared the horrible truth about his past.

If she was staying to listen to him, did that mean she still cared for him, even a little?

"Thanks for telling me your story, Ward. Now, I understand a little better the reason you unexpectedly left college years ago." Jane sighed heavily.

Her violet-blue eyes lifted until her gaze held onto his.

"Ward, I'm sorry you were blackmailed." She hesitated.

A crease formed between her brows as she studied him.

With shaky fingers she tucked a stray tendril of hair behind one ear. "But I still don't understand why you didn't say anything to me back then. All you told me was that you had decided to leave and transfer to another college. I was devastated, confused, and hurt when you suddenly left."

"I'm so sorry for leaving without a word, Jane. I never

wanted to hurt you." Regret flooded him. "I regret it. I don't have any excuse for how I treated you. All I can do is explain, if you want to hear it."

"I do." Hurt lingered on her features.

Ward longed to pull her into his arms. He yearned to make things right between them.

He ached for her forgiveness.

"It was insecurity and fear that stopped me from telling you the real reason I left college." Ward rubbed the back of his neck. With a shaky voice he continued to explain, "I was afraid that if I told you about my past — my secret shame — that you would reject me and leave me."

Jane sucked in a quick breath. "You believed if I knew about your terrible childhood, I would reject you?"

"I did." Swallowing quickly, he nodded and looked down at his sandaled feet.

From his flawed and broken childhood, he had learned the hard way that when people love you, it could be used against you.

He learned that when you were vulnerable with people you loved, it only led to pain and heartache.

Jane's eyes widened in understanding.

She hadn't known until today that Ward had deep scars and unhealed trauma of shame and rejection.

He had always been a very private person. Only sharing details about himself that were necessary.

After listening to Ward describe his terrible childhood suffering, the fears he referred to began to make sense.

"I'm sorry you believed I would have rejected you, Ward. Reflecting on our relationship back then, I think I would have listened, sympathized and been supportive of your decision," Jane continued.

Ward nodded. "I regret that I doubted you, Jane."

She sighed. "Thank you for that. However, now that I understand what happened, perhaps it goes to show how very little trust we had between the two of us in our college years. And maybe it also shows that a relationship between us wasn't meant to be."

Jane was surprised by the downcast look on Ward's face.

He looked down at his empty hands, a crease between his brows. Unexpectedly, his dark eyes fastened with a fierceness onto hers.

"I don't believe that, Jane. Maybe, years ago, it wasn't the right time for us, but in the years since, we have both matured and grown. I can't help but believe that maybe we've been given a second chance," Ward murmured.

Jane sighed heavily. "I'm not convinced of that. You see, I found out the hard way from my ex-husband that love can be cruel. And it not only affected me, but my son, Noah."

A flash of pain crossed over his features. "I am truly sorry to hear that, Jane."

He leaned closer. "But not all relationships are like that. It doesn't have to be that way."

"So I've been told by my sisters." Jane didn't know how

she could ever come to believe again in a love that was real, after the abuse she suffered from her ex-husband.

"If you give me another chance, Jane, I believe I can convince you that we can establish trust again." Ward persisted, "I would like for the two of us to grow in friendship and learn to trust each other again. Perhaps in time, that could grow into something more."

Jane could only shake her head. "I don't know, Ward. I don't think I'm ready for a relationship. There's too much pain from my past to consider that now. Not only that, but I don't want my son to be hurt by a man in my life. I've been very protective of Noah."

"That's understandable." Ward stared at her for the longest time, deep in thought.

"I'm truly sorry for how I abandoned you and caused you pain, Jane. I hope someday you can forgive me." His voice trembled with the fervency of his longing.

Jane sighed heavily. "You hurt me, Ward. I do wish you could have trusted me enough to tell me what was happening to you back then, Ward."

"After listening to what happened to you in college, now I understand better why you left. I do forgive you. But, to be honest with you, I think it will take some time for us to trust each other again."

His head bowed for a long moment before he finally looked up.

Ward's dark eyes searched hers and he spoke in a low voice, "I understand. And I will take whatever you have to offer me, Jane. I do want us to get to know each other better again. I am quite determined to be a help and support to you. I want to be there for you no matter what."

There was a new resolve in his tone of voice that surprised her. "I must tell you, I am very determined to win you back, Jane."

She couldn't help but smile at his determination.

Jane hesitated for a moment as she thought over his words. "Maybe we could go slow and begin to grow our friendship again, Ward. Perhaps, in time, that might lead to the beginning of trust."

"I'm happy to hear you say that, Jane." He smiled broadly. Reaching for her hands, he kissed the inside of her palms. "I really want to know how I can begin to earn your trust."

Heat rose up to her cheeks at his show of affection.

She liked his compliments a little too much.

Maybe this was the right time to warn him about her situation.

"In all honesty, you might change your mind about me," Jane began, trying to find the courage to tell Ward about her biggest fear.

"I've decided to move back to the island with my son, but you might find trouble in the wings, if you choose to be my friend. You might not like the drama that surrounds my life."

"I'm confident I won't change my mind about you, Jane. But I'm curious. What do you mean by drama?" He leaned close, his brows creased together.

"I have lots of drama coming and going in my life. Over the years, my life has become a little more complicated. I have mysteries that I need to solve and somebody who is a threat to me and my son. I don't think you'll want to get too close to me, because it might involve trouble."

Ward shrugged. "I would rather stay by your side and help you, then worry about you, Jane. First of all, what mystery are you referring to?"

Jane hurried to explain. "My parents' death years ago. The police said the case was solved and labeled it a boating accident. But my late grandmother asked us sisters to dig deeper in the journals she left behind for us to read."

"That's interesting." Ward rubbed his fingers on his chin as he thought. "If you're digging deeper into what happened the night your parents died, I want to help."

Jane raised one eyebrow in surprise. "Are you sure you want to do that, Ward? It might be risky. In fact, Lizzie asked me to talk to you about helping us, but I thought it was too much to ask."

"It's never too much to ask, when the situation involves danger to you, Jane," Ward insisted. "So, tell me, how did your sister think I could help?"

She shrugged. "Lizzie thought you might be willing to talk with Officer Shelton. He was your friend years ago."

"Neville and I are still good friends." Ward added, "Why do you want me to talk to him?"

"Lizzie believes that if we can talk with a police officer who works in the same department as Officer Ryan Hart and Sheriff Hart, that we might be able to uncover some information. For instance, why does the Sheriff still refuse our request to reopen the case? Is he afraid of something?" Jane's fingers rubbed her arms as a sudden gust of wind blew in her direction.

Ward was silent for a long while. "Those are tough questions. But I will have that talk with Neville. Maybe, he'll be able to help us out."

"I hope so too. My sisters and I really want answers to what really happened to our parents years ago." Jane ran a shaky hand through her blond hair.

"You also mentioned there is somebody who's a danger to you and your son. Who is that?" A deep crease of worry formed between his brows.

Jane hurriedly reached into her pocket and pulled out her smartphone. After a minute she showed him an old photo.

Fear coiled in her belly as she stared at the photo. "This is the guy. My ex. At some point, Devon will most likely find out I've moved to the island. I can't help but think he'll follow me here, when he learns where Noah and I are. He's a terrible man. I wanted to warn you now. I don't want you to be hurt or worse because of your friendship with me, Ward."

One of Jane's biggest fears was that her son, or somebody she cared about, would be hurt because of her ex-husband.

Ward slid his thumbs into the belt loops of his pants and replied with a firm voice, "I refuse to be afraid of your ex-husband. This is the same man who abused you. He can try to harm me, but he'll fail. Don't worry about me."

He reached for her hand and squeezed it softly.

She smiled slowly in response.

Ward went on, "One other thing, if your ex-husband tries to hurt you, Jane, you can be sure I'll do everything in my power to protect you."

Her heart skipped a beat at his words of protection and care.

It was strange how her mind was numb and analytical while her emotions were alive and reawakening.

"You would do that for me?" Jane began in a shaky voice that trailed off.

It had been so very long since any man had offered to care for, and protect her.

A strange warmth flooded every cell of her body.

"Don't you know that I'd do anything for you, Jane?" Ward's lips slowly descended to meet hers.

Her knees weakened as his lips moved against hers in a series of slow, shivery kisses.

She was shocked at her own eager response.

Suddenly, he pulled away, his dark eyes staring into hers.

Her senses reeled and her mouth was left burning with fire.

Ward slipped one arm around her shoulders, pulling her close to his side.

Together they watched the sunset on the ocean.

Standing by her side, Ward whispered softly, "All I ever wanted was to hold you in my arms again, Jane."

Her heart fluttered at his words, which shocked her.

She didn't want to feel anything for this man other than a slight friendship.

But Ward's romantic words of care, protection, and his longing for a closer relationship with her, stirred her heart.

Yet, at the same time, fear pushed its way back.

Fears and mistrust plagued her, and she was convinced

she would be hurt again if she allowed this man into her life.

Her worries of abandonment, rejection, and pain were at the top of her list of reasons to avoid a relationship with this man.

For now — until she was sure that she could trust him — she chose to push down the stirrings of attraction.

Until proven otherwise, Ward Hampton was off limits.

She needed reasons to trust the man who jilted her. That trust would need to be earned.

ane

"Yesterday, I talked with a wealthy couple who want to buy your grandmother's heirloom jewels, Jane." The agent with whom she had listed the jewels spoke over the phone with her.

The man explained, "Under our security team's watchful eye, they've already seen the jewels first-hand. They are ready to sign the papers and send you payment."

Jane sucked in a breath. "Wow. That was quick. They are willing to offer the appraised value?"

"Yes. They're eager buyers," the agent added.

"Alright then. I'm ready to sell my grandmother's jewels," Jane agreed. It was time. She needed to sell those beautiful gems so she could fulfill her part of the bargain with her son.

She desperately wanted to do everything in her power to give Noah the real home he longed for.

In the past few years, Noah had often talked about his desire for her to marry a man who would be kind to both of them so they could be a family.

Noah yearned to have a dad in his life who would accept him, play ball with him, a dad who would love him.

Jane was hesitant. She had already been hurt by one man, she didn't think she was ready to try again.

Ward's words from their walk on the beach circled round and round in her mind.

I am very determined to win you back, Jane.

His words of regret and heartfelt apology, for how he had suddenly left her in college years ago, had touched her heart.

When Ward had explained the reason he left so quickly — and the classmate who tried to blackmail him — she had been horrified that anyone could be that mean.

However, just because she forgave Ward and his words had touched her, didn't mean she was ready to begin a relationship with him.

No, she wasn't about to jump into a relationship a second time until she was sure she could trust him.

Maybe, as they spent time together to learn more about the mystery of how her parents died, trust between them would grow.

Time would tell.

A WEEK LATER, Jane walked beside Lizzie to *Yarn Around the Cove*, the quilt and yarn shop on Main Street.

She adjusted her wide brimmed hat so it hung low over her eyes. It was an everyday habit to hide her identity.

"Did you get everything settled with the sale of Grams' jewels?" Lizzie asked as they neared Mrs. O'Connor's quilt and yarn shop.

Jane nodded. "Yes. I'm still surprised how quickly a buyer was found. I feel good about it."

"I'm glad." Lizzie turned to her. "Have you decided if you're going to lease the Peterson's house?"

She grinned. "Yes. I called Mrs. Peterson last night and went to sign the papers to lease the house."

"Oh, Jane. I'm so happy for you." Lizzie slipped one arm around her shoulders. "Now you'll be living close by. How is Noah feeling about the move?"

Jane recalled her son's smiling face when she told him the news. "Noah is excited. He keeps asking for us to stay for good and make our home on the island. And he's making friends at school."

"Jane, I think your son's plan for the two of you to stay in our island community is a wonderful idea. You should consider buying the Peterson property after you have the money from the sale of Grams' jewels."

Searing pain from the past few years clenched like a knot in her belly.

Her words rushed out in a hoarse whisper, "I know Noah's plan is to stay, but I don't see how it would be possible, Lizzie. The reason why I only rented the Peterson house was because I was sure I would need to move away again. Devon is sure to find me and Noah. I don't know when, but I wouldn't be surprised if it's sooner rather than later."

Lizzie stopped in her tracks and turned her way. "Jane, look at me. I understand you're afraid of the past catching up with you and of what Devon might do to you or your son. But, I really think it's time for you to stop running. Even if your ex-husband found you here, what could he do? You have more protection by staying here on the island than you would if you lived anywhere else."

"Maybe. I just don't know." Unshed tears misted Jane's eyes.

Lizzie went on, "I believe it's time, Jane. And one other thing. If you've been thinking of setting up your business license here as a wedding planner, I think you should set it up in your real name."

Jane gasped. Her blue eyes grew large with surprise.

"I don't know how much Devon knows about me. He did find where I lived in San Diego, even though I used my fake name. I admit, I'm still scared that it'll be easier for him to find me if I use my real name." Jane swallowed back fear.

"He might find you. But we would do everything possible to ensure the safety of you and Noah," Lizzie whispered. "Jane, you could finally get rid of those sunglasses, the black wig, and your oversized hat. You could finally be who you are. You are braver than most women I know, dearest sister. I believe you could do this."

A shiver of fear ran through her at Lizzie's words.

In her heart, Jane knew that her life of constantly

running away needed to end. If she couldn't do it for herself, she needed to do it for her son.

Could she give up the self-made protective barriers she had placed around her and Noah?

Was it possible to finally be who she really was meant to be? After all these years could she finally be herself?

Jane turned to her sister and looked her in the eye. "I will think about what you've said, Lizzie. It's very difficult for me to think of getting rid of the protective barriers I've placed around me and my son. But I promise I'll think about it."

Lizzie hugged her and whispered, "Good, I'm glad. Now, let's go enjoy some time with friends and stitch another memory quilt."

GRAMS' long-time friend Mrs. O'Connor had started *Yarn Around the Cove* when the weekly craft meetings at her home had become much too large.

There were many folks in the Sweet Beach Cove community who loved to quilt, sew, knit, crochet, and create different kinds of crafts.

The older widowed woman sold yarn, sewing material, and all sorts of accessories for the crafters in the area.

She glanced around the large room.

Rows of shop shelves were filled with many different types and colors of yarn. Knitting needles and crochet hooks of many sizes hung on pegs on a nearby wall.

As her gaze lifted higher, she noticed two walls

covered with baby quilts, wedding quilts, and memory quilts.

The shop was a testament to the dedication that the crafters of their community had to creating their art.

For some reason, it inspired Jane. It stirred her emotions.

It also unnerved her.

It reminded her of the day she quit on her own dream.

Memories and regret flooded her. She had been so in despair when Ward abandoned her that she quit everything important in her life.

Somewhere from deep inside rose up a longing inside Jane for her dreams to be re-kindled.

But, as soon as that hope rose to the surface, she tamped it down.

Her dream wasn't possible for her. Not anymore.

Jane had learned from the last seven years of constantly trying to outrun her ex that nothing in her life was safe or constant.

She had stopped expecting things to turn out differently.

So she would enjoy the fleeting moments of being with the community, like tonight's quilting bee, when she could.

Her musings were interrupted by her best friend.

"Hello, Jane," her friend Kenna called out to her, waving.

She turned head and waved back.

Kenna finished her conversation with a few ladies from the Sweet Beach Cove community quilters. She had always been so good at connecting with others.

Hurrying towards her, Kenna wrapped one arm around her shoulders before she said, "Jane, I'm grateful you could make it today."

Jane whispered to her friend, "Thanks, Kenna."

Her fingers shook a little as she touched the black wig.

"Stop worrying. Tonight, you're with neighbors and friends you've known since childhood. What could be more wholesome or safe?" Kenna grinned.

Jane nodded. "You're probably right."

Even as she said that, she couldn't help glancing around the shop once more.

She reminded herself that she had told her sisters that she would try to step out farther away from fear and into faith.

The room was filled with many people she knew from years ago. Ida Cantrell was here along with her daughter Nettie Cantrell and her granddaughter, Ava Cantrell-Worth.

Ida's sister-in-law, Florrie Cantrell-Jones, was there with her daughter Linda Hart.

Jane wasn't surprised to see both younger people and the older generation, like widow Jean Bellanger and retired doctor, Grace Waverly, at the quilting bee.

Her sisters Lizzie, Alex, and Charlie were in conversation with their friends. It was nice to catch up with friends like Debbie McVay, Becca Weatherstone, and Charlie's good friend Angie Dickson.

She spotted Lizzie's daughter, Annie, chatting with Sarah O'Connor and Debbie's two daughters, Emma and Olivia.

It did her heart good to see the younger women at the quilting bee.

Mrs. O'Connor stepped over to speak into the microphone. "Ladies, I'm glad you could all join us tonight. If you're ready to begin, find a spot around one of the square quilting frames. We will have four to six women at each quilting frame. That way, when each large square piece is finished, we'll be ready to sew all the squares together to form a large quilt."

The women walked towards the eight quilting frames that were located in the middle of the large craft shop.

Mrs. O'Connor spoke again into the microphone, "Tonight, we'll be starting another quilt for one of the first families that came to Sweet Beach Cove. It's a secret for now, but don't worry, all will be revealed soon enough. Remember, ladies, this is a memory quilt stitched with love from all of us in our community. Let's enjoy working together and have fun."

The ladies each began to find the quilting square they would work on for tonight.

"Come, Jane, let's find a spot." Kenna slipped her hand through her arm and steered her towards a quilting frame in the middle of the room.

Kenna sat down at the farthest edge and next to her sat a woman she didn't recognize.

"Adele Hayes, I want to introduce you to my best friend, Jane Stafford," Kenna said.

A twenty-something woman with brunette hair and large brown eyes turned to her.

She nodded with a shaky smile. "Nice to meet you, Jane."

Jane pulled out the chair and sat down next to Adele. Turning, she looked over at the younger woman.

Her brows creased in a frown of what looked like worry. Her fingers fiddled nervously on her lap.

"This is my first time stitching in a long time. Do you like to quilt?" Jane whispered softly to the young woman.

Adele nodded slightly. "Sort of. Violet Hayes insisted that I come tonight. I'm trying to please my new mother-in-law, so I thought I would come to the quilting bee."

"That's good of you." Jane was trying to remember who Adele married. "You must have married Ron Hayes then?"

"Yes, I did," the young bride whispered. "We married one year ago."

"Congratulations on your marriage," Jane spoke softly.

Adele nodded and whispered thanks. But then she noticed the young woman quickly glance over to where Violet Hayes was seated.

The young woman seemed to visibly shrink inside herself at the sight of her mother-in-law. Or was she imagining things?

Jane was about to say something else, when a woman on her other side spoke to her.

She turned her head to see the much older widow Jean Bellanger sitting on her other side.

"Jane Stafford, I hardly recognized you. It's wonderful to see you back on the island."

"Thanks, Mrs. Bellanger. It's good to be back home," Jane replied. She wondered how the older widow woman was keeping. "How have you been?"

"I'm well enough. The odd aches and pains act up every once in a while, but it never keeps me down for long," the older lady replied. "But never mind about me, tell me about you. You've been away from the island for a long time, Jane dear. Tell me how you've been."

The older widowed lady gently patted her hand, much like her late grandmother used to do when she wanted to talk.

Emotion swelled up inside Jane and she blinked back the prick of tears that threatened to overcome her.

A vivid memory returned swiftly of Mrs. Bellanger as she sat on the deck beside Grams, drinking sweet tea.

The memory brought with it the inescapable feeling of acceptance, belonging, and love.

The older lady looked at her, seemingly concerned.

Jane's voice cracked a little when she replied, "I *have* been away for a long time. But I'm back for the foreseeable future. I have my son, Noah, with me as well."

"Good. Your son will like the island. I know Matty did. He had so many good friends. Your father, John Stafford, was his best friend. Did you know that?" Mrs. Bellanger asked.

"Grams wrote in her journal that my dad's best friend was your son, Matty. I'm sorry for the loss of your son, Mrs. Bellanger." Jane couldn't imagine the heartbreak of losing Noah.

"Thank you, my dear. It was a very long time ago, but a mother never forgets her children. For me, Matty's loss was a wound that never fully healed. I still miss him." The older widow's eyes misted with unshed tears.

"I'm sure you do." Jane hesitated and then asked, "You know, my sisters and I are trying to find more answers about what happened the day our parents died in that boating accident. But I also question if the police investigated the death of Matty enough to find out the real truth. I would like more answers to those questions."

"I've often wondered that as well." The older lady nodded. "Well, if you have questions you want to ask me, feel free to do so. I'll tell you what I remember."

Hope ignited in Jane's heart. Maybe learning more details of Matty's death would somehow reveal more about what happened to her parents.

Jane nodded. "I really appreciate that. I did want to ask you a few questions. For instance, are there details you remember about the day Matty and his friends went diving for treasure? Anything that seemed strange?"

Mrs. Bellanger leaned over and whispered, "I thought it was strange that Matty agreed to go when he knew Ted Cantrell, Bobby Sutton, and Jerry Hart were part of the group. Matty had always told me he never really got along with them. However, Matty told me many times that John Stafford — your father — was his best friend."

Jane thought about that for a minute. "That is odd that your son would agree to go along with their plan if he didn't really want to spend time with the other three boys."

"I think Matty wanted to please your dad, Jane. Matty always said how loyal and helpful John was to him. My son would have done anything for him," Mrs. Bellanger whispered softly with a gentle smile.

Jane couldn't help but be pleased that her dad was such a good friend to Matthew Bellanger.

"Was there anything else that seemed odd about that

day?" Since they were on the subject, Jane thought she might as well ask.

"Now that you mention it, there was one other thing," the older lady said softly. "I explained it to the sheriff at the time, but he told me it wasn't important. I told the sheriff it was very difficult for me to believe that my son, Matty, died by drowning."

The widow continued to explain, "You see, my son was an excellent swimmer. In fact, he had just completed his life guard certification and had already saved many people from drowning. He was as good on water as he was on land. That's one of the reasons I found my son's death so hard to believe."

Jane sucked in a breath.

That really did seem strange. *How could Matty have died by drowning when he was an excellent swimmer? Was there foul play involved with Matty's death?*

Jane quickly asked. "Did the police say they found evidence of a head wound that could've rendered him unconscious?"

The older widow shook her head, "No, they simply told me my son had drowned."

"Who was the sheriff at that time?" Jane felt like she needed more answers.

"Sheriff Elias Hart. Jerry Hart's father," the older widow replied.

Jane couldn't help but ponder that bit of information.

"Did Matty say anything else about his friends that you remember?" Jane asked.

"Not to me. But, before my son died, he had written in a journal every day since he was ten years old. If you're curious and would like to read his journal, I'd be happy to lend it to you, Jane." The old widow smiled.

"Would you? That would be very helpful. Thank you, Mrs. Bellanger." Jane sighed in relief. Maybe it would be possible they would find some answers to the mystery behind her parents' deaths after all.

"You're welcome, my dear. Stop by my house anytime and you can pick it up." The older widow turned to her with a smile before she began to stitch her row on the quilt.

Jane pulled the yarn onto her needle, a feeling of uneasiness flooding her at the new information Matty's mother had just revealed to her.

She could only hope Matty's journal would reveal more answers to secrets that the island community, so far, had refused to surrender.

MOST PEOPLE WERE JUST LEAVING the quilt shop, when Jane stopped and talked with some of the women she remembered from her childhood.

Miss Sadie walked towards Jane with her older sister, Miss Hattie. These two beautiful African American women had been really good friends of her beloved grandmother.

"Jane Stafford, I hope you are back on this island for good." Miss Sadie reached over and gave her a hug, as did her sister Miss Hattie.

She couldn't help but feel welcome and valuable as she talked with these two women.

"Just this morning I agreed to rent the old Peterson house. So, I guess I am hoping to stay on the island, Miss Sadie." Jane smiled.

Miss Sadie leaned closer. "Sugar, there ain't no hoping you'll stay. There's only deciding. Your dear grandmother, God rest her soul, would always tell me she longed for the day that all her granddaughters would move back to the island to stay. Ain't that right, Hattie?"

Jane sighed. She'd forgotten how formidable the two sisters were when they tag-teamed each other in a conversation.

"That's right, Sadie. Jane, you've got to decide to stay. Be bold and make a decision. Ain't no use letting fear hold you back. Fear never did anybody no good anyhow. Have faith, be brave, and decide to take what you want. Take back what you lost." Miss Hattie placed her hands on ample hips, her brown eyes focused on Jane's, "It's your time to return to our community. It's time to come back home to stay."

Tears pricked the back of Jane's eyelids and she quickly blinked them away.

"I know you're both right. My sister said the same thing earlier today." She stumbled a little over her words. "Things are so complicated in my life right now. But you're right, I have lots of fears about coming back to live on the island for good."

Miss Hattie leaned close and whispered, "Don't let fear do the decidin' for you, sugar. Instead, let love and faith be stronger than fear. That's when you'll know you're going in the right direction."

Jane nodded, swallowing back emotion. "I remember

Grams told me the same thing. Coming back to the island brings back so many painful memories. Like my parents' deaths in that boating accident."

Miss Sadie slipped an arm around her shoulders. "We know, sugar. But perhaps the island is where you need to be to heal from the past."

Jane shrugged. "Maybe. It's difficult when the island is the place where I have most of the painful memories. One of the biggest questions I have is, "What really happened to my parents?"

"Are you looking for an old journal or some old pictures or something, Jane?" Miss Sadie asked.

Jane nodded. "Yes. Something that would help me dig deeper into the details of what happened."

"My sister has been taking photos of folks and land-marks on this island most of her life." Miss Sadie grinned. "Hattie isn't just a wonderful cook at my diner, she's also a memory keeper with her large collection of pictures."

Miss Hattie sent her a gap-toothed smile. "I surely am. You need to come visit me sometime, Jane. I have lots and lots of pictures to show you. It might help bring back some memories. Maybe some of them will help bring the truth to light."

"Maybe that's true." Jane offered a shaky smile.

"That's good then, sugar." Miss Hattie grinned. "Come visit me next week. We'll have tea."

Jane's smile widened. "Thanks, Miss Hattie. I'll do that."

"Oh, I just saw another friend we need to chat with," Miss Sadie said. "We'll talk with you later, Jane."

Jane watched as the two sisters walked away.

She couldn't help but feel hopeful that, as she looked through Miss Hattie's photos, she might find one or two things that would help to uncover another missing piece of the mystery.

Jane turned and began walking towards the outside door, when she was stopped by the kindly face of an older woman.

"Jane Stafford, is that you?"

Jane smiled warmly.

Suddenly, she remembered the reason this woman's face was so familiar. "Hello, Mrs. Morrison. How nice to see you again. How have you been doing?"

"Not as well as I'd like. But that might be because my three children have married and are living so far away. I'm all alone in my home now. I miss when you and my daughter Shelly would stop by after school and come inside for freshly baked cookies," Mrs. Morrison sighed. "Oy, I'm sorry. I'm just rattling on and on. How are you doing, Jane? Are you married?"

Jane shifted on her feet.

This was a common question that almost everyone asked now that she returned. She couldn't help but feel uncomfortable having to explain herself. In the end, she told people the shortened version of her story.

"I'm no longer married, Mrs. Morrison. But I do have a twelve-year-old son, Noah." Jane smiled.

"Oh my, how wonderful that you have a son. My husband died when we were only married for ten years. And I was left with my three daughters. But Shelly, my youngest daughter, moved away last year. You're so blessed to have your son with you, Jane."

"Thanks, Mrs. Morrison. He's a wonderful boy. I'm thankful for him," Jane replied.

The grey-haired lady asked, "What are you doing for work, now that you're back on the island?"

"I was thinking I would set up my business license as a wedding planner. I've done that for the past few years. It's work that's familiar to me," Jane replied.

She explained, "Although, I'm not sure how I'll keep busy with that and keep an eye on my son as well. Sometimes, as a wedding planner, evenings and weekends can be busy. So I guess I'll need to figure out how to make that work."

The widow suddenly smiled. "Well then, I have the perfect solution for you, my dear."

"What's that?"

"I would be willing to be your housekeeper and cook, Jane. It would be an honor to take care of your son each day after school." The older woman smiled wide.

Jane thought for a moment, and was thrilled with the idea. "That would be wonderful. But do you have the time?"

"Oh, my dear. I have nothing but time. Having a young boy to look after and cooking for the two of you would make me feel useful again. I wouldn't be so lonely. Taking care of you both would be my pleasure," Mrs. Morrison prattled excitedly at the prospect.

A surge of warmth flooded Jane.

"I would really like that, Mrs. Morrison." Jane grinned. "I will let you know if the Sweet Beach Cove community accepts my application for a business license. If they do, I'll be calling you."

"Your business application will be approved, Jane." Mrs. Morrison grinned. "I have no doubt about that."

"Thanks for your vote of confidence, Mrs. Morrison. I appreciate that." Jane looked around and saw her sister Lizzie waiting by the door for her. "I've got to go, but I'll see you later, Mrs. Morrison."

"Of course, my dear. I'll talk with you later," The kind-hearted widow said softly just before Jane walked outside.

As she walked home with Lizzie, Jane couldn't help but smile.

"You know, Lizzie, I had some very good conversations tonight." Jane explained about her talk with Mrs. Bellanger, Miss Sadie, Miss Hattie, and Mrs. Morrision. "I have a feeling we will be able to learn more answers about the mystery surrounding our parents' boating accident after all."

"Jane, that's amazing. I can hardly believe it. Let's hope and pray that we'll find new answers to our questions soon." Lizzie slipped one arm around Jane and together they walked down the path toward the beach cottage.

Jane released a sigh of contentment and leaned her head against her sister's shoulder.

Could it be possible that moving back to the island might be a new beginning for her and Noah and a deeper relationship with her family?

Her fingers gripped the pearl dangling at the end of her necklace.

Jane could only hope that her dreams of a deeper and closer relationship with Noah and her sisters would come true.

CHAPTER EIGHT

WARD'S MIND was on Jane as he uploaded and saved the latest video to his YouTube channel.

He needed to call her about what he had just learned.

Reaching for his phone, he dialed Jane's number.

Ward hoped she would be happy to hear the latest news.

"Hi, this is Jane," her sleepy voice answered his call.

"Jane, this is Ward. I'm sorry if I woke you." Regret flooded him. He didn't even bother to look at the time.

It was quite late in the evening.

"That's alright, Ward. Why did you call?"

Ward replied, "I wanted to tell you the news. Neville called me. He asked if we could come over to his place tomorrow. He has those documents."

"That was fast. Alright, let's meet him tomorrow evening." Jane's tone of voice grew more alert at the news. "I hope we learn something that will help us fill in the missing pieces."

"I do too. I'll pick you up, Jane. We can drive to his place together." Ward suggested.

"Sure. Thanks, Ward."

"Happy to do it. I'll see you tomorrow, Jane. I hope you'll be able to get back to sleep," he whispered.

"I will, don't worry. Good night, Ward." Jane's soft words only increased the ache in his heart to have this beautiful woman by his side forever. Perhaps, by helping Jane find more clues about the mystery of her parents' deaths, it would help to gain her trust.

With all his heart, he hoped she would open up her heart to him.

He was determined not to give up.

It was just after the evening meal that Ward stopped by to pick up Jane.

She was waiting for him on the front deck at Lizzie's beach cottage.

Ward thought she looked beautiful in her purple t-shirt and jeans. He was still trying to get used to the black wig she always wore.

He hoped, in time, Jane would feel safe enough with him that she could be completely herself with him.

As they arrived at the condo building, Ward parked in the visitor's parking lot.

"Are you eager to learn what Neville discovered?" Ward asked Jane as they took the elevator to the police officer's top floor condo.

"I am. But I'm also a little worried about what we'll discover," Jane replied as they walked down the long hallway.

Ward stopped at the door at the end of the hallway and knocked. "I guess we're about to find out."

Officer Neville Shelton looked different without his police uniform.

"Ward and Jane, come on in."

They followed him to the kitchen table. On top of the table was a large screen computer monitor.

"Have a seat. And I'll show you what I've found." Neville pointed to three chairs facing the computer screen.

Neville sat on the chair in the middle and began to click the mouse. Documents began to appear on the computer screen. "Just so you know, I could get in trouble for sharing this information with you. So please don't tell anyone where you got it from."

"Of course," Jane said.

Ward nodded in agreement. He certainly didn't want his friend to get in trouble. Neville was putting his career on the line to help them out.

His friend clicked on the mouse, scrolling until he found the archived document.

"I have documents here as far back as when your parents died and up until last year." Neville turned towards Jane. "When I searched the archived files, Jane, this is what I found."

"Here's some handwritten notes about this case: *The Sweet Beach Cove police investigation into the deaths of John and Anne Stafford took six months and revealed the following:*

The night of September twenty was when the boating accident occurred near the Cove.

It was a stormy night and there was only one other boat on the water besides the Stafford boat. The second boat belonged to Fergus McGee. At first, Mr. McGee was thought to be a suspect in the deaths of John and Anne Stafford. Mr. McGee's skill as a diver, his long-time experience with boats, and his location near the damaged Stafford boat gave him opportunity.

However, a few weeks after the initial report, a witness came forward who saw Fergus McGee on his boat in front of his waterfront property around the same time that John and Anne Stafford died.

After learning of Mr. McGee's alibi, the charges against him were dropped. Shortly thereafter, Sheriff Jerry Hart concluded that the deaths of John and Anne Stafford were an accident.

"That's all that was documented about my parents' deaths?" Jane's eyes widened in surprise. "It doesn't seem like a very thorough police investigation."

Ward nodded. "I agree. What do you make of it, Neville?"

A crease of worry dug deep grooves between Officer Shelton's brows.

"This short note about what the police found worries me a little. I find it strange that, after six months of searching, they only found one suspect, who later it was discovered had an alibi." The police officer sighed heavily.

"Everything is too neat and clean in this report. I'm forced to question whether there was someone in the police force at that time who hid something from the public?" Neville rubbed his chin.

Ward couldn't help but agree. "Maybe. I wonder if we

could find Mr. Fergus McGee? I'd be interested to hear what he remembers about that night."

"So would I," Jane added.

Neville scanned through the next few pages in the document on the screen.

"Wait just a second. I see something." Jane pointed to the bottom of one of the last pages. "It looks like the hand-written notes on this page are about Officer Ryan Hart."

Neville looked closer to the screen. "Yes. It's simply saying that Officer Hart was transferred years ago to the narcotics division in the police department. That's the drug related offenses department."

"That's interesting. But I guess that's not relevant to finding clues about what happened to my parents." Jane grimaced.

Neville replied, "No, it isn't. Sorry about that, Jane."

"That's okay." Jane sighed.

"I'll scan the rest of these pages to see if I can find Fergus McGee's location," Neville continued to look closely, until finally he found the address.

"At the time of your parents' deaths, he was living on the island. He might have moved since then. However, I can give you his last known home address," Neville added.

"That's great." Ward took out his smartphone and began typing down the address of Mr. McGee.

"Thanks, Neville. You've been a big help today," Jane said as they walked to the door. "Maybe we're one step closer to learning what happened to my parents."

Neville nodded. "I hope so, Jane. I really do."

As they drove away, Ward looked at Jane and said,

"Let's see if we can find Mr. Fergus McGee. Maybe he'll be able to give us some answers."

⸏

JANE SIGHED as Ward drove the small car towards the address he'd added to his smartphone's GPS.

It didn't take them long before they arrived at a small, older looking bungalow.

They parked the car and walked toward the house. Jane spoke softly, "I really hope we can find some real answers."

"Me too." Ward stopped at the door and turned towards her. "But, even if this is a dead end, I won't stop until we have some real answers."

A small smile lifted the corners of Jane's lips. "Thanks, Ward. That means a lot."

Ward knocked on the door.

It was a few minutes before the door opened.

Standing in front of them was a gray-haired man who looked to be around seventy-five years old.

"Yes? What do you want?" The low, gravelly voice of the old-timer spoke sharply.

His irritation at their arrival caused a knot to form in Jane's belly.

Ward replied in even tones, "We're looking for Mr. Fergus McGee."

"I'm Fergus. Who are you and what's this about?" The man's gruff tone of voice sent a spurt of anxiety through Jane.

Ward introduced them both. "My name is Ward Hampton and this is Jane Stafford."

Fergus McGee's brows bunched together and he stared at Jane for a long time.

His words were softer this time. "You have the look of your mother. You are John and Anne Stafford's daughter?"

"Yes. They're my parents." She swallowed back emotion that rose to the surface. It surprised her that, even after all these years, memories of her parents affected her so strongly.

"Well, come on in then." The old man rubbed the whiskers on his chin. "No doubt you're here to ask about what happened the night of the tragedy. I'll tell you what I know."

"Thanks, Mr. McGee." Jane sent the older man a hopeful smile.

Ward lifted one eyebrow in surprise. "The old-timer seems to like you, Jane. I hope he can tell us something helpful."

"I do too." Jane nodded and they walked into the old home.

As she walked into the small house, she stepped around papers and boxes that were scattered on the living room floor.

"Go ahead and sit down." The old man pointed to an old sofa on one side of the room.

"Thank you." Jane sat down and glanced around the room. Paintings and photos covered the wall of boats, ships, and lighthouses of their island.

One picture frame held an old photo of Sweet Beach

Cove. It was the same Cove that was very familiar. It was an important piece of land to the Stafford family.

"See something you like?" Mr. McGee studied Jane as he waited for her to speak.

Jane nodded. "That photo of the cove. It's lovely. That's the same place where my great-grandfather Captain Henry Stafford's ship sank years ago. My late grandmother had photos of the area in her house."

The older man simply nodded. "That tale is well known on this part of the island. Everybody knows the Stafford family and the story of how Captain Henry Stafford won that sixty acres of waterfront property from Ike Cantrell in a game of chance."

Jane shrugged. "Well, that was many years ago, so it's not really relevant today."

"Isn't it?" Mr. McGee rubbed his chin whiskers again and looked over at her. "But that's not the reason you came today. You want to know what I remember about the night your parents died."

"Yes, if you could tell us what you remember that would be helpful," Jane added.

"Alright. But in order to do that I'll have to take you back in time," the older man explained.

A little shiver ran up Jane's spine. She couldn't help but wonder what past memory the old man was about to share with them.

Fergus McGee began to tell his tale.

"I remember when all us boys were teenagers. I got along well with John Stafford and Matty Bellanger. They were good friends of mine."

He shook his head.

"But I had difficulty getting along with Ted, Jerry, and Bobby. They were always trying to test the boundaries of good society. Not to mention that at that time — as teenagers — they were always trying different schemes, trying to strike it rich. Anything to make a buck."

"Anyway, on that day when Matty drowned, the fact that those five teenage boys went diving for treasure on your great-grandfather's sunken ship, didn't surprise me," the old man explained.

"Growing up, Ted Cantrell seemed desperate to do whatever he needed to do in order to make his father, Eli Cantrell, proud of him. Eli Cantrell died when Ted was just entering his teenage years and I think Ted went a little crazy."

"Of course, Jerry Hart looked up to Ted and so did Bobby Sutton. So those boys went along with whatever Ted planned.

"Those three boys ended up dealing drugs and shoplifting from an electronics store. I knew about the drugs because my stepfather, Harry, was the one who sold the drugs to them. I was supposed to look the other way. I didn't say anything, but it stuck in my memory."

"Of course, old Sheriff Elias Hart didn't want his only son, Jerry, to have a crime record, so he found a way to make the problem disappear."

"Those boys continued their crime spree throughout their teenage years. Maybe they stopped when they went to college, I don't know."

"Jerry Hart threatened me that if I ever told that I saw him or his friends doing drugs, he would ruin me."

Fergus McGee sighed heavily as he finished telling the

tale. "I never told anyone until now. I'm telling you, Jane, because your parents died and you deserve to know the truth."

"Thanks, Mr. McGee, for telling me." Jane turned, her hands shaking. Ward's eyes were wide, stunned at the tale the old man just shared.

Ward asked, "Do you believe your memories of Jerry, Ted, and Bobby, relate to the night of Jane's parents' deaths?"

The older man ran a shaky hand through his grey hair. "Well now, that's the same question that ran through my mind when Sheriff Jerry Hart had me brought into the police department the day after the boating accident."

Jane asked, "What did Sheriff Hart say?"

"He tried to pin the deaths of your parents on me, of course. But, even though I was out on my boat that night, I wasn't responsible. However, I do remember that night. I could tell a storm was coming on, but I wanted to try out my new boat to see how well she did on the rough waters. So I took my boat out on the water that night."

The older man had a faraway look in his grey eyes as he remembered.

"I was out on the water when I saw John Stafford pass me in his boat. I could see Anne was beside him. It seemed like she was motioning for John to turn back because she kept pointing back where they'd come from. I could see John shake his head in disagreement. Wherever John was going, he was determined to get there."

"Then I remember the storm really picked up. My boat shook in the wind and I crawled closer to the shoreline.

Finally, I was able to set my boat on the sandy beach in front of my friend Theo Rowland's beach house."

The old man explained, "That night, Theo was setting his boat inside his boat shed. I waved at Theo and he walked out to talk with me on the beach and that's when I heard a loud blast. I turned and saw fire coming from John and Anne's boat. I remember seeing wood pieces flying through the air and landing in the water."

Jane sucked in a quick breath as the vivid image the old man described imprinted into her mind's eye. What happened to cause a fire on her parents' boat? They must have been so scared that night.

"So, when I was hauled into the sheriff's office the next day, I explained what I saw. Sheriff Hart said I was a suspect in the investigation. A few days later, they charged me. However, it was only a few weeks later, after the police talked with Theo Rowland, that the police finally realized I had a solid alibi for that night."

Ward shook his head. "It seems so strange."

Jane nodded in agreement, trying to make sense of it all.

Mr. McGee went on, "What's really strange is that the police decided to charge me again ten years later, when investigative reporter Sean O'Connor died in a boating accident."

"They tried to charge you for Sean's death?" Jane shook her head, trying to understand.

"Yeah, they did. But, again, I had an alibi. This time I was boating with another guy. He was in his boat and I was in mine. Sean was about a quarter of a mile ahead of us. It looked like he was heading in the direction of the

Cove. I could be wrong, of course, but that's what it looked like to me. I saw what looked like a fire on Sean's boat, but it was too far away to see much else."

Jane shook her head. "Maybe the Cove is cursed. With my great-grandfather's sunken ship, then Matty's death there, and then my parents and Sean O'Connor dying nearby. That place must be cursed. There have been too many senseless deaths along the Cove."

"I wonder. You may be right," Mr. McGee replied.

"You said you heard a loud blast and then you saw fire on my parents' boat. Do you think my parents died from a boating accident, Mr. McGee?" Jane held her breath. Did she want to know the answer?

"Honestly, I don't believe your parents' deaths or Sean O'Connor's death were accidents as the police labeled them." The older man went on to explain, "It seemed to me that Sheriff Hart and his police officers tried desperately, both times, to find reasons to make me look guilty. I think they were trying to hide something. Something that they didn't want folks on the island to find out."

Ward commented, "Do you have any ideas about what they were trying to hide Mr. McGee?"

The older man shrugged. "There are a great many things they might have wanted to hide. My guess? It was something illegal that Jerry Hart and his police officers were desperate to hide."

Jane asked, "But what would the police's illegal activities have to do with my parents? Did somebody want my parents dead?"

The older man shook his head. "That's the question

that has worried me for years, Jane. And the honest answer is, I don't know. I suppose it's possible, but I can't think of one reason why somebody would deliberately want to harm good people like John and Anne Stafford."

"Well, my sisters and I are going to dig until we find out the truth. My late grandmother asked us to get to the truth and somehow we will." Jane couldn't help the swell of emotions and the strong sense of justice that rose up inside her.

"You have your late grandmother's fierce spirit for justice, Jane. I believe you will find the answers you're seeking." A smile lit up his eyes.

Jane stood to her feet. "Thanks, Mr. McGee, for talking to us today. Hearing you tell your story helps me understand some things better about what happened that night. I appreciate it."

"You're welcome, Jane. Stop by again if you have any more questions." The older man waved as Jane and Ward left his house and walked to the waiting car.

As Ward drove her home, all Jane could think of was all the details Fergus McGee had shared with them.

It seemed strange to her that, with the boating accidents of her parents and later with Reporter Sean O'Connor, that the sheriff tried to place blame on an innocent man both times.

She was deep in thought as they drove the main stretch in Sweet Beach Cove.

It was the start of November and their island community was bursting with Christmas decorations.

As they entered Main Street, there were wreaths on the doors of the library, coffee shops, and clothing stores.

Old-fashioned street lamps were decorated with red and green Christmas lights that brightened the narrow streets.

She stiffened at the sight of Christmas decorations strewn around the businesses and street corners.

Christmas.

How she hated this holiday.

It was supposed to be a holiday of faith, hope, and love.

Yet, for most of her adult life, it had been a holiday filled with the opposite. For Jane, it was filled with hopelessness and fear.

She continued to look at the different shops as Ward drove down the street.

Out of the corner of her eye she spotted a familiar sight.

All of a sudden, she took in a quick sharp breath.

Two child-sized wooden rocking reindeers were placed on the sidewalk in front of a Christmas store.

Similar to a wooden rocking horse, these reindeers each had a large red bow around their necks.

These were Christmas toys for children.

As Ward slowly drove the car, she could make out the faint logo with the letters: *HCE.*

Her body jerked against the car seat in shock.

"Jane, is something wrong?"

Ward's deep voice barely registered, as shock sent a shiver of fear up her spine.

"He's here. My ex-husband is selling his children's Christmas toys to our island community." Jane swallowed the bile that surged from her belly up her throat.

"He's found me and my son."

Ward pulled the car over and gently touched her arm. "What do you mean, your ex-husband is here, Jane?"

"I saw the wooden rocking reindeers in front of that Christmas store. They have his logo on them," Jane whispered.

"Maybe he's simply trying to sell his toys to more stores. It doesn't mean Devon is here on the island, honey." He rubbed the top of her hand in an effort to calm her fears.

Jane shook her head. "No. You don't understand. This is what Devon always does. First he brings his children's toys to a retail store to sell them. Then he buys the store. When he buys it, he moves somewhere close so he can get the store profitable."

Jane reached up and ran one hand along her throat.

Ward gently reached for her hand and pulled her close.

"Jane, even if that's true, your ex-husband is not going to harm you." He kissed her forehead and looked deeply into her eyes. "I promise to do everything in my power to protect you and your son."

"Thanks, Ward." Jane shuddered. "But, that man is evil. What if he finds a way to hurt Noah or me anyway? Maybe I need to leave again."

"No, Jane. This time we'll see this through together, alright?"

Slowly she nodded. "Alright."

Jane only hoped she would be able to keep her word.

Because, right now, all she wanted to do was to take her son and run as far and as fast as she could away from the island.

 ane

"Moving to this house and staying on the island is not a good idea." Jane rubbed tired eyes.

All night she had tossed and turned and woke up several times in a state of panic.

Thoughts of her ex caused fear to race through her all night long.

"How can Noah and I possibly stay here now that my ex-husband has returned?" Jane ran a shaky hand through her blonde waves as she turned to her sisters.

She hardly slept last night after seeing her ex-husband's Christmas children's toys at one of their community stores yesterday.

"Jane, we don't know if he has returned. You only saw

the toys he makes. And second, I really believe you need to stop running, Jane. If he does show up on the island, you need to stay and face him once and for all. He's the one who is in the wrong, not you." Lizzie's tone was unshakable and firm.

"I agree with Lizzie, Jane. It's time to stay and stand up for Noah and for yourself," Alex declared.

"And I agree too," Charlie chimed in.

Jane studied each of her sisters one by one. She heard unshakeable resolve in their voices and it gave her courage. However, it was the compassion in their eyes that was her undoing.

"Alright. I don't know if I'm crazy or just hopeful that you're right, but I'll stay. I'm only doing this because you all are there to help me." Jane sighed heavily.

"Don't doubt it, Jane. All of us are here for you," Lizzie agreed.

Jane forced a small smile. "Well then. I guess it's time to move Noah and my things into our new home."

"Gladly." Charlie reached over and grabbed her into a big hug. "I'm glad you're staying, Jane."

"Me too." Jane watched as each of her sisters took a box from the back of the van.

Finally, she took the last box.

All she could do was hope she made the right decision.

THE DAY WAS UNUSUALLY mild and warm for the last Friday at the end of October.

Jane was grateful for the warm weather.

It was a perfect day for her and Noah to move into their new home.

For an added surprise, all her sisters had shown up this weekend to help her and her son move.

"Jane, it's good to see you without that black wig or hat. Your lovely face is no longer hidden from the world." Charlie grinned as she took another box from the back of Lizzie and Jonathan's van.

"Thanks, Charlie." Jane ran shaky fingers through her naturally blonde hair. "I must admit, I feel very nervous without my usual accessories."

The idea of giving up the hat and wig that had hidden her and kept her safe had seemed impossible for such a long time.

Even now, she was worried about the consequences of her actions. Would her ex-husband find them?

But she had willed herself to find inner courage.

She would force herself to be brave and come out of hiding for her son.

More than anything she prayed for her son's safety.

Today, they had a chance to start fresh and have a real home.

She was grateful.

Today, she chose to be thankful and stop worrying every waking moment.

According to advice from her sisters and from Kenna, it was time for Jane not to live in constant fear.

She had already started. Today, she decided not to put on the black wig or the hat.

However, was she brave enough to step away from the curtain and present who she really was to the public?

She was scared to make a decision that could harm her son.

Lizzie walked past her, and turned to her. "Jane, there's no need to feel nervous. You're home now. All of us here today have your back. I'm happy you've decided to begin to shed the old layer of you that was only a veneer, Jane. This new, real you looks beautiful."

Jane shuffled the heavy box in her hands. As she stared at her oldest sister, she questioned how Lizzie could make being the real her sound so easy?

A big fear she'd always had was that someone would pull back the curtain and scream: *You're a burden to everybody. You're one of the kids that shouldn't have been born. You're not worthy of love.*

In tandem with those thoughts, a vivid image of cruel words from her mother's younger brother, Uncle Tony, haunted her memory.

Her hands trembled. The box slipped a little in her fingers.

Just at that moment, Ward hurried towards her. He took the heavy box from her hands.

Leaning close, Ward whispered, "I agree with your sister, Jane. The woman you are, wrapped in your original packaging, is beautiful."

Heat crept up her neck to her cheeks at his compliment.

"Thanks, Ward," she whispered, her voice raw.

Once again, her former boyfriend managed to surprise her with charming words of praise.

Jane swallowed back emotion.

Insecurities and self-doubt plagued her. Beautiful was certainly not how she saw herself.

When she looked in the mirror, all she saw were flaws and imperfections.

Jane had always been convinced she wasn't good enough in the eyes of others.

Doing her best to shake off the negative thoughts, she stepped into the kitchen.

Lizzie's young adult children, Annie and Jake, were busy helping with the move. Annie scrubbed the kitchen counters and Jake was helping Noah haul his mattress to his room.

As her son walked by her, he turned her way with a grin. "Look, Mom. Jake and I are going to set up my new bedroom."

"I'm glad, Noah. I'm excited you'll be able to sleep in your own bed and your own room from now on." Jane blew her son a kiss as the two of them walked towards the bedrooms.

"Noah sure is excited about moving here," Annie commented as she turned to Jane. "I'm glad we get to celebrate his birthday today too."

Jane grinned. "Me too. I think Noah will be surprised by his birthday gift."

For the past few weeks she'd been thinking about the special gift she was about to give her son.

"Annie, you have no idea." Jane chuckled. "All he's talked about for weeks now, is the two of us living in a real house and having a dog of his own."

"It's nice for you two to be settled into your home. And

I think a lot of boys have a love for dogs." Annie grinned. "I'm glad you and Noah are back on the island."

"Me too, Annie." Jane took a clean rag and dipped it in the soapy bucket Annie was using to wash the countertop. "So tell me what's new with you?"

"Well, I'm still living at mom's beach cottage. I've been helping with The Vineyard Inn's website design. And I've been doing quick fixes whenever there is an issue with guests who register to stay at the inn," Annie commented.

Jane smiled. "Your mom told me you've been a huge help to her."

"That's good to hear." Annie smiled. "My other news is my boyfriend, Christopher, and I have been back together now for the last three months. He has recently moved to Martha's Vineyard. He started his own business building houses. Jake is joining him as a subcontractor with his carpentry work. It's nice to have Chris back in my life again."

Jane smiled. "You're glowing. I wondered if there was romance in the air. You seem happy."

"I am happy. I feel like things are getting more serious between the two of us. I feel ready for the next level." Annie grinned. "Is there a man in your life, Aunt Jane?"

Jane glanced out the kitchen window and saw Ward standing on the front lawn talking with Sam and Jonathan.

"There is the possibility of a relationship, Annie. But I've been a little gun-shy." Jane sighed.

Just at that moment, Lizzie, Alex, and Charlie walked into the kitchen. Lizzie stopped and turned towards her. "Jane, it's time for you to embrace love again."

Her oldest sister turned to the other women. "Look at us. We've each been given a second chance with men we love. I've seen how Ward watches you all the time, Jane. That man is smitten. I think he's changed. Give him a chance, Jane."

"I'm trying. And I agree, he seems to have changed. He's more patient and kind than before. But I feel like I need to see more of that change. That he truly loves me and is ready to be committed. That he won't abandon me."

Jane sighed.

Lizzie turned to her with a warm smile that lit up her face. "I believe Ward will show you how much he loves you, Jane."

A warmth started in her belly and spread upwards. One of her biggest longings was to be loved for who she truly was.

Jane began to clean the walk-in pantry. It was a large room with more than enough shelves to hold a vast amount of canned goods.

Alex followed her inside and began to clean the shelves on the other side. "Jane, have you decided if you're going to continue as a wedding planner?"

"I was thinking of applying for a business license in Sweet Beach Cove. I'm not sure. Being a wedding planner is the one thing I seem to be good at which — when you think about it — is incredibly ironic." Jane grimaced.

Alex smiled. "I don't think it's ironic. I think the reason you're good at planning weddings is because you have a passion to help people who love each other to finally find happiness. It's the same longing you have. Don't give up.

Your wedding day to the man you love is coming, dearest sis."

"I hope so, Alex." Jane scrubbed harder against the difficult stains on the shelves.

Alex turned to her. "I think it's good that you'll be applying for your business license. Will you use your real name?"

"To be honest, I've been so worried. I'm afraid to promote this business using my real name. I just don't know what to do," Jane whispered. "If I use my real name, it's the same as placing a target on my back. However, I've come to realize, I can't live my life afraid. If I choose not to be courageous, what kind of example am I setting for my son?"

Alex nodded. "I agree. I think you should go for it, Jane. You are brave. The courage you need is inside of you. Step out in faith, not fear. Do it for your son."

Jane stopped cleaning and turned to face her sister.

A sudden longing to be free of the fear that held her down for so many years, burst through her.

"I think you're right, Alex. It's time I begin to stand tall and embrace who I am. My son needs me to be brave. I will use my real name as the public face for my business." Jane could feel her heart rate accelerate as she heard her own words. But it's what she needed to do.

Her fingers touched her pearl necklace. Grandmother's words swirled in her memory.

Remember Jane, during difficult times, hold onto faith, hope and love.

Despite the fear coursing through her veins, Jane decided she would plunge ahead.

She would force herself to be brave for her son.

*

"Since our men went to pick up the last load of Jane's stuff, I thought we could take a few minutes to read from Grams' journal." Lizzie walked towards the kitchen table in Jane's and sat down.

All the sisters soon followed.

Annie was outside with Noah. They were playing a game together.

"I'll pour the sweet tea." Jane poured seven glasses of the delicious drink and set them on the table.

Charlie raised her glass. "Today has felt like how it was being at Grams' cottage on a Saturday afternoon. Drinking this sweet tea makes this day perfect."

Lizzie turned to Jane. "Now that all of us sisters are together again, there have been new developments. Jane can tell you what's been going on with our search into the mystery of our parents' deaths."

Jane set her glass on the table. "There have been a few new details that have been helpful."

She started to explain, "I had a chance to talk with Matty's mom at the weekly quilting event. Mrs. Bellanger talked about how surprised she was that her son drowned that day when those boys went searching for treasure."

"Matty had recently finished his training to receive his life guard certification. He was an excellent swimmer. As we talked, Matty's mother agreed to let me look at Matty's journal from when he was a teenager. Maybe we'll find something there."

"I hope so," Jules said. "This search into the mystery of our parents' deaths is beginning to feel like one of those murder mysteries in my favorite novels."

Alex sighed heavily. "I'm beginning to wonder, when all is said and done, if we won't discover that for years there has been a cover-up. Possibly, even people we've known all our lives might have been involved in or responsible for the deaths of our parents."

"I hope not." A coil of fear tightened in Jane's belly as she thought of Alex's words. It would be terrible to learn that a good friend or someone they knew could have had a hand in the deaths of her parents.

Jules asked, "Did you find out anything else, Jane?"

"Well, I had the chance to talk with Miss Sadie and her sister, Miss Hattie." Jane thought about her conversation at the quilting event. "Turns out, Miss Hattie has been taking photos on the island ever since she moved here fifty-five years ago. Miss Hattie said I should come to her place and look at some photos. Her suggestion, that it might help us in our search about our parents' deaths, made sense."

"That's a good idea. I didn't realize anyone on the island had been taking pictures for that long. That's amazing." Charlie took another sip of sweet tea while Lizzie began to speak.

"Every few steps forward helps in our search. Thanks, Jane." Lizzie smiled warmly her way.

Jane was pleased that she could be of help in some small way to her sisters' search for what truly happened to their parents.

"Let's begin to read another chapter from Grams' journal." Lizzie pulled out the well worn leather journal.

Opening the worn pages to the next chapter, she began to read out loud.

I was talking with William at supper about what I'd learned earlier today.

"I talked with Linda Hart at the grocery store today." When my husband puckered his eyebrows, it was my sign he didn't remember who I was talking about.

"Linda is Florrie Cantrell-Jone's daughter. Linda is newly married to Jerry Hart," I explained.

William nodded and grunted at me (sometimes I'm convinced I am doing ninety percent of the talking in our marriage.).

Anyway, when he didn't comment, I went on to explain the conversation I had with Linda.

I said, "Are you enjoying your first year of marriage?"

Linda looked at me and shrugged. She said, "It would be easier if we didn't need to visit Jerry's mom and dad so much. Elias Hart, my father-in-law, is constantly muttering on and on about how he never should have sold that waterfront property to the Petersons."

"I didn't realize that the Harts owned that place before the Peterson family bought it," I commented.

Lina shook her head and said, "Between you and me, I think his dad regrets that he sold the place, but does he need to bring it up every time we come over to visit?"

"Sorry, I guess that would be frustrating," I replied.

Linda must have been very upset, because she continued talking about her frustrations. "My husband, Jerry, is also upset that his dad sold that property. But, for Jerry, there's a bigger reason for his frustration than simply missing out on owning a waterfront property. He won't tell me the real reason he's upset though."

I told her I was sorry to hear that. And encouraged her that perhaps someday her husband would open up and tell her the truth.

Linda replied, "And pigs might fly. My husband, Jerry, is as hard-headed as his father, Sheriff Elias Hart. They're both as stubborn as the day is long. So I doubt I'll ever find out the real reason."

Without saying anything more, Linda Hart walked away.

I told my William, "I wonder if there's more to that story about the property the Harts sold to the Petersons? Perhaps they left something behind that now the Hart family wishes they would have taken with them."

Finally, my William commented softly, "Elizabeth, you are making a mountain out of a mole hill. The simple reason the Harts regret selling that property to the Petersons, is because that piece of land is a nice spot on the island."

"Maybe." I still thought it was strange.

"Perhaps Jerry Hart is reliving the memories he had being next door neighbors with the Sutton family. I'm glad that Jerry and Bobby are good friends. They were neighbors throughout their growing up years. Maybe Jerry is feeling nostalgic about the good memories he had on the Cove with his friend Bobby Sutton," William added.

"Maybe. That area of our waterfront property that connects to the Peterson property is the same Cove where your father Henry Stafford lost his ship. I wonder if that cove is cursed?" I couldn't help but explain what I was thinking.

"Now, Elizabeth. Let's not go thinking that way. It's good

land and a great area along the beach. Sure, it has rough waters now and again, but I don't think the place is cursed." William finished eating and soon left to go read in the den.

Later on, as I washed the supper dishes, I couldn't get it out of my head.

I wonder if there is some bigger reason why old Sheriff Elias Hart and his son, Jerry, regret that they sold that property to the Petersons. Perhaps I should try to find out when they sold that property? It's possible I'll learn more from that information.

However, I might never learn the answers to all the questions I write here in my journal. And I suppose I'll have to be satisfied with not knowing all the answers.

"This is a journal entry that Grams wrote from when Linda first married Jerry Hart. At this point in their lives, all of us sisters would have just lost our parents and we were living with Gramps and Grams," Lizzie explained.

Charlie commented, "That makes sense." She paused before continuing, "Grams mentions the waterfront property along the cove that former Sheriff Elias Hart sold to the Petersons. This is the same place Jane is now renting from the Petersons. I wonder what Grams could have meant when she wrote about a bigger reason why Elias Hart and his son, Jerry, regretted selling this piece of land?"

Jane nodded. "That's a very good question, Charlie. This land is along the cove and it's next door to the land that the Sutton family rented for years from our grandparents. That's why Bobby Sutton and Jerry Hart were good friends. They grew up together along the cove."

Torrie commented, "Yes, the Sutton family moved out last year. That land Bobby Sutton grew up on is Stafford land. It's the ten acres of land that Grams bequeathed me in her will. There is no one living on those ten acres now. Maybe soon I'll be able to move there. It's a nice spot on the cove."

Jane smiled. "It's a beautiful property, Torrie. We could be next door neighbors."

Torrie grinned. "That would be perfect."

The sisters sat together quietly for a long while.

All of a sudden, Alex said, "I can't stop thinking about what Grams wrote in her journal. I wonder if there is a bigger reason why Elias Hart and Jerry Hart regretted selling this piece of land? Did they leave behind something that they now wish they had kept? Did they use that area by the cove for something?"

Jane replied, "Good point, Alex. Maybe we need to research what was going on along the cove at the time that Sheriff Elias Hart sold this land to the Petersons. That might help give us some answers to our other questions. I'll look into that. Hopefully, we'll uncover more answers soon."

The truth was, Jane worried about what she and her sisters would find when their questions were finally answered.

Would they discover that someone they knew and trusted played a part in their parents' deaths?

That thought was much too dreadful and frightening to imagine.

A COUPLE HOURS LATER, her sisters, their husbands, and Annie and Jake were gathered around the table.

An outside picnic table spread over the deck. It was just large enough for them all.

"Thanks for the pizza, Jane." Alex turned to Jane.

Jane grinned. "You're welcome. This is simply my small way of saying thank you to each of you for helping us move today. Besides, it is Noah's birthday today and one of his favorite meals is pizza."

Noah finished his last bite of pizza. "Yup. This is my favorite food."

Annie leaned close, whispering to her young cousin, "Mine too, Noah."

Jane couldn't help her wide smile as she glanced around the table.

There were so many reasons to be grateful.

Her family, for her son, and that they now had a real home.

"We were happy to help you, Jane. That's what family does." Charlie grinned.

Soon, everybody had finished their meal.

Jane looked over at Ward and nodded.

She had asked him earlier if he could help bring Noah's gift when the time came.

As Ward walked away, Jane turned to everybody. "I'll go get the birthday cake."

"Does that mean it's time to open presents, Mom?" Noah's blue eyes sparkled.

"Yes, it does." Jane grinned as she hurried inside the house. She could tell her son was excited. This was the first time Noah was able to celebrate his birthday with his aunts, uncles, and cousins.

Jane pulled out the ice cream cake from the freezer.

This was her son's favorite treat.

She set the candles on the cake and lit the sparklers.

As she carried it outside to the table, Noah's eyes grew wide and he clapped his hands.

Setting the birthday cake on the table, Jane said, "Noah, I hope this birthday will be the start of many more memorable and fun birthdays for you."

Glancing over, she saw Ward was walking towards the table with a dark blanket thrown over his arms. He had picked up the gift she planned to give her son.

She lit the candles.

Everyone sang the happy birthday song and Noah blew out the candles.

Suddenly, the loud bark of a dog could be heard behind them.

A surge of warmth shot up Jane's spine at the sound.

She watched as her son turned his head.

Ward lifted the blanket off of the cage, revealing a small brown and white Saint Bernard puppy.

"Happy birthday, Noah!" Jane smiled.

Her son's jaw dropped and he squealed in surprise. "Aww… Mom. You got me a dog!"

"I did. It's the kind of dog you love." Her eyes misted over at her son's look of absolute delight.

Noah hurried towards the puppy. Ward grinned and bent down. He held the leash and let the puppy run to Noah.

Jane put her hand on her chest, filled with happiness as her son caught the furry dog in his arms.

Noah hugged the puppy close.

As the family talked between themselves, Jane walked towards her son and Ward.

"Looks like you couldn't have made a better choice for your son's birthday present," Ward leaned over to whisper.

Jane smiled. "He's been talking about a dog of his own for years. It seemed like the timing was perfect. Especially now that the two of us are moving into our first real home."

"I'm happy for you Jane. You deserve it," He said softly.

Just at that moment, Noah carried the furry puppy over to her. "Mom, look at this dog's big paws. Jake told me this is a boy dog. What's his name?"

"You get to choose this puppy's name, Noah. He's yours to keep." Jane ran one hand along the dog's fur.

"I do?" Noah thought about it for a few minutes. He toyed with the oversized paws for a minute. "Okay. I think I'll name him Buddy. He's going to be my new furry friend after all."

"That's a great name, son." Jane said softly.

Noah set his new dog on the grass and the dog took off running. After a few minutes, her son finally caught the leash.

"It's so good to see Noah happy. And he loves to spend time with his cousins too." Jane loved watching as Jake and Annie played catch with Noah and his dog.

"It's good Noah has cousins whom he adores," Ward added. "You know, Jane, if you want your son to meet more kids his age, I can help with that."

"It would be good for Noah to get to know more kids his age." Jane turned to him. "Tell me. What are you thinking?"

Ward rubbed his chin. "I don't think I told you, but I coach the middle grade students' basketball team. It's an after school sports program for students who are interested in learning the game. If you are alright with the idea, I could add Noah to the team."

Anxious thoughts flooded her like they usually did whenever she thought of Noah going places by himself.

"You would be willing to look out for him?" Jane turned to him.

Ward nodded. "I would. The boys meet at the gym for a two hour practice time twice a week. I think he would enjoy basketball and make new friends."

"Alright then. I'll agree if you're there to watch him. Maybe you're right. It might be good for Noah," Jane added.

She couldn't help but worry a little, but if Ward was there to watch over her son, what could go wrong?

"You seem worried, Jane." Ward turned towards her, a crease forming between his brows.

"Maybe a little. But you'll be there at each practice with my son. So I'm sure he'll be fine." Jane sent him a tremulous smile.

"He will be." With gentle fingers, Ward tipped her chin upwards. Her heart skipped a beat at the intense expression in his eyes. "I think it would be good if you could find time to relax and enjoy yourself."

Jane squirmed a little at the intense expression in his dark eyes. "I'm not sure I know how."

"Let me help. I know of one of the best ways to relax," Ward suggested.

"What do you have in mind, Ward?"

His dark eyes danced in merriment. "The annual Christmas barn dance is this Saturday evening."

'I remember the community had the Christmas barn dance every year during my childhood. But I didn't realize they kept it going."

"They do. The community celebrates Christmas two months early on the island." Ward chuckled. "What do you say, Jane, do you want to go with me?"

Dark memories circled around and around in her mind.

Her ex-husband had betrayed her on Christmas. He had abused both her and Noah on Christmas Eve.

For Jane, there were so many reasons she hated Christmas.

Ward was asking her to try to leave her son to go to an event that celebrated a holiday that served as a reminder of her painful past.

Jane stammered as she thought of the first excuse that came to her mind. "I don't think I should go. I can't leave Noah all alone at home."

Ward studied her for a long time before he replied, "Jane, I really think a night out would be good for you. Plus, I already checked with Mrs. Morrison. She's happy to begin her duties as housekeeper and caregiver. You won't need to worry about Noah. He'll be well taken care of."

She smiled. "You planned ahead. You must have been sure I would agree to this."

Ward grinned. "I was hopeful. So, will you come with me?"

Jane could feel her resistance breaking down. He'd always had a way of winning her over to his side.

"Alright, I'll go with you to the Christmas barn dance, Ward," Jane said softly.

"I look forward to it. I can't wait to hold you in my arms again, Jane. We'll dance the night away just like we did years ago," Ward lowered his head, speaking softly in her ear.

Jane's heart turned over in response to his whispered words.

She remembered being in Ward's arms during the Country Christmas dance years ago.

That was the night she had fallen in love.

Was her heart about to repeat the same folly as last time?

CHAPTER TEN

ane

THE NEXT EVENING, the women in the quilting circle had their meet-up at *Yarn Around the Cove.*

Jane was pleasantly surprised by the turn out.

In the past week, so many things happened.

She had boldly changed both her and Noah's legal names back to their original names. Also she submitted her application for a business license on the island.

Her nerves had been on edge ever since making the decision to use her real name.

Fear had caused her belly to twist into a tight knot last night.

She had tossed and turned, imagining the worst.

It wasn't hard to imagine that her ex-husband would

soon be living on the island. Or, perhaps he already was here.

Once again, fear formed tight knots in her belly.

She forced her thoughts to return to the truth.

But she wasn't going to dwell on all the negative "what ifs" and her fears.

Her sisters had convinced her to do this — to be brave for her son's sake.

Her thoughts turned to Ward.

Jane was grateful he had taken her son under his protective wing.

Noah had already been to one after school basketball practice at the school gym.

When she picked him up at the school, her son was all smiles. Noah had made some new friends. Ward had taught Noah the game of basketball and he was happy to be learning.

As Jane sat at the quilting frame, she couldn't help but be grateful that her son was beginning to find friends and settle into this friendly community on the island.

Jane turned her head to one side and noticed Adele seated next to her like last time.

"Hello, Adele. I'm happy we get to work on the quilt together again," Jane commented.

The young woman turned, glancing up hurriedly. "Hello, Jane."

At that moment, Jane caught a glimpse of a dark purple bruise on the side of her neck, just below one ear.

Without thinking she asked, "It looks like you've been hurt. Are you alright, Adele?"

Adele's cheeks stained red and she quickly pulled her shoulder-length brown hair so it covered her neck.

"I fell down the stairs and hit the side of my neck on the railing on the way down. I'll be fine," Adele whispered hurriedly, before turning back to focus her attention on stitching the quilt.

Jane stared at her for a moment, unsure of what to say. So she simply said, "I'm glad you're okay."

However, she admitted to herself that the fact that Adele blamed the bruise on her neck from a fall down the stairs, raised questions.

From past experience as she volunteered at women's shelters, Jane remembered many women who used the excuse that they fell when what really happened was they were abused.

What was really going on in Adele's life?

Jane started to stitch the next row on the quilt, her thoughts swirling with worry for her new friend.

The loud scrape of the chair beside her interrupted her thoughts.

The older widow Mrs. Bellanger sat down on her other side.

"Jane, I'm glad you came to quilt with us tonight." The older woman sat down, setting her tote back on the floor next to her chair.

"This memory quilt feels important. And it's stitched together by ladies in this community. I wanted to be a part of it." Jane stitched beside the older woman as they talked.

The older woman stopped stitching and reached into the tote bag she'd brought for the evening.

"I brought something for you." Mrs. Bellanger pulled

out an old, well worn leather journal. It was a thick journal that had yellowed pages from years of use.

She handed it to Jane with a shaky hand. "This was Matty's journal from when he was ten years old. I thought it would be easier for you if I brought my son's journal to our weekly quilting time."

Jane's eyes widened and she reached out to take the leather journal from the old widow's shaky hand.

"Thank you, Mrs. Bellanger. I will take good care of it. After I've read what Matty wrote, I'll return the journal to you," Jane replied and felt the weight of responsibility of stewarding this precious gift.

The final words of this beautiful woman's dead son were now in her hands.

"I know you will, Jane. And I'm happy to help with anything that will help make sense of my son's death all those years ago," the older widow said softly.

They didn't say much after that, but each woman continued to stitch side by side. Everyone was quiet at their quilting frame until Mrs. O'Connor spoke into the microphone to call an end to the evening.

Jane said her goodbyes and had just started to walk toward the door when Madison Hayes stopped to talk with her.

"Jane Stafford. It's good to see you back in our Sweet Beach Cove community." Madison swished her auburn hair so it fell across her shoulders. She was Violet Hayes' daughter and had been closer to Lizzie in age growing up on the island.

"It's good to see you as well, Madison. How are you

doing?" Jane tugged her tote close to her side as she looked at the tall, slender woman.

"Oh, you know me. I'm always busy. Real estate takes up most of my time of course. However, I have other news. I recently was engaged to be married." Madison showed Jane her the large diamond on her left hand.

"How exciting. Your ring is beautiful. Congratulations, Madison. So, when's the big day?" Jane asked, forcing herself to be patient, when all she wanted was to go home.

"In one month."

Jane smiled. "Well, I hope you have fun getting ready for your big day."

She was just about to make her excuses to leave, when Madison surprised her.

"Jane, speaking of my wedding, I wanted to ask for your help." The woman's words stopped Jane in her tracks.

"Help with what, Madison?" Confused, Jane's brows creased together.

"To plan my wedding, silly." Madison giggled. "I know you're an amazing wedding planner. And I desperately need you. I'd like to hire you."

Jane's eyes widened.

So many things had seemed up in the air, and now it seemed she would be getting her first client.

"I don't know what to say."

Madison grinned. "Say yes, Jane. Please, I need your help."

Jane swallowed. "Your wedding is in thirty days. Do you have a venue planned for the event?" In Jane's experience a place for the wedding, as well as the reception, needed to be planned months in advance.

"I have the church and the country club booked for the last weekend in November. I sent out the wedding invitations a couple months ago. I also have my wedding dress. However, nothing else has been planned." Madison shrugged. "You can see how far behind I am, Jane. Please say you'll let me hire you."

Jane sighed heavily. "I would say yes, but there's one small matter of getting my business license. I haven't set up my business as a wedding planner on the island. The trouble is, I think it takes a bit of time to get approval for a new business from the board of selectman."

Madison waved her hand. "Oh, don't worry about that. It's no trouble at all. The board voted for my mother to take Vera Cantrell's place on the board of selectmen. I'll put in a good word for you, Jane. You'll get your business approved quickly, trust me."

"Thanks, that sounds great."

Madison grinned. "When the board meets the first week of the month, I'm sure they'll approve your business."

"I hope so." Jane smiled.

"So, will you plan my wedding, Jane?" the woman asked.

Jane nodded. "I will."

"Oh, thank you. I know with you planning everything, Jane, this will be the best wedding the island has ever seen." Madison clapped her hands together. "Here, let me add my number to your phone. That way you can call or text me with any questions."

Jane handed her phone to Madison and she quickly typed in her name and phone number.

"Thanks, Jane. This is going to be fun. My fiancé is waiting outside, so I must go. I'll call you soon." Madison waved and hurried out the door.

Jane waved at Madison, who left like a whirlwind. She shook her head, surprised by the fact that — in a matter of minutes — she had just agreed to plan a wedding in thirty days.

As she walked out the door towards her car, Jane swallowed nervously at the thought of submitting her business application.

It looked like she was about to face the public, and experience the consequences of that decision — whether good or bad.

NERVOUS TINGLES RAN up and down Jane's arms as she walked beside Ward across the grass towards the sounds of the country music band.

The annual Christmas Country Barn Dance was in full swing.

Country songs filled the air, sung by a popular island band. A dozen couples danced together in the center of the wooden dance floor.

Looking around the large space, Jane flinched visibly at the sight of all the Christmas decorations.

"Are you alright?" Ward leaned over, his dark eyes studying her closely.

Jane nodded slightly. "I'm fine."

He hesitated, seemingly unsure. "Alright. If you're sure. But if there's something you want to tell me, Jane, I hope you know you're safe with me."

Jane turned to him and saw the heartfelt sincerity in his dark eyes. Swallowing back emotion she whispered, "I appreciate that, Ward."

As they walked into the center of the barn area, she realized the man beside her had changed.

He was becoming a more thoughtful and compassionate man than she'd ever known.

Tiny white lights criss-crossed above along the wooden rafters. Above them were handmade signs with the words, joy, faith, hope, and love.

The tall Christmas tree against the far wall was surrounded with sparkling lights, red bows, and topped with a large white star.

Jane couldn't believe she was once again surrounded by reminders of Christmas.

This was the holiday in which she had come to expect heartache.

At least, that's what past experience had taught her.

Her shoulders tensed at the thought of being surrounded by people who loved Christmas.

Tonight there were so many people.

The large barn was crowded.

They said hello to familiar faces as they weaved their way through the crowd.

Her sisters Alex and Lizzie danced with their husbands. Her sister Charlie danced with Zach Whetstone. They were friends from years ago.

Annie and Christopher danced together. It warmed her heart to see her niece with a big smile on her face.

Jake was dancing with Emma, and Lizzie's oldest son, Will, had also arrived. He was dancing with Sarah O'Connor.

Other familiar faces included the Cantrells, Suttons, Harts, and the Hayes family. Mrs. O'Connor was helping with the food and drinks along with her daughter Althea. Becca Weatherstone was handing out coffee and desserts together with her daughter.

Jane stopped and said hello to some of the women she saw weekly at Yarn Around the Cove.

She stopped to talk with Nettie, who sat beside her mother, Ida Cantrell. As usual, Ida was wearing her gray hair in a bun with a stylish hat. This time it was a deep red to match the Christmas colors on the stylish green and red dress.

Violet Hayes, her daughter Madison, and daughter-in-law Adele were seated next to them.

After Jane said hello to Violet and Adele, Madison stood to her feet and grabbed her hand. "Jane, I have a friend I want you to meet. I've told her about all the wonderful work you've already done to organize my wedding. She recently got engaged and wants to talk with you."

Madison led her to the punch bowl, where a blonde-haired woman was talking with Ryan Hart.

"Brandi, I have someone I'd like you to meet." Madison went on, "This is the gal who is doing such a great job planning my wedding."

Jane stared at the pretty woman. She was well dressed in the latest style and everything about her looked expensive.

"Jane, I've heard Madison go on and on about the beautiful plans you have for her wedding. I recently got engaged to be married."

"Congratulations. Is your fiancé here with you?"

"No, sadly. He needed to get some business details wrapped up before we moved here to the island. But I'm glad Madison introduced us. I wanted to ask if you could possibly find room in your schedule to plan my wedding? I would be so thrilled if you would," Brandi gushed.

"I might be able to do it. When were you thinking of having the wedding?" Jane asked.

Brandi sighed. "We were thinking about Christmas. You know what, I think Christmas Eve would be the perfect day for our wedding."

Jane's mind shifted into planning mode. "That gives us about seven weeks. What do you have planned so far?"

"Well, I already have a church for the wedding. And I booked the country club for the reception. But that's as much as I've done." Brandi grinned. "So, will you agree to plan my wedding?"

Jane nodded. "Yes. I'll be happy to."

"Oh, I'm thrilled." Brandi reached over and pulled Jane into a hug. "I'll be in touch soon."

She nodded and smiled. "Sounds good."

"Jane, soon you'll have more clients than you can handle. I'm glad." Madison spoke quickly, "I need to go, but I'll talk to you soon."

Jane nodded, and looked around the crowded barn

dance area. She was in a daze wondering how she got a new client so quickly.

She began to look for Ward, when suddenly, Ryan Hart appeared by her side.

"Jane, you look beautiful as always." Ryan leaned closer. "I hear the band switching to a slower tune. Will you dance with me?"

Jane hesitated. "I don't know if I should. I'm expecting someone."

"I know you came tonight with Ward Hampton. But he's busy talking with his friends. Which leaves you available to dance with me."

Heat stained her cheeks. "Alright then, lead the way."

She could admit to not being very comfortable dancing with Ryan Hart. He'd always been unpredictable and a little crazy.

And since she'd learned about the boxes the other day — and his possible connection to her ex-husband — that really disturbed her.

Ryan held her hand and slipped one arm around her waist as the band leader crooned a familiar country Christmas song.

"I could get used to holding you in my arms, Jane." Ryan leaned down, whispering in her ear.

Jane didn't know what to say.

He'd always been charming.

However, she didn't want to encourage his attention, so she said nothing.

"Did you enjoy boating with me the other day?" Ryan asked.

"It was very nice. It had been too long since I've

enjoyed time on the water. Were you able to get those boxes delivered to your mother's store?" Jane asked, curious as to what happened to them.

Ryan's quick intake of breath surprised her. "We did get my mother's product order to her store. She told me customers were waiting for the new Christmas products, so she was happy they arrived."

"That's good." Jane quickly asked, "Does your mom often have new products delivered via boat to her store?"

Ryan sighed and tightened his grip on her waist. "No, this was a special delivery from a new business partner of my moms. He specifically asked that his products be delivered by boat."

"Oh." In Jane's mind it seemed strange. "Do you help your mom with deliveries often?"

"Sometimes." Ryan pulled back from her a puzzled expression on his face. "Why all the questions, Jane? I was hoping we could focus on dancing."

Jane sighed heavily. Her impulse to ask Ryan questions had backfired. "Sorry. I have a tendency to ask too many questions."

She decided to switch to a safer topic. "I'm enjoying this country music. It's nice for dancing."

"I do too. I enjoy dancing with you, Jane." Ryan pulled her close.

Her body tensed.

She didn't want to get close to this man. Truth be told, he might be handsome and charming, but a part of her had always known not to trust Ryan Hart.

She sighed in relief when the music for the dance stopped.

At that moment, Jane saw Ward.

She could sense the simmering anger from Ward.

He was talking with Zach Whetstone, but when he glanced over at Ryan, there was obvious dislike.

If Ward was jealous, that certainly hadn't been her intention.

Before Ryan could ask for another dance, Jane blurted, "Thanks for the dance. I need to go talk with someone. See you later."

"Alright. See you later, Jane." She couldn't help but overhear Ryan's frustrated sigh as she walked away.

Ward pulled himself away from his friend at Jane's approach.

Jane smiled. "Did you enjoy your talk with Zach?"

"I did. Zach told me he's retired from the Coast Guard. Now he's decided to stay on the island and help his father as he gets older," Ward commented.

"Sounds like someone else I know." Jane chuckled at the similarity between Zach and Ward. They were both men who had moved back to the island to help their fathers in their senior years.

"Yeah, it's true. Maybe that's why we get along so well." Ward smiled.

"I talked with a few friends earlier. Madison introduced me to another woman who asked me to help plan her wedding." Jane went on to tell him the details.

Ward nodded. "Sounds like you're getting new clients all the time."

"Yeah. I'm keeping busy."

"It's good that you talked with friends. I noticed you

and Ryan dancing together. Did you have a good talk?" Ward peered over at her, waiting for her answer.

Jane nodded. "It was alright. I went boating with him a few days ago. I had the chance to ask a bunch of questions."

At Ward's look of confusion, Jane explained what she saw the day she went on Ryan's yacht.

"I'm worried. Anytime my ex-husband is involved in something, I get suspicious about what's really going on." Jane swallowed back emotion.

Ward nodded slowly. "Now I understand. I was beginning to believe you were interested in a relationship with Ryan."

Jane shook her head. "Never. Ryan might think that's the case, but nothing could be further from the truth. However, I do want to find out what's happening with this business between my ex-husband, Ryan Hart, and his mother, Linda Hart's, store."

"That makes sense." Ward expelled a sigh. "I want to help you get to the bottom of your questions, Jane. But what do you say we enjoy dancing together first?"

Jane nodded. "Sure, that would be nice."

Ward enclosed her small hand in his. Leaning down he whispered, "I'm relieved to hear you have no interest in dating Ryan Hart. I admit that the green-eyed monster of jealousy had already overtaken my thoughts."

Jane simply smiled. "You don't need to be jealous of him, Ward."

"I'm glad." Ward tightened his grip on her waist. "The band has switched the music to a slow song. My favorite kind for dancing."

Heat flooded her cheeks.

Her nerves were tightly strung. She didn't know if it was because of finding out about her ex-husband's involvement with business on the island or if it was being in Ward's arms that made her nervous.

Most likely it was both.

He slipped his arm further around her slender waist and pulled her closer.

The band leader crooned the slow Christmas country song "I'll Be Home For Christmas." Their harmonies sounded similar to the Rascal Flatts' version of this popular Christmas country song.

The beautiful melody drifted across the room, like a light sprinkling of snowflakes.

Soft lyrics enveloped Jane in a gentle hug. The words of the song spiraled around her and, without warning, her eyes misted.

"It truly feels like Christmas now that you've come home to the island, Jane." Ward's warm breath whispered against her ear.

Jane offered him a wobbly smile.

She didn't know what to say to that.

"This Christmas country barn dance always brings with it the joy of Christmas. The holidays warm people's hearts with hope, faith, and love. Being with you makes all the feelings of Christmas come alive in my heart. Tonight, it seems like the holiday magic is waving a sprinkling of fairy dust over everyone."

Despite her firm resolve not to enjoy Christmas or this evening, Ward's words spread over her like warm honey.

She could sense a tiny shift taking place inside her chest.

It was strange, because tonight's theme was all about Christmas. Normally, she hated everything about this holiday.

Yet, tonight she could sense the hard shell around her heart beginning to form cracks.

What was this new feeling all about?

"It doesn't get any more perfect than holding you in my arms, Jane." Ward's warm breath whispered against her ear.

Her fears of being in a relationship began to dissolve. Jane was beginning to feel truly cared for by this man.

She could sense her heart opening up to the possibility of a relationship with Ward.

Just as those thoughts were beginning to churn new emotions inside her, loud voices filled the air.

A woman's cry filled the air. "Stop it, Roy! You're hurting me!"

Jane turned to see who it was and what was going on.

"That's Adele. She's in my quilting group." Jane gasped and covered her lips with one hand. "That man dragging her across the room is her husband, Roy Hayes."

Ward shook his head. "He's drunk. Nobody should get away with treating their wife, or any woman, so cruelly."

Taking swift action, Ward hurried towards Roy as they were nearly at the exit door.

Jane followed him. She winced at Adele's cries for help.

"Roy, I think you should listen to your wife. She's crying for help. Everybody in this room knows that you're hurting her. Whatever your argument is with your wife, it can be solved after you sober up." Ward's firm tones only made Roy angrier.

Roy let loose a few cuss words at Ward and continued to drag his wife across the room.

Ward hurried after him. "If you won't listen to your wife, then perhaps we need to solve this man to man."

In a drunken rage, Roy's fist flew at Ward. However, Ward responded quickly with a few jabs of his own.

It didn't take long before Roy was lying on the floor, drunk and moaning about his bruised body.

There were many people in the room who cheered Ward for standing up to Roy Hayes.

Jane had heard many folks say Roy was a bully when he was drunk.

In the middle of it all, Jane hurried over to Adele, who now stood against the wall, her body shaking all over.

"Adele, how are you?" Jane spoke softly, so as not to scare the younger woman.

"I— I'm scared. I don't like to be near my husband when he's drunk like this. He tends to take out his anger on me," Adele whispered in a shaky voice. "I'm scared to go home with him."

"He'll most likely be forced to spend the night in jail. I see the sheriff talking with Roy now. Looks like they're taking him away." Jane tried to calm her fears.

"Yes, but this has happened to me more than once," Adele whispered. "When he comes home the next day, he'll remember things and then he'll beat me up telling me it's all my fault."

Jane belly tightened in knots of fear for this woman's

safety. "Do you have any place you can go where you'll feel safe?"

"I only have Roy's family on the island. Both of my parents have passed away. Sadly, I don't think there is anyone around here whom I trust," Adele rubbed her shivering arms. "Right now, I'm scared to go back home."

Jane thought for a moment about what to do. How could she help this young woman?

Suddenly, an idea formed in her mind.

"Do you want to come stay with me for a while, Adele? You would be welcome to stay in my home as long as you like. At least until you feel safe again," Jane reached for the young woman's trembling hand.

Adele's eyes widened in surprise. "You would do that for me?"

"Of course I would. I know what it's like to live in fear of my own husband. I have a little idea of the torment you're going through right now. If you want to come stay with me, you are very welcome." Jane offered again.

Adele nodded quickly. "I would like that. But I should warn you, Roy won't like it. Neither will the Hayes family."

"That's alright. I am more concerned about your safety than how people might respond," Jane smiled warmly. "Ward's coming this way. I think we can go home now."

Ward was surprised when Adele walked with them to his waiting car. As Adele got in the back seat, Jane quickly explained.

He nodded and said, "I'm glad. You have a compassionate heart, Jane. There will be folks who won't understand, but I'm glad you're offering Adele safety."

Jane thought about Ward's words as they drove back to her place.

She was sure she would get backlash from her actions today, but she realized she cared more for Adele's protection than whatever mean words were flung her way.

For once in a really long time, she was proud of her decision to be brave.

CHAPTER ELEVEN

ane

Jane woke up to the savory smell of freshly made pancakes that drifted in the air from the kitchen to her bedroom.

As she dressed, her thoughts were of Noah and Mrs. Morrison. How would they react to Adele staying with them?

It turned out she didn't need to worry about it at all.

"Adele, do you want more pancakes?" Mrs. Morrison's gentle voice could be heard as Jane walked down the hallway towards the kitchen.

"I'm full, but thanks for the delicious breakfast, Mrs. Morrison," Adele replied.

Jane sat down next to Noah at the table.

"Mom, did you know we have a guest staying with us?" Her son asked in between bites of pancakes covered in syrup and blueberries.

Jane smiled. "I do, Noah. What do you think of Adele staying with us for a while?"

"I'm glad she's here. Even more so, because she loves Buddy as much as I do." Her son's reply made her smile.

Jane chuckled and winked at Adele. "Well, that's very important. Because your new puppy needs all the love he can get."

"I love dogs." Adele offered a bright smile.

At the sound of his name, Noah's Saint Bernard puppy got up and hurried to the spot between Adele and her son.

His tail was wagging and his dark brown eyes seemed to be asking for more affection from the two of them.

Affection they willingly gave.

"Jane, it's almost time for Noah to leave for school. Would you like me to drive him?" Mrs. Morrison offered.

Jane had just started eating her breakfast and hadn't realized how late it was.

"That would be wonderful, if you wouldn't mind?" Jane looked over at the older woman.

"I don't mind at all. I'll clean up the dishes after I come back," Mrs. Morrison replied.

A few minutes later, Noah and Mrs. Morrison left the house.

Jane was busy texting back and forth with Madison and her newest client Brandi about wedding details.

Adele began to clean up the dishes. "Jane, you look busy. Is there something I can do to help you?"

Jane turned to her and an idea sprouted. "Do you

know anything about sending emails with invoices or about setting up social media accounts?"

"I do. I'm good at all of them. Can I help you set up yours?" Adele offered.

"Yes, that would be amazing. I've been so busy with wedding planning details that I haven't done much as far as getting the word out about my business. Thanks so much for your help, Adele. You're a lifesaver." Jane smiled.

The morning and afternoon flew by as Jane gave ideas to Adele of what she was looking for with her email newsletters and the social media branding. Adele was a very quick learner and soon had everything set up.

By the evening, Jane was ready for a video call with her sisters. She needed to talk with them tonight.

❧

A COUPLE OF WEEKS LATER, after a busy week putting the finishing touches to the details of Madison's wedding, Jane finally had a chance to call her sisters.

Adele had been super helpful planning her social media marketing and sending out her newsletters for new clients. She was a great help to Jane.

The bruises on Adele's arms were now healed. But she still didn't want to return to live with her husband, even with Roy's repeated attempts at calling her and demanding she return home.

Adele asked Roy if he would be willing to go to marriage counseling with her so they could heal what was broken in their relationship.

He flatly refused.

Her mother-in-law, Violet Hayes, told Adele, in no uncertain terms, that she needed to return to her husband.

But Adele told Jane she wanted to know that her husband was sorry for hurting her. She wanted to hear from Roy's lips that he was committed to changing to be a better husband and a better man. Adele also wanted her husband to agree to getting help through counseling.

Jane had received nasty phone calls from Roy and Violet.

However, it wasn't Jane who was stopping Adele from going back to Roy. Jane had mentioned to both of them that Adele was looking for a change of heart from her husband and a commitment to working at healing their relationship before she returned home.

Sadly, Roy still hadn't met Adele halfway.

With everything that was going on, it was late in the evening before Jane could finally rest on her bed and call her sisters.

They talked over a live video call on an app on their phones.

It was nice to see her sisters' faces even if it was only a virtual call.

"Hello, Lizzie. Hi, Alex and Charlie. Hey, Jane, Katie, and Torrie. I'm glad you could all talk tonight." Jane smiled as she got comfortable leaning back against the headboard of her bed.

They all talked a little, giving updates on their families, before they got down to the real reason they had all agreed to a live call.

"So, Jane, you wanted to talk to us all tonight. I gather you have news?" Lizzie asked.

"Tell us, Jane. What have you been up to since we last talked?" Charlie asked.

Jane thought about that for a minute.

"I'm not sure where to start. However, since our last talk, I've been digging deeper into the details about the Peterson property, trying to understand more about why the Harts regretted selling that land," Jane explained. "First, I asked around and looked at files from the Historic Registry of the Peterson's property on the island."

She continued, "I was surprised to learn that a little more than a hundred years ago, they had considered this parcel of land as a place where the Sweet Beach Cove community might build a lighthouse."

"In the historical documents they said this area along the island had an expansive view looking over the cove and the water. They wrote that, in the past, this was an area where ships had floundered, or capsized and sank." Jane explained.

Lizzie commented, "That is interesting. It seems like there were more ships than our great-grandfather's ship that went down near the cove."

"That's what the documents say," Jane went on to explain. "I also learned that when Sheriff Elias Hart sold the land to the Petersons, not long after the sale was completed, that the land by the cove doubled in value."

"Maybe that's why both Elias Hart and Jerry Hart regretted selling their land to the Petersons." Charlie added, "It makes sense they would be upset. Because if they would have kept that land, the Hart family would have received double the original sale price."

"Wow. That's a big difference." Torrie's eyes widened in surprise.

Alex went on to say, "I wonder if that's the only reason Sheriff Elias Hart and Jerry Hart regretted selling that land? I keep thinking there might be more to it, but I can't put my finger on it."

"Maybe," Jane replied. "Also, it is interesting to note that Sheriff Elias Hart sold their land to the Petersons not long after our parents' boating accident."

Alex raised one eyebrow. "Hmm, I wonder. What was the reason the Hart family decided to sell their property at that time?"

"I don't know." Jane sighed. "Maybe we'll find more clues in Matty's journal. I have it with me tonight. Earlier, I read through it, and I added bookmarks to different spots that stood out to me."

"Go ahead, Jane. We're listening." Lizzie prompted.

Jane began, "This excerpt is from when Matty was ten years old."

"I started to get to know John Stafford better today at school. His family lives in the big beach house on the waterfront. John is one of the few boys that is nice to me. We're going to go hiking on Saturday."

"I bookmarked Matty's next journal entry. This was written when he was twelve years old." Jane continued reading, *"In the past few years, John Stafford and I have hung together a lot. I like John, he's a good friend. But, the problem is, John's also friends with Ted Cantrell, Bobby Sutton, and Jerry Hart. I don't think they are very good friends to John, because I overheard Ted say something strange when they didn't realize I was listening."*

"Ted said, 'All of us need to keep being friends with John Stafford. His family owns that waterfront property where his grandfather's ship sank years ago. Sometime soon we must go diving for that treasure.' I hate to say it, but I think John's friends are using him."

"But those boys aren't very nice to me either. Sometimes they have strange ideas. For instance, just the other day Jerry was excited that his dad, Sheriff Elias Hart, bought a waterfront property by the cove. Jerry says it has a great view and, best of all, the cove is a great place to hide boats. He says you could drop off stuff there that you didn't want other folks to see. But why would Jerry want to drop off stuff along the cove?"

"Here's the last journal entry from Matty's diary." Jane read on, "*Being sixteen is fun. Now I have a little more freedom. But I won't be getting into bad habits like John's friends, Ted, Bobby, and Jerry. My other friend Fergus McGee says that he's seen Jerry buy drugs from his stepfather. I think those boys might be buying drugs to sell them. But I don't have any proof. At least, not yet. John says he won't ever get into drugs or smoking and he doesn't want to take any chances. He needs to be in good health to do the type of work he wants to do.*"

"*We go swimming together a lot. John is as good a swimmer as I am. This coming weekend John asked me to go with him and his three friends to dive for treasure. They want to dive down to his grandfather's ship at the place where it sank along the cove. I recently passed my lifeguard certification, so I'm confident of my swimming skills. But I would rather not spend time with Bobby, Ted, and Jerry. In the past year they seem to always be chasing the next scheme to strike it rich. Sometimes, it makes me wonder how far they'll go to get all the money they're desperate to get their hands on.*"

Jane looked back up at the video. Her sisters looked like they were deep in thought. "That's all of Matty's journal entries that I found that were relevant to our search for what happened to our parents. What do you think?"

"I think Matty's journal only confirms what Fergus McGee told you, Jane," Alex replied. "Fergus said he didn't trust Ted, Bobby, or Jerry and that they were buying drugs. Were they doing drugs or were they selling them? I don't know. But, at any rate, it sounds like there were some things those teenagers were doing that weren't on the level."

Torrie added, "I agree. Maybe you'll find new information when you go to Miss Hattie's place to look at those photos. When do you think you'll get a chance to visit her, Jane?"

"I plan to visit Miss Hattie later this week," Jane replied, her thoughts already wandering to what she would discover in all of Miss Hattie's old pictures. "I'll let you all know what I find."

"Sounds great, Jane," Lizzie said. "Thanks for reading through Matty's journal. It's definitely eye-opening. I feel like pieces of the mystery puzzle are starting to be put in place."

The rest of her sisters agreed and they all said their goodbyes.

As Jane got ready for bed, she couldn't help but wonder what new details she would discover when they looked at Miss Hattie's photos.

❧

LATER THAT WEEK, Jane went to visit Miss Hattie's house.

Miss Hattie opened the door, and welcomed her inside with open arms. "Sugar, ain't you a sight for sore eyes. I've been waiting for this day. I told Sadie, 'If I'm going to have one of the Stafford ladies in my house this week, I'd better clean up the place.'"

Jane chuckled. "Miss Hattie, you have a beautiful home. And, just so you know, I'm the one who is honored to visit you, not the other way around."

"Ah, you is too good to me, Jane dear. You is just as sweet as your beloved grandmother, God rest her soul." Miss Hattie led her into the wide open space of the living room.

As Jane walked into the spacious room, she glanced over, surprised to see Miss Sadie sitting on the large sofa.

"Miss Sadie, you're here too." Jane walked over and was soon enveloped in the gentle arms of the large, beautiful, African American woman.

Being hugged by Miss Sadie and Miss Hattie was refreshing to her soul.

"I couldn't help myself, Jane. I wanted to be here as you paged through all these old photos my sister has taken over the years. I was so curious about what you might find, that I couldn't force myself to stay away." Miss Sadie chuckled.

Miss Hattie laughed at her sister. "Sadie, you always were the curious one between the two of us. But you know I'm always glad to see your smiling face."

"It's true." Miss Sadie grinned.

Miss Hattie started walking towards the next room, waving for them to follow. "You both might as well come with me to the kitchen. I've got a table big enough to feed a large family. You can see I already started with some early photo albums."

Jane's eyes widened in surprise as she stared at the many photo albums placed on the shelves in the room.

Photos were part of the room decor and they added an old-style charm to Miss Hattie's house.

"You can see each album has the years from when the photos were taken. I started with this album here, because these photos were taken during the time when a childhood friendship developed between Matty and John." Miss Hattie pointed to a large brown photo album.

Jane looked over at Miss Hattie. "I'm so excited to browse through the pages."

She sat down at the table, with each sister sitting on either side, and began to turn the pages.

The first few pages in the photo album were of familiar places like the communities of Aquinnah, Edgartown, and other small towns on the island.

As she turned the pages, suddenly she stopped. "This looks like a photo of my dad swimming with Matty Bellanger in the cove."

"Yeah. The water was blue that day. It's one of my favorite pictures," Miss Hattie replied.

There was something wonderful about seeing her father in his childhood simply swimming and having fun with his friend.

She continued turning the pages until she came upon a photo of her dad with his four friends Matty, Ted, Bobby, and Jerry, with their diving gear, standing on the beach in the cove.

Jane whispered, "This must have been the day those five teenage friends went diving for treasure."

Miss Hattie nodded. "Yes, that day I was out walking as usual and I saw them along the cove. So, I began taking photos." She shook her head. "You know, I thought I had a few more photos from when those boys were done diving. Because I remember that day. It was warm outside and I had a picnic lunch. I sat there eating my lunch, waiting until those boys returned to the surface. I remember I took a few more photos afterwards, but I can't seem to find them now."

Jane turned her head. "If you ever do find those pictures, Miss Hattie, I would really like to see them."

"I'll search for them, sugar, and let you know," the older lady promised.

As Jane continued to turn the pages a few details caught her eye. "You know, there are some details in your photos that are interesting, Miss Hattie." Jane turned back a few pages and then forward again. "A couple details I've noticed. Some parts of the landscape on the island change with each passing year."

"Like what?" Miss Sadie took a closer look at the photo album.

Jane pointed to two photos. "This looks like a photo of what used to be Sheriff Elias Hart's property. On the edge of the property, that looks onto the cove, but in this earlier photo, there are no trees. Then later, in this other photo, I see an image of Jerry Hart with his father standing by tall trees at the corner of the land closest to the cove."

"That *is* interesting," Miss Hattie replied.

Jane continued to explain, "I also noticed that on my grandparents land, the place where Bobby Sutton's parents rented a house for years, originally there was no wood shed on the corner of that property."

She added, "Then, a few years later, I see a photo of Jerry Hart with Bobby Sutton, and those two boys are standing next to a new wood shed. In a photo taken later on, I can hardly see the shed because now it's surrounded by thick bushes."

"You have keen eyesight, Jane," Miss Sadie commented. "I don't believe I would've noticed those changes."

Jane shrugged. "I used to take photos all the time. I guess I can't help but notice details. It almost looks like someone tried to alter the landscape. I wonder if someone might have wanted to hide something?"

She continued to look through the next photo album that Miss Hattie had set on the table for her to page through.

Jane focused on the details in the old photos, "Here's one more thing I've noticed. It's interesting that, throughout the years, as Miss Hattie took photos, there is a woman that is photographed along the beach near my grandmother's old beach cottage. This woman is elegant and wears a wide-brimmed hat. It's almost like this same woman appears in the background of events, across the years. But she's always in the same location along the shore."

"The problem is we never see the woman's face. We don't know who she is." Miss Hattie commented, "You're right, Jane, that is very interesting."

Jane replied, "I don't know who the woman is, but sometime soon I would like to find out."

She continued to browse through the next photo album. "You also have a photo of Investigative Reporter Sean O'Connor standing next to his new boat." Jane took a closer look. "It looks like Sean named his boat, *Island Pearl.*"

Miss Hattie chuckled. "I remember that day. I had asked Sean to stand beside his new boat. He was happy to do it. He looked as proud as could be. That day, Sean told me he named the boat after his daughter, Sarah." Miss Hattie shook her head, a sadness forming on her features. "It was terrible when he died. A boating accident, the police said. I don't understand what happened."

Miss Sadie commented, "It was horrible. Sean's mother, Mrs. O'Connor, his sister Althea, and his daughter, Sarah's, hearts were broken when he died so suddenly."

Jane spoke sadly, "I remember that time. It was about ten years after my parents died in a boating accident. It's so strange that the police described Sean's death as a boating accident as well."

"Here are two more photos of Sean O'Connor. This first one he's digging in the ground with a shovel. It looks like it's on the edge of Peterson's property with all the trees. In this second photo, Sean has the door open to that shed that's hidden by trees. I wonder what he was looking for?" Curiosity surged through Jane as she stared at the photos.

"I remember when I took those photos. I thought it

was strange at the time." Miss Hattie nodded. "Maybe you and Ward will be able to dig up more information."

Jane nodded. "Maybe."

The older woman stood to her feet and pulled out two more photo albums.

"Sugar, I don't want to keep you here all day. But I think you should look at these last two photo albums." Miss Hattie set the large albums in front of her. "The top binder is during the years when your dad and mom were newly married and so were their friends. The second binder is full of photos that were taken in the last five years or so."

Jane opened the first photo album, eager to see pictures of her parents from when they were younger.

"Here's a photo of my dad and mom walking down the beach holding hands by Grams' beach cottage. They look young. Most likely this is around the time they were first married." Jane's heart melted. It was beautiful to remember her parents happy and loving each other.

Her eyes moved on to other pictures. Jane stopped as her eyes caught one photo in particular. "I see Jerry Hart and his mother-in-law, Florrie Cantrell-Jones. In the picture it looks like Florrie is handing Jerry a thick envelope."

Miss Hattie commented, "I remember when I took that photo. I'd overheard those two in a heated argument and then Florrie handed Jerry Hart the envelope. Jerry was a police officer at that time, not the sheriff. I don't know what was in the envelope, but I've always wondered if it was money."

"Hmm... I wonder." Jane was curious too. She'd think more about that later.

Jane picked up the last album that Miss Hattie had set on the table.

Opening up the album, she noticed these pictures were taken in recent years.

"The first photo looks like Officer Ryan Hart, along with Officer Miles Carter, carrying boxes as they walk along the beach on the cove. They seem to be walking towards Ryan's yacht. In the next photo, it looks like a bag of something is falling out of the box." Jane turned to the next page. "Miss Hattie, here's a photo you took on the cove with Ryan Hart and a man in a Fedora hat. They are transferring boxes from one boat to the other boat."

A shiver of fear shot up her spine. "That last photo, I believe, is a picture of my ex-husband. He has always worn a Fedora hat just like that one. I wonder if Devon is selling his products to Ryan Hart's mother's store."

Jane explained to Miss Hattie and Miss Sadie what she had learned from that day trip she took on Ryan's boat.

"So your ex-husband is on the island then?" Miss Sadie asked.

Jane tucked blonde hair behind one ear. "I haven't seen him yet. But I have this feeling he's here somewhere."

She shivered.

"This next photo is even more telling." She felt as if her breath was cut off as she stared at it. "I have a feeling that both police officers Miles Carter and Ryan Hart might be involved in something that they'd rather folks didn't know about. I can't help but wonder what they're up to?"

"Heavens. Do you think our own police officers might

be doing something illegal?" Miss Hattie's eyes grew large at the thought.

"Maybe. But I don't have any proof." Jane rubbed her forehead, feeling a headache coming on. "I'm curious about why they are carrying those boxes. I want to know what's inside. One thing is for sure, I'm going to ask Ward for his help to find out what's going on."

She asked, "Miss Hattie, do you mind if I borrow the photos we looked at today? I would like to take them to Officer Shelton and Detective Sullivan. They can make copies. I think it would be helpful for them to look through the photos. They might even need to use them as evidence."

Miss Hattie nodded. "If it helps to solve a crime, of course. Whatever you need, Jane."

"Thanks." Jane stood to her feet and hugged both sisters before she walked to the door.

"Just don't be getting yourself into any trouble, sugar," Miss Hattie said firmly. "Asking too many questions is a good way to get the wrong folks angry at you. And then maybe they'll be chasing you to try to shut you up."

Jane's heart rate accelerated at Miss Hattie's words.

"Promise you'll be careful, Jane. We don't want you getting hurt," Miss Sadie commented.

Jane nodded. "I promise to be careful. Thank you again for sharing your photos with me, Miss Hattie. It was wonderful to spend time with the two of you sisters again."

Jane waved goodbye and hurried down the front steps towards her car.

As she drove back home, she had so many questions

about how Miles Carter fit into Ryan's plans. What did the two of them have going on?

She would need to talk to Ward.

But then she remembered that tonight Ward was at the school gym coaching the middle school basketball team.

So far, Noah was enjoying being on the team and learning so much.

She would need to talk with Ward later tonight.

They needed answers. So much was at stake.

For instance, her ex-husband's business dealings with Ryan Hart — was everything on the level? How did Officer Miles Carter fit into this whole picture? And what about the other photos?

Why did she have this feeling, from the photos she saw today, that some landscapes along the cove were deliberately changed, almost as if the people involved had something to hide?

Jane needed answers and was more determined than ever to find them… whatever it took.

CHAPTER TWELVE

ard

WARD PACED UP and down the sidelines of the basketball court in the school gym.

He was doing what he could to offer encouragement and direction to the middle school boys team.

Ward's deep voice was loud, "You boys chose the team name, *Island Sea Lions,* because you are formidable and strong. Don't slow your pace now. You can do this!"

Ward did his best to encourage Sweet Beach Cove's grades seven and eight boys basketball team.

He watched Noah stumble with the ball in his hands. Yet he didn't give up. Jane's son grabbed the ball again. This time he caught it and pivoted. He ran down the court and passed the ball to the point person, who took the shot at the basket and scored.

Noah was learning. Not only that, he was making friends. It was encouraging to see him thrive.

Jane's son was smiling and laughing a lot more lately than when they first moved to the island.

Her blond-haired boy was a handsome young man and it was good to see a smile light up his face more often nowadays.

Now that he was friends with Noah, Ward hoped to win his mother's heart. He had loved her for years. He was doing his best to try to earn her trust and love.

Maybe he needed to be bolder.

Loud voices of parents, cheering their children from the bleachers behind him, interrupted his musings.

Soon, the game was over, with the Island Sea Lions winning by only a hair.

The boys formed a line and slapped hands with the opposing team before heading to the showers.

Ward was in the middle of helping clean up basketballs when a man approached him.

The stranger was about Ward's height and wore a baseball cap. In the dim light of the school gym, the man's skin was pasty and white and he wore sunglasses to hide his eyes.

"Are you the coach for the Island Sea Lions?" the man asked.

Ward nodded. "I am. My name is Ward Hampton."

The man held out his hand. "I'm D.J."

The stranger looked around the basketball court. "I was watching the team. There are lots of good players on this middle school team."

"Yeah, there are. We're grateful to have so many good

players. They make mistakes but they are willing to learn and grow. And they have good attitudes. To me, that's an important factor in a winning team," Ward explained.

D.J. rubbed his chin. "I like the sound of that. A winning team. I have some friends who have kids on this team. I've decided I'd like to sponsor the Island Sea Lions. I'd like to purchase new uniforms for your middle school team with your logos and anything else you need. Would that be something you could use?"

Ward raised one eyebrow, surprised. "That would be great. As it happens, the team uniforms are a little old. Some new team uniforms might be just the thing to spark motivation in these boys. Thank you for your generosity."

"Of course. Do I bring my check to the school?" the man asked.

Ward nodded. "Yes. Just go to the receptionist and tell her you're sponsoring the Island Sea Lions middle school basketball team and she'll give you a receipt."

"Sounds great." The man waved and walked out of the school gym.

Later, as Ward walked towards his car, his thoughts returned to the conversation with the stranger. New uniforms for his team might be just the thing to bring them out of this slump.

"Noah, you did a good job on the court today," Ward spoke to Jane's son as they began the short drive to his home.

"Thanks, Coach." Noah shrugged. "Most of the other guys on the team are better at basketball than I am. I fumble the ball and make mistakes a lot."

Ward parked his car in front of Jane's home.

As they got out of the car, he placed one arm around Noah's shoulders. "Noah, it's all right if you fumble the ball and make mistakes. Everybody on the team has days like that. The important thing is that you are willing to keep learning. That you are willing to keep trying and practicing."

Noah grinned. "I do want to get better, Coach. I want to be one of the best players on the team."

"And you will. Just keep coming to basketball practice and keep learning. You'll soon see all your consistent practice pay off."

"Thanks." Noah opened the door to the house. "Do you want to come inside? I think my mom is here."

He grinned. "Thanks, Noah. I would like to talk with your mom. I'll come inside for a minute."

Ward didn't have to wait long before he saw Jane.

His heart raced at the sight of her.

"Ward, I'm glad you stopped by." Jane's hands fidgeted, a nervous gesture. "A lot has happened in the last few days."

"Like what?" Ward asked.

He listened as she explained about what she learned from reading Matty's journal. And then she talked about the images she'd seen from Miss Hattie's old photo albums.

Jane rubbed the back of her neck. "I think we need to learn more about what's going on. Those photos of Officers Ryan Hart and Miles Carter hauling boxes of stuff onto Ryan's yacht are puzzling."

"I'd also like to talk with Officer Shelton and Detective Sullivan. I'd like to show them Miss Hattie's photos. That way, they can zoom in and get a closer look. Perhaps that will shed light on any missing details." Shivers crept up his spine and his arms suddenly grew cold.

"I can't shake this feeling that there might be something Ryan Hart and Miles Carter are doing that isn't on the level."

Ward grimaced. "I can understand that. Perhaps the two of us should take a walk along the edge of the Peterson property. We could get a good view of the beach area along the cove. You never know what we might find."

"That's a good idea." Jane sighed. "Let's stop by Linda Hart's store tomorrow. I'm busy planning Madison's wedding, but we'll find the time," Jane explained.

"Sounds good. Pick you up for lunch?" Ward offered.

Jane walked to the door and opened it. "Thanks, I'd like that."

Ward stopped on his way out the door. "You're very beautiful standing there in the doorway."

Placing a large hand on her waist, he drew her body to him.

He leaned down and kissed her and whispered softly, "I look forward to seeing you tomorrow, Jane."

Ward was still smiling as he drove down the long driveway away from Jane's place and back to his home.

He couldn't help the thrill that zipped up his spine when Jane didn't pull away.

The fact that she stayed in his arms was a hopeful sign.

He looked forward to kissing her sweet lips once more.

Like an eager schoolboy on his first date, Ward's smile lingered even after he got home later that night.

JANE'S HEART raced at Ward's words.

Her knees turned weak when he slipped his large hands around her waist.

Her traitorous heart was beginning to soften towards this man.

It was doing the very thing she worried might happen.

She could sense the stirrings of vulnerability. She could sense the stirrings of love.

But, for some reason, those feelings didn't flood her with fear like last time.

Today, the usual panic she felt when a man came too close, wasn't there.

This time, she could breathe.

So, she stood still with her back against the door, and waited.

Inch by inch Ward lowered his head until finally his lips touched her own.

She sighed from the warmth of his kiss.

When he stepped back, she felt the loss of his touch.

Ward's whispered words that he would see her tomorrow caused a rush of warmth to flood her body.

Jane waved as he drove away and sighed as she closed the door.

Later that night she lay in bed, her thoughts whirling from Ward's kisses.

Why did her heart betray her by softening towards Ward now, when she had to deal with so many other problems?

One thing was for sure, she would be in close proximity to Ward for the foreseeable future as he helped her solve this mystery.

Somehow, she would need to be able to handle his closeness without dissolving into a puddle of messy emotions.

THE MOMENT he watched Noah get in the car with the basketball coach, he was caught off guard.

Where was the coach taking his son?

There was only one way to find out.

He would follow the coach's car.

He needed to know where the coach was taking his son.

The coach turned off a side road that he realized led onto Peterson's land.

Careful not to be seen, he parked his car on a side road and walked through the trees, continuing to keep an eye on the slow-moving coach's car.

He was surprised when the coach parked the car on Peterson's driveway.

This waterfront acreage was on land connected to the cove.

He knew the place well. He'd been bringing his boat to the cove for a few years now. Business there was very lucrative.

But the question that lingered in his mind: *Why were the coach and his son at this house?*

Watching, he saw Noah enter the house, the coach behind him.

He waited and watched.

Finally his patience was rewarded.

The door opened and he gasped.

There she was — Jane Stafford.

His headstrong ex-wife who escaped him years ago, taking his only son.

Now the coach was kissing her.

Jealousy consumed him.

It looked like he had even more reason for revenge.

Since he knew where she lived, perhaps it was time to do what he planned.

It was time to get back at Jane for taking his son away.

Very soon he would take his son. Noah would be back with him — exactly where he belonged.

THE NEXT DAY, Jane stepped outside and waved at Ward, whose car just drove onto the yard.

She was busy locking the front door behind her, when she looked downwards.

A gasp escaped her lips.

Plopped against the bottom of the door, was a torn old Saint Bernard plush stuffed dog, with soft white and brown fur.

Her eyes widened in recognition.

It was the same stuffed dog that Jane had desperately tried to find in her hurry to escape her abusive ex years ago.

Jane searched but couldn't find it anywhere, so she had to leave it behind. Only five years old at the time, her son had cried himself to sleep for weeks after they left their home.

Noah had named this stuffed dog Buddy. The same name he gave the real dog she recently gave her son for his birthday.

Her son had been heartbroken, believing that his beloved stuffed dog, Buddy, was lost to him forever.

But now, unexpectedly, his beloved stuffed animal appeared on her doorstep.

Crouching down, Jane got a closer look.

Picking up the stuffed dog, she noticed the tear on Buddy's neck that she had stitched up. This was definitely her son's fluffy dog.

The fact that it had shown up on her doorstep, could only mean one thing.

Her ex was not only back on the island, but he knew where she and Noah lived.

A knot of fear formed in her belly. Her grip tightened on the stuffed animal.

Without warning, her fingers caught on a red ribbon tied around its neck.

Leaning closer, she saw the attached note.

On the white note card words were written in bold: *You're not the only one who can hide. I know where you live. You are being watched.*

Icy fear twisted around her heart.

She choked back a cry.

Footsteps sounded on the stairs leading up to her front door. "Jane, is everything alright?"

Swallowing back tears, she stood to her feet.

Holding out the stuffed dog she began to explain what happened years ago.

"I'm sorry I never told you, Ward. But there's no doubt this threatening note is from my ex. He is not only on the island, but he knows where my son and I live." Jane covered her mouth, but not before a soft sob escaped her lips.

Ward slipped his arms around her and pulled her close. "Shh, sweetheart. It's going to be alright. He's just trying to scare you."

"It's working." Her voice trembled. "I'm scared of what Devon might do. I'm scared I won't be able to protect Noah." Jane pulled back, tears running down her cheeks.

"Then we'll make sure we're more protective of your son," Ward whispered into her hair.

"That will help. But don't you see, Ward?" Her lips trembled. "I'm the one to blame for this. I used my real name for the business license. Everybody knows who I am now. Anyone can track me through public records. Now my ex has returned to the island and knows where I live." A shiver ripped up her spine. "My son's life is being threatened and it's all my fault."

"No, honey, it's not your fault." Ward's hand moved in slow circles along her back. "It's Devon who is at fault. He's the man who started abusing both you and Noah years ago. He's a bully and an abuser who must be stopped."

Jane swallowed and nodded slowly.

She thought of her innocent son and how he had asked if they would keep running away for the rest of their lives

— or if they would finally settle into a real home of their own.

She knew her answer.

Her ex was not going to get in the way of her giving her son his dream.

A new resolve and determination rose up inside her.

Quickly, she wiped tears from her cheeks. "You're right, Ward. I won't lie down in defeat. I won't give up. It's Devon who must be stopped. There must be a way to do this. Will you help me stop him, Ward?"

"You know I will, Jane." Ward nodded with a grin. "I can see that fire in your eyes that I've come to love. Alright, what's the next step?"

Jane thought for a minute. "I'll put this stuffed animal inside. I'll need to ask Mrs. Morrison to pick up Noah from school."

Jane opened the door to her house. She hurried inside to talk with Mrs. Morrison and, after explaining, she handed the older woman the stuffed animal.

The older woman shook her head in worry and made the sign of the cross. "Oh my, dear. Don't worry. I'll pick Noah up from school and take care of him. We'll keep him safe here at home."

"Thanks, Mrs. Morrison, I appreciate that." Jane knew her housekeeper had a mother's heart that wouldn't rest until she saw her son back home and safe.

"I will be spending time with Ward for a few hours. But I'll be home later today." Jane waved as she hurried out the door.

Ward drove them to an Italian bistro for lunch.

He looked out the window, nodding to a store across the street. "I thought it might be a good idea to eat here today. We can enjoy lunch and continue to watch Linda's store across the street."

"That is a good idea." Jane took a sip of water, her hand shaking slightly as inner worry gnawed at her.

As the waitress brought their food, Jane barely managed to eat a few bites. She fought to control her swirling emotions.

Ward reached over and held her hand. "I can see you're really worried."

"I am worried. Sorry, I'm a poor lunch companion today." Jane swallowed a last bite and pushed her plate to the side. "I'm sorry, I just can't eat another bite."

"It's alright, Jane." Ward was just finishing his lasagne when Jane looked out the window.

Her face clouded with uneasiness. "Ward, look across the street. Ryan Hart is walking into his mother's store."

Ward raised one eyebrow. "I see Miles Carter is just stepping out of his cruiser parked nearby. He's going inside store, too."

"Let's go. Maybe we can learn something today." Ward stood to his feet and grabbed Jane's hand. Quickly, he paid for their meal.

Together, they hurried out of the bistro and across the street.

Ward opened the door and Jane stepped inside the store.

Immediately, her eyes widened.

The store was filled with Christmas themed decorations and products.

Jane stared wordlessly as she looked around. The vast amount of products on the shelves was amazing.

"At least half of these products are made for children. And more than half are Christmas items," Jane whispered to Ward.

He chuckled. "Didn't you see the name of this store?"

Jane shook her head. "I didn't even look. What is it?"

"The store's name is, Made For Children." Ward shrugged as he looked around. "It sort of explains all the children's products."

Jane bit down hard on her lower lip, frustrated to be surrounded once again by Christmas themes. "I guess. Well, let's look around and then we can get out of here."

Ward squeezed her hand.

She knew the man beside her was trying to reassure her, but it wasn't really doing much good. At least, not with the way she felt today.

They continued walking down the aisles until suddenly Jane stopped.

"Most of these children's products have Devon's logo on them," Jane whispered.

"What do you mean?" A crease formed between Ward's brows.

Jane pointed to a rideable wooden reindeer. "On the side of the wooden horses and reindeer you can see the logo, *HCE*. That's one of Devon's company's names."

"What do the initials stand for?" The man beside her traced the engraved letters on the neck of the wooden toy.

"Hollingsworth Children's Emporium." Jane sighed. "It's always been Devon's way to make everything he does as convoluted as possible. He likes to have his name on everything. He's the biggest narcissist I know."

Ward shook his head. "Sounds like your ex is a control freak."

"He is." Jane looked over to the front counter where the woman was busy talking on the phone to a customer.

As she looked behind the counter, she spotted a large sign leaning up against the back wall.

"Do you see that sign behind the front counter?" Jane's eyes widened. "It has Devon's name painted on it. I wonder if he has already bought the store from Linda Hart?"

Ward murmured. "Hmm. That sign does look like your ex has taken over control of the store."

She bit her lip.

Jane was suddenly anxious to escape the store.

The reminders of those years with her cruel ex-husband were too much for her to dwell on.

"Maybe we should leave..." Jane started to say, when Ward stopped and leaned towards her.

"Let's wait for a minute." Ward turned his head as if listening. "Do you hear those voices in the backroom of the store?"

Jane strained to listen. "Yeah. It sounds like the voices of two men arguing."

"Exactly," Ward whispered. "I see the sales girl is busy behind the counter. Let's wander over to the aisle of products that is closest to the door that leads to the backroom. Maybe we'll overhear something that will be helpful."

Ward grabbed her hand and led her over to the aisle of products that was closest to the closed backroom door.

The sales girl began to walk towards them, busy chewing her gum. "Can I help you find something?"

She looked to be a twenty-something girl with short blonde hair and brown eyes.

Jane smiled. "We're just browsing right now. If we need help, we'll come get you."

"Alright. Just let me know." The girl turned and hurried back to her workspace behind the counter.

Ward whispered, "Let's move a little closer to the products at the end of this aisle. That way hopefully we'll be better able to listen to the conversation."

"Sure," Jane whispered and moved towards the end of the aisle. "I can hear what they are saying now."

She glanced uneasily over her shoulder, looking at the closed door, overhearing what the low male voices were saying.

It sounded like the conversation was between Officers Ryan Hart and Miles Carter.

She held a children's toy in her hand, pretending interest, as she leaned closer to listen to the men's conversation in the other room.

The first man's voice complained, "I don't see our contact here. Wasn't he supposed to meet us today? I need him to be here. I'm running out of the supplies and people will start getting angry."

The other man's voice replied, "He called. He told me he ran into a bit of trouble. He said he was going to go on a run to get more packages. Tell your clients a new shipment is on its way. It should be here tomorrow. That should make them happy."

The first man's voice said, "Ryan, I don't like it when our ability to get supplies falls behind schedule. That's usually when I get yelled at by clients."

The other man's voice, apparently Ryan Hart, sounded irritated as he spoke. "It can't be helped. Our contact told me he needed to change his plans a little because a woman from his past had resurfaced. Now, he says he'll need to figure out some new plans."

Jane sucked in a quick breath. It was Ryan's voice. When he talked about his contact, did he mean Devon? When he mentioned the woman from the past, was he talking about her?

The first man muttered, "Well, our contact should plan his life a little better and leave his personal stuff out of his business with us."

Ryan spoke angrily, "Listen, Miles. It couldn't be helped, okay? Don't go saying stuff like this when we see our contact next time. Right now, this guy brings in at least eighty percent of our income."

The first man – apparently Miles Carter – interrupted, "I know. But we do have ten percent of our income coming from 'helping ourselves' from inside the depart-ment." He chuckled. "We're earning big cash right from under their noses. You gotta love the irony."

Ryan responded in a firm voice, "Yes, I do appreciate the irony, Miles. But it's important that you remember what I'm telling you. Don't say or do anything that will make our contact regret doing business with us, alright? Or I'll make you regret it."

Miles agreed, his voice subdued, "Alright, alright. I'll stop."

Suddenly, all was quiet in the backroom. The only sounds were the cutting open and movement of cardboard boxes.

Ward whispered, "I think we should get going. Before those two guys come out of that backroom and see us."

"Sure. Let's go." Jane followed Ward until they were outside.

Ward held her hand as they walked out of the store. They were about to cross the street when they saw another car pull up and park along the sidewalk.

Jane glanced over and gasped.

The fedora hat on the tall man's head was a dead giveaway.

Her heart raced like it was going ninety.

"That's my ex-husband. He's here," Jane whispered in low, urgent tones.

Just as they started to walk across the street, Devon turned and saw them.

A deep crease formed on her ex's forehead as soon as he spotted Jane. He looked back at the store and then back at her.

Jane turned to Ward. "Let's hurry."

Finally they reached the car.

As Ward began to drive away, Jane sighed. "I can't believe Devon saw us come out of the store."

"Maybe he'll assume we were shopping," Ward suggested.

Jane shook her head. "No, he'll be suspicious. I know

him. He'll wonder what we were doing in the store. He'll assume we're up to no good."

"Well, let him stew. It's our business what we were doing." Ward grinned. "And speaking of what we were doing in that store, care to share your thoughts on that conversation we heard?"

Jane began to share her perception of what they had overheard.

"I think the two men talking were Ryan Hart and Miles Carter." She turned to Ward.

"I do too. But their conversation was troubling," Ward added.

Jane nodded, swallowing. "When the one man talked about his contact, I think he meant my ex. And I couldn't help but believe that the woman from his past was me. He said he needs to figure out new plans."

To her dismay, her voice broke slightly.

Ward reached over and gently held her hand. "I believe what you're saying is true, but don't be afraid, Jane. I'm with you in this. Together we'll deal with your ex and whoever else is trying to hurt you. I promise to do everything I can to protect you and your son."

"I know you will. Thank you, Ward." Jane chewed on her lower lip and stole a look at him. "I do have one other thing that worries me."

Ward turned to her. "What's that?"

The nagging in the back of her mind refused to be stilled.

Jane explained, "When the one guy said that ten percent of their income came from helping themselves from inside the department. He said he loved the irony that they were earning big cash from under their noses. Which department do you think the man was referring to?"

After a long pause, Ward answered without wavering, "I think they might have been talking about the police department."

Jane gasped. "The police department is supposed to be catching the bad guys. If this was Ryan and Miles talking, what do they mean when they say they are helping themselves inside the police department. What are they doing?"

Ward shrugged. "I don't know. Except, I'll say this. Whatever those two are doing, it's got to be related to whatever 'business' they have going on with Devon. And, whatever they are doing inside the police department, I question whether it's legal since most of the other officers don't realize they are doing it."

"We need to find out what those two are doing. What should we do now?" Jane asked as he parked in front of her house.

"We bring this information back to Officer Shelton. Let's hear what he has to say." Ward paused and turned to her,"You and I should take that walk along the cove. I'm curious if we'll find anything that will help uncover the mystery as to why Jerry and Bobby, and later Sean O'Connor, had an interest in that shed on the property the Sutton's lived on years ago."

His words inspired confidence in Jane. They would do this together.

"Yes, that's what we should do, Ward. I'm having coffee with Kenna later tonight, but we should plan to talk with Neville soon. Thanks for all your help with this, Ward. I'm beginning to realize how much I need you." Jane leaned over and kissed his cheek. "Thank you."

Hearing Ward's contented sigh as she got out of the car, caused an unexpected smile to turn up the corners of her lips.

Jane

HER BEST FRIEND'S eyes grew wide as Jane shared all the details of what she had recently discovered.

They sat at a table that was located on the outside patio in front of *BeansWithBooks.*

They enjoyed another chance to spend time together.

"Those photos Miss Hattie had of Ryan and your ex seem to tell a sobering story. Then, the fact that you and Ward overheard Officers Ryan and Miles whispering together in the back room of Linda Hart's store makes me wonder what they are up to?" A deep crease formed between Kenna's brows.

Jane took a sip of her tea before setting down the cup. "I've been asking myself the same questions. Ward suggested we bring Miss Hattie's photos to Officer Shelton and Detective Sullivan so they could take a look."

"That's a great idea, Jane." Kenna leaned close to whisper, "You know, the police department does have forensic analysis that they use on photographs. You never know, they might find some new clues."

Jane rubbed the back of her neck.

"That's true. I guess we'll see." She shrugged. "We haven't gotten the answers we need yet. On top of that, now I have an even greater worry of what my ex might do."

She told her friend about Noah's old stuffed dog that Devon had left on her front step. "I wonder if he's trying to scare me into leaving?"

Kenna shook her head. "It's possible. Most likely your ex is letting you know he sees what you're doing and knows where you live. That sort of thing is cruel and vindictive."

Jane cleared her throat. "I think you're starting to understand Devon. I have to admit, it's got me worried. However, I'm grateful Ward and Mrs. Morrison have each agreed to watch out for Noah. I feel better knowing that."

A thoughtful smile curved up Kenna's lips. "Hmm. Ward Hampton. He seems to be constantly by your side lately, Jane. Have the two of you grown closer?"

Jane smiled to herself as she spoke, "We have. There's still a part of me that is scared to let myself be vulnerable with him."

She shifted uneasily on her chair.

Her friend replied, "I think you're afraid to fall in love again. Ward is a good guy, Jane. Give him a chance.

Choose to break the walls around your heart. Let yourself fall in love."

"Maybe you're right." Jane nodded tentatively.

Later that evening, as she drove back home, her friend's words continued to tumble around and around in her mind.

Perhaps Kenna was right.

Ward had been so faithful with helping her solve this mystery and protecting her son. Her heart knew he was a good and trustworthy man.

Maybe it was time for her to open up her heart again.

Maybe it was time for her to be vulnerable again.

Maybe it was time for her to love again.

THE NEXT DAY, she and Ward walked together towards the police station.

Jane's heart thumped madly as they grew near the place.

Would Detective Sullivan be willing to listen to what they had to say?

She could imagine the difficult position they were placing him in because of what they overheard at the store and saw in the photos.

If those crimes were proven true, it would implicate two fellow police officers.

She chewed on her lower lip and stole a look at Ward.

He turned, and the warmth of his smile successfully disarmed the tension in her body.

Reaching over, he held her hand and gave her a reassuring squeeze as they entered the building.

The simple touch of his hand holding hers calmed her worries. She had a lot to be grateful for with the way Ward had faithfully been helping her to search for answers.

Leaning down, Ward whispered, "It'll be alright, Jane. Neville said Detective Sullivan is one of the good cops and is easy to talk to."

Jane smiled over at him, grateful Ward was at her side.

As soon as they talked with the officer behind the counter, they were ushered down a hallway to the detective's office.

After Jane knocked, he immediately called for them to enter.

"Thanks for agreeing to see us today, Detective Sullivan." Jane's fingers gripped the brown envelope in her hands as she sat on the other side of the desk and faced the solemn features of the detective.

She was still surprised that, somehow, Ward managed to get an appointment to talk with the detective.

"It was Officer Shelton who assured me you had an important matter to discuss. Tell me, what's this about?" The detective's voice was low with a depth of authority.

Jane turned quickly to look at Ward. He nodded and smiled to encourage her to continue.

"As you might know, my sisters and I have been asking questions of folks who knew my parents. We've been trying to find answers to the mystery of their deaths years ago," Jane started to explain.

"Yes, if I remember correctly, your sister Alex was

resolved to get more answers last year. That was even after the Sheriff informed her he wasn't going to reopen the case. I must say, you and your sisters are determined, I'll give you that." Detective Sullivan's grin of amusement settled her nerves.

"We get that persistence from our late grandmother, I'm afraid. Grams never could let an idea go when she got a bee in her bonnet about something." A grin overtook Jane's features.

"I knew your late grandmother. I believe you're right." The detective winked at her in merriment. "Let's get down to business. What do you have for me?"

Jane cleared her throat nervously. "Miss Hattie offered to show me pictures she has taken on the island over the past few decades. When I sifted through the photos in her album, I found images that raised some questions and are frankly worrisome. Photos of Police Officers Ryan Hart and Miles Carter moving barrels and boxes from one boat to another along the cove."

A crease formed between the detective's brows. "Let's take a look."

Jane handed Detective Sullivan the envelope. "All the photos are inside. Miss Hattie wrote the date on the back of each photo."

Soon, the detective was looking through the photos. A furrow deepened between his brows the longer the detective studied the images.

Finally, he looked up at the two of them.

"I have to admit, these photos don't look good for these officers." Detective Sullivan released a heavy sigh. "Do you have anything else you want to tell me?"

Ward's concerned voice broke into silence. "Yes. After Ryan Hart told Jane that he often made deliveries to his mother's shop, Jane and I decided to check it out."

"I see." The detective sighed. "And did you learn anything new?"

Ward smiled. "We saw Ryan Hart and Miles Carter enter the store and a few minutes later we followed."

Detective Sullivan's eyes widened. "You confronted them?"

"No, we didn't. We pretended we were ordinary shoppers and began to roam the aisles. After a few minutes we overheard male voices. They came from the back room and the voices sounded a lot like Ryan Hart and Miles Carter."

The detective folded his arms across his chest. "Go on."

Nervously, Jane bit her lip. "I believe the man in the fedora hat in those photos is my ex, Devon. In their secret conversation, they mentioned their contact. From the photos, I think Devon is involved with Ryan and Miles and those boxes and barrels they bring to Linda Hart's store."

"What we overheard seems unbelievable, but we needed to tell you anyway." She paused before blurting out the rest of the story, "Ward and I overheard Miles tell Ryan, 'We have ten percent of our income coming from helping ourselves from inside the department. We're earning big cash right from under their noses. You gotta love the irony.'"

Detective Sullivan ran a shaky hand through his hair. "You believe they were talking about the police department?"

Ward nodded. "Yes. It sounds crazy, but that's what we overheard."

The detective rubbed the back of his neck and a look of tired sadness passed over his features.

"It's difficult to believe." Detective Sullivan shook his head. "But, these photos, along with what you overheard the men saying, is evidence against them. However, I still don't think that'll be enough proof of wrongdoing."

Ward leaned closer and spoke in low tones, "Maybe not. However, Officer Shelton had one more idea. He was curious what Ryan and Miles are doing inside the department that is bringing the extra cash."

He turned to Jane and then back to the detective. "I told him it's possible they are trafficking drugs."

Detective Sullivan shook his head. "I hope not. Those two would be locked away for a very long time if that were true."

Jane nodded. "They would. But still, it's important to find out the truth. So then, how do we find the evidence we need?"

Ward whispered in low tones, "Officer Shelton mentioned you have an evidence locker inside the police department."

"We do." A frown formed on the detective's forehead. "What's your plan?"

Ward shrugged his shoulders. "I suggest we use video to track their movements, to see what they're up to."

Detective Sullivan spoke in low tones. "We already use recorded video that tracks the movement of people coming in and going out of the evidence locker."

Jane asked. "Do those videos show the faces of which officers enter the room and what they do there?"

"Let me take a look." The detective opened up a file on his computer and was able to access the videos of the evidence locker room. "From these videos I don't see any officers entering the room later in the evening from the previous week."

Jane whispered, "Is it possible that someone took the video and edited the parts they didn't want anyone to see?"

The detective nodded. "Yes. However, they would need to be a police officer to get access to the videos. I suppose that would mean, either Officer Ryan Hart or Officer Miles Carter would have access."

He ran a hand through his hair, a worried look crossing his features. "Things aren't looking good for those police officers."

Ward spoke in low tones, "We need to figure out what's going on. I have an idea. Why don't I figure out a way to plant a video camera so it's hidden somewhere in the evidence locker room. We'll soon find out if there's something fishy going on."

Detective Sullivan sat motionless behind the desk for a long while before he spoke, "I don't like the idea of spying on our own police officers, but I think your idea is a good one, Ward. I can't mention this to Sheriff Hart for obvious reasons."

The detective added, "And I don't know who on the police force is compromised. So, despite the fact this idea of yours might be borderline illegal, I can't see any other way to get the evidence we need. Let's do it."

"Alright. I'll have Officer Shelton let me inside that room later today to take a look," Ward replied.

The detective said, "Make sure you get in and out of there fast, preferably without the other police officers seeing you."

Ward grinned. "They won't even know I've been there."

Jane stood to her feet. "Before we go, there is one other thing I should tell you."

"What's that?"

"When we walked out of the store, we saw my ex get out of the vehicle and walk into the store. I think there is a good chance he's involved in all of this." Jane shook her head in dismay.

Detective Sullivan asked, "Did your ex see you?"

Jane nodded. "He did. And the look he gave me was very hostile. I think he might have noticed that we had just been inside the store. So, he might try to get back at me. He's been trying to scare me lately. I just thought you should know."

She told the detective about the stuffed dog left on her doorstep with the threatening note.

"Jane, I think you should be very careful. Watch yourself and keep an eye on your son. If your ex-husband is involved in all of this, he might lash out to try and scare you so that you'll back off."

Unshed tears filled her eyes. "I know. And I will do everything I can to protect my son. I won't stop trying to find answers to any details that might be connected to my parents' deaths."

Detective Sullivan stared at her for a moment, before a

slow smile appeared. "Then I'm here to help you to find those answers."

"Thank you for your help, Detective," Jane replied as Ward walked to the door with her.

He opened the door, speaking in a low voice, "I'm happy to help. It's important we get to the truth. Let me know how things go."

"We will," Jane assured him.

As they drove away from the police station, her thoughts were on all they had discovered so far.

There were definitely strange things going on.

Ward turned to her. "I hope the video recorder we plant inside that room will be something that will give us proof about what those officers are up to."

A cold shiver went up Jane's back. "I do too. Yet, I can't help but wonder if there will be more folks who live in the community who will object to all our efforts to search for the truth."

"If they object, that can't be helped. We need to keep digging until the truth comes out," Ward added.

"I suppose so." Jane squirmed uneasily in her car seat. She didn't like the idea of folks on the island attacking her for searching for answers behind her parents' deaths. But maybe it was like Ward said, it couldn't be helped if they wanted to get to the truth.

"If we want to dig deeper for answers, I think I know where our next stop should be." He parked his car in front of Jane's house and turned to her with a grin.

"Where's that?"

"The edge of the Peterson property leads down to the cove. I have my video camera with me. I think we should see if we can uncover any secrets." Ward smiled as he stepped out of the car.

Jane got out of the car, feeling hopeful. "Sure, let's do it. I just need to grab my camera."

She dashed into the house and hurried to where Ward stood leaning against the car.

The wide camera strap was behind her neck and her camera hung low on her belly. She had attached a zoom lens in case she needed close-up shots.

Jane was eager to learn whatever new information there was that would lead to solving this mystery.

ane

As Ward and Jane neared the edge of the Peterson property, they ran into a large cluster of trees.

She stopped and looked up, one hand shielding her eyes from the rays of the sun.

"It's strange, but when I was a young girl, and my sisters and I would walk towards the cove, I don't remember seeing these trees." Jane turned to Ward.

He was in the middle of adjusting his digital video camera when he stopped.

Glancing up at the trees, he said, "Maybe those trees weren't here when you were a child. You should ask Miss Hattie if you can take another look at her old photos. That way you could see a timeline of what the landscape looked like along the cove from when you were young."

"That's a good idea." Jane nodded and took pictures of the trees near the cove so she could compare the past and present day photos.

Next, she snapped a photo of the view from the cliff's edge of the Peterson's property.

The view was incredible from this location.

Jane could see much farther than she imagined. A wide expanse of blue water surrounded the island. In the distance, she could see Lizzie's cottage.

Farther still, she could see waterfront properties she recognized, like old man Theodore Montgomery's place and other folks that had been fixtures on the island for as long as she could remember.

Memories of the strong community support and peace that she enjoyed during her childhood years returned. She longed to feel like that again, now that she was living back on the island.

As the two of them walked slowly down the slope towards the beach, Jane continued to take photos.

Her mind was busy as she thought about all they had uncovered so far in their search for the truth.

With the new details that had been revealed, Jane was compelled to capture even more pictures so they wouldn't miss any more details.

She looked downwards towards the cove.

"I'm surprised there aren't any boats by the cove today," Jane commented to Ward as she continued to look.

Ward scanned the area, recording it with his video

camera. "Yeah, that is strange. Perhaps our guys like to do their business after the sun goes down."

"Maybe." They reached the flat area near the sandy beach and continued to walk.

"Somewhere around here is where your great-grandfather Captain Henry Stafford's ship sunk, right?" Ward turned towards Jane.

"Yeah. Grams and Gramps took us girls a few times after we went to live with them. She said it was right near that large rock that Captain Stafford's ship sank." Jane added, "Some folks on the island are convinced that there's a pink diamond somewhere on that ship."

Ward grimaced. "Sometimes I wonder if that gem will ever be found."

"Me too. But, knowing my sisters, they'll want to keep searching for it." Jane sighed. "Let's not worry about the pink diamond today."

She turned and looked over at the property that joined Peterson's land.

"Let's go scout out this place. This is where the Sutton family lived for a lot of years. This has been Stafford land ever since Henry Stafford won this waterfront property in a game of chance from Ike Cantrell decades ago." Jane walked beside Ward and continued to snap photos as they climbed the small hill.

Together they reached the property line and spotted the yellow bungalow style house in the distance.

"This home is where Bobby Sutton spent his childhood. You can see the place in Miss Hattie's photos." Jane began walking along the land.

Ward stopped the video camera for a moment and turned to her. "Isn't this the land that your late grandmother gave your younger sister as her inheritance?"

Jane nodded. "It is. I remember coming here once as a child. It was the year after my parents died. My grandparents wanted to have a day that was in memory of our parents. I remember my mom's younger brother, Uncle Tony, also was with us. It was a nice day and we decided to enjoy a family picnic."

Shivers rippled through Jane as she vividly recalled that day.

Feelings of worry deepened the crease between her brows.

She wasn't going to think of that now. "We didn't come here very often because another family was always renting the property."

"What's the matter, Jane? You look worried." Ward looked over at her, a puzzled expression on his face.

Jane shook her head. She wasn't ready to share the intimate details of her past with this man. At least not yet.

"Sometimes I get a creepy feeling about this place, that's all," she whispered.

Memories of what happened in this place did give her an unpleasant feeling.

His dark eyes were tender with understanding as he looked over at her. "In that case, we won't stay long."

Looking around, he held up his video camera again and pivoted.

Ward turned to get a wide range of view of the area when, suddenly, he stopped. "There's a large grove of trees in that corner. I wonder if that's where the shed is located that you saw in Miss Hattie's photos?"

Jane's pulse raced at the thought. "Maybe. Let's take a look."

Soon, they reached the poplar trees. The foliage was so thick that they were forced to push back branches.

They went about twenty feet before they stumbled upon an old shed. The rustic building looked really old, built with mismatched sizes of plywood and long pieces of two by four planks.

The building was about fifteen feet long and ten feet wide and looked like the wood might snap in pieces if the wind was too strong.

"So, this is the shed that they tried to hide." Ward rubbed the back of his neck. "Ready to look inside?"

She shoved down the fear that pierced her veins at the thought of being inside that enclosed space once more.

"Sure," Jane replied automatically, even though her emotions were floundering in an agonizing maelstrom.

They walked up to the wide, weather-beaten door.

Ward pulled the handle, but the door wouldn't open. Finally, he put his full weight into it and slowly it creaked open.

The musty smell, combined with the dust floating through the air, made both of them sneeze.

"I don't think anyone has used this shed for a real long time," Ward commented as they walked inside.

Jane swallowed. "You're probably right."

Looking around, she saw broken old wood pieces.

"I remember seeing all this wood as a little girl. Now,

years later, as an adult, I see it differently. I'm curious about all that's inside this shed," Jane whispered.

The one window at the back of the shed was wide enough to allow a ray of light to brighten the room.

Ward was busy pivoting slowly to record everything in the room with his video camera.

Jane took a few photos as she tiptoed through the scattered wood pieces to reach the far end of the building.

Crouching down, she reached into her pocket and pulled out a set of light gloves, quickly pulling them on.

She didn't want painful wood splinters on her skin.

Reaching over, she began to lift the different sized wood pieces one at a time.

It was a few minutes of lifting and discarding into a new pile before she came upon a piece of shattered wood.

Faded words from years ago were etched onto the wood.

Jane reached down and lightly removed the dust and dirt with her gloved hand.

She leaned closer so she could see the words clearer.

The letters written in script were barely visible.

Island Pearl.

Her eyes widened.

She could hardly believe it. Just to be sure she was seeing correctly, she wiped the wood a second time, in an effort to clear any remaining debris.

Tracing the letters with a finger, she read the same words again.

Looking over at Ward she said, "You are not going to believe what I just found."

He looked over at her and hurriedly turned off his video camera.

Pivoting on his feet, Ward began to carefully walk among the pile of debris until he reached her.

"What is it?"

Jane pointed at the jagged piece of wood with the faded words. "Do those words mean anything to you?"

His mouth dropped open and he sucked in a breath. "That was the name of the boat that Sean O'Connor owned. What's it doing here?"

She shrugged. "Your guess is as good as mine. However, since this shed is hidden from public view, I am curious why someone would want to hide the debris from the late Sean O'Connor's boat — in what the police told the public was a 'boating accident?'"

Ward raised one eyebrow. "Probably because Sean O'Connor's death wasn't an accident after all."

"Bingo." The groove between Jane's brows deepened. "But what's strange is that, according to the timeline of Miss Hattie's photos, the trees around this shed were planted not long after my parents' deaths."

"Sean O'Connor died ten years after my parents. And the police determined that the cause of death, for both, to be a 'boating accident.' Because of that, I'm curious if we might find debris from my parents' boat somewhere in this shed as well?"

Ward whispered in a low voice, "Wouldn't that be something?"

"It would be something alright," Jane mumbled, feeling nervous and overwhelmed. She touched the broken wood again and she ran her hand along it. All of a sudden, her finger caught on a nail.

"Wait, there's something here." Jane leaned down for a closer look. "It's a nail, but there's a piece of cloth attached to it."

Ward sucked in a breath. "I don't think we should touch the cloth as that could be some sort of evidence. We should bring a few of these wood pieces to show Detective Sullivan."

"Are you thinking maybe the police can get a DNA test done?" Jane turned to Ward.

He nodded. "I think it we should ask for a DNA test. We'll see what the detective has to say about that. Meanwhile, there might be more old wood pieces that might give us clues."

Jane agreed. "Yeah. We might as well take a look and see what we can find."

Immediately, Jane got busy reaching for the pieces of wood debris that lay on the shed floor.

Soon, Ward began to help.

They developed a system. Each of them tossed all the wood pieces they had already looked at into the corner.

It wasn't until there were only a few wood pieces left on the floor, that Jane spotted another partial wood piece that had faded words written on it.

After wiping off all dirt, Jane looked closer.

"There's two words that I can't quite make out. The words written here are, *Lady Anne.*" Jane gasped and a hand flew to her throat. "I think this broken piece of wood is from my parents' boat when they died. My father named his boat after my mother."

Ward shook his head in disbelief as he stared at the faded words on the piece of wood in Jane's hands.

Shock, fear, and anger, caused a knot to form in her belly. "It's hard to believe that this was where the scattered pieces of my parents' boat were hidden all these years. It's starting to look like somebody out there has been trying really hard to hide the truth of what happened years ago."

"I agree." Ward nodded, swallowing. He gave her a sidelong glance of utter disbelief.

Ward took his video camera. "I want to explore outside the shed to see if there's anything else we missed."

"Alright." Jane watched him leave. He didn't close the shed door, but instead left it wide open.

She didn't mind since it increased the amount of light in the room. The one small window at the back of the small shed, made the space feel quite dark.

Jane shivered.

It was time to get to work.

Grabbing a bag from her backpack, Jane placed the two wood pieces with the faded boat names inside the bag.

She would take them to Officer Shelton or Detective Sullivan.

Jane was so preoccupied with her thoughts, that she jerked back when a gust of wind suddenly slammed the shed door shut.

The wind blew hard and rattled the only window in the enclosed space.

A shiver ran up her spine.

Suddenly, horrible memories swirled in her mind of

that windy day she'd endured locked inside this very building years ago.

When she was a little girl, her Uncle Tony played a mean trick on her.

To this day, it was the reason she was terrified of being stuck in a small space.

There was no way she could relive that nightmare again.

Hurrying to the door, she tried to open it.

The door was stuck.

The door handle on the outside must have slammed down and locked her inside.

A chill of fear swept up her spine.

Now she was stuck.

"Help, Ward!" Jane called loudly. All she heard was the straining of the wind through the trees.

After she'd called out a third time, panic welled in her throat.

It took about ten minutes of calling Ward's name before she could hear the sound of someone pushing and pulling on the door handle.

Finally, the wide wood door flung open.

Ward stood motionless as he stared at her.

Her body shook. She couldn't stop swallowing back the fear that consumed her.

His dark eyes grew wide with what looked like worry.

Without thinking, she flew at him, throwing her arms around his neck.

Immediately, his strong arms wrapped around her slender body.

"Jane, you're shaking," Ward whispered, his breath

warm against her hair. "Shh. You'll be alright. I'm here now."

His whispered words calmed her.

"Let's get away from this shed." Ward wrapped an arm around her waist, holding her close as they walked.

They didn't stop walking until they came to a clearing in the yard by the house.

Leaning against the side of the house, Ward turned to her.

With one hand he began to gently draw soothing circles on her back. "Now, tell me what happened."

She pulled back slightly and, with hurried movements, wiped tears from her cheeks before she replied.

Her voice erupted in a broken whisper, "The wind grew fierce and, suddenly, the door of the shed slammed shut. I was locked inside. It was very dark all around me."

"And…" Ward gently prodded. "What happened?"

Jane stepped out of his embrace, that familiar fear rising up inside of her. She shook her head and whispered, "And I was scared, that's all."

Ward clenched his mouth tighter in frustration.

He ran trembling fingers through his hair.

Finally, his low whisper got her attention, "No, that's not enough. I know there's more to it or you wouldn't have been so afraid."

She swallowed back emotions, yet remained silent.

He leaned closer and stared at her, his eyes dark with intensity. "Please don't leave me guessing, Jane. You've told me you want to build a life here. You've told me you're ready for us to be together. But you keep shutting the door every time I try to take a step inside your heart."

Her thoughts circled the hamster wheel of fear until she ran out of strength to keep a tight rein on her secrets any longer.

Jane, you need to tell Ward the truth. How can you expect him to understand the real you, if you don't tell him about who you really are. It's time. Be brave.

"You're right, Ward." Her voice sounded hoarse to her own ears. "It's time I told you. The truth is, I've kept a lock and key around the hurt and shame. It's because I didn't want to give you a reason to abandon me. I didn't want you to see what a mess I am. I didn't want you to look at me the same way my Uncle Tony did during my childhood."

Jane blinked back sudden tears that pricked the back of her eyelids.

Ward gently touched her cheek. "I won't see you that way, I promise. Just give me a chance, okay?"

Awkwardly, she cleared her throat and nodded slowly. "Alright, I'll tell you. The moment the shed door slammed unexpectedly, a terrible memory returned from when I was a little girl."

Ward studied her face, the crease of worry deepening as he listened. "What did you remember?"

Jane shivered with vivid recollection. "I was always curious about things and places as a little girl. So, when my grandparents took all us girls to the cove one summer day, I was glad to go. As a family, we took Gramps' large boat to the cove that day. We went there to remember the deaths of my parents. My late mother's youngest brother, Uncle Tony, had arrived the day before to visit my grandparents, so he came with us."

A cold shiver spread over her as memories of that painful day returned.

"It was after we spent some time by the cove, remembering my parents, that we had a picnic. I remember I accidentally knocked the sweet tea over and made a mess. I apologized to Grams and cleaned up my mess. But my emotions were raw and I needed to get away for a while. So, I went exploring."

"I'd seen a small building up the embankment from the cove and I was curious. So, I walked to the place. It was a building that looked like it had recently been built. I enjoyed breathing in the new wood smell. I opened the door and walked inside. Suddenly, the door slammed shut behind me. When the door handle was slammed down, I turned quickly. That's when I heard his voice."

"Whose voice did you hear?"

Her misery was like a steel weight as memories returned.

She looked down at her hands and spoke in a rush. "My Uncle Tony's voice. He was a teenager and I seemed to be the niece that he liked to pick on. Except, this time, his words and actions really hurt me."

Ward held her hand and squeezed gently. "What did he say?"

"Uncle Tony stood on the other side of the door and taunted me, "Jane, all you ever do is make mistakes. Like spilling the sweet tea today. Can't you do anything right? You're a burden to everybody in this family."

"You're one of the needy kids. You're one of the ugly kids. You're not worthy of love. You need to learn to pay for your mistakes. I'm going to lock you inside this shed until I think you've learned your lesson. By the way, it won't help yelling for help, because no one will hear you and come and save you."

Jane squeezed her eyes shut for a moment.

The painful memory created a sick and fiery gnawing in her belly.

"I'm so sorry you were treated like that, Jane." Ward wrapped his strong arms around her and held her even closer to his heart. "Your Uncle Tony should have been horse whipped for saying all those hurtful words to a little girl."

She could feel the tense anger in his body as he held her close.

Pulling back, he studied her. "Did your uncle eventually come back and unlock the door?"

Jane shook her head and sighed. "No, it was my oldest sister, Lizzie, who came to my rescue. If my uncle would have had his way, he'd have left me alone and locked up in that shed all night."

Her bottom lip quivered. "That horrible experience is the reason I've been terrified of being stuck in small spaces all my life."

Ward nodded solemnly. "I'm so sorry, honey."

Tears pricked the back of her eyes.

Jane blinked quickly, refusing to cry any more tears. "My Uncle Tony's degrading words really changed me. From that day on, I believed I made too many mistakes to be of value to anybody."

She ran a shaky hand through her hair. "I believed I wasn't worthy to be loved. Which was why, after that day, I made a decision to make every effort not to make any more mistakes. I tried my hardest to remake myself into as perfect a woman as I could be. But I was never able to reach that goal."

"Oh, sweetheart, you've been too hard on yourself for so many years." Ward's gentle hand reached under her chin, lifting it up so she could look into his eyes. "I want to tell you something and I hope these words sink down deep into your heart."

Jane's heart hammered foolishly with anticipation.

Ward's low whisper sent a shiver up her spine. "You are valuable. I want you to know I don't see imperfections or flaws. I see you as perfect, just the way you are. And more importantly, you are worthy to be loved, Jane."

This time she shivered, but not from fear.

His words melted any resistance she had left.

This time, as his dark eyes met hers, her heart turned over in response.

Ward was a man who had been a faithful friend. He'd been there for her, helping, encouraging, and being her friend, ever since they were school-aged children.

Jane's heart swelled with a feeling she had thought long since dead.

In the beginning, she had been convinced she'd never be able to trust Ward again.

She assumed she wouldn't be able to trust any man ever again.

With all the pain she'd suffered at the hands of her ex-husband, it had placed a deep chasm of mistrust that she thought she'd never be able to cross.

However, in the past few weeks, as Ward had

continued to encourage, support, and help her, he had won her trust once again.

Her heart had shifted.

She could no longer deny herself. She longed to be close to him.

Jane knew her heart was beginning to fall in love with him once again.

The admission was dredged from a place beyond logic and reason.

His words had touched the deep recesses of her heart.

Swallowing back emotion, she whispered in a shaky voice, "Your kind words and belief in me have truly touched me, Ward. Most of all, thanks for saving me today."

"My pleasure. You know I'd do anything for you, Jane." His low whisper sent her pulse pounding.

With gentle fingers he traced her cheeks, finally tracing her full lips.

His dark eyes burned with passion and, looking deep into her eyes, he whispered, "Because I love you with all my heart, Jane."

She was struck motionless by his words of love. "I love you too, Ward."

Then, there wasn't time to say anything else.

He pulled her close and his lips slowly descended to meet hers.

Jane could feel her knees weaken at the sweetness of his kiss.

As he caressed her lips in a series of slow, shivery kisses, her emotions whirled and skidded.

She slipped her arms around his neck, shocked at her own eager response to his coaxing kisses.

As the kiss ended, Jane buried her face in his neck.

Her thoughts spun with worry and questions.

However, the most important questions she asked herself were this:

Would their new relationship cause changes in their everyday lives? Would Ward truly be willing to stick by her side and not abandon her like last time?

❧

HE WATCHED his ex-wife in the arms of another man.

Since he was hiding behind an outcropping of trees a distance away, they couldn't see him.

That was just the way he wanted things to be.

The expensive binoculars he bought recently had paid off.

What was Jane doing at the cove? And why did she bring that man with her?

He didn't like it that Jane was near the place where he worked his most profitable business deals.

He couldn't afford for her to find out all the pieces of the pie he had his hands in.

Anger flooded him.

Not only was Jane getting in his way, but he could see she was kissing that man.

He wasn't just any man either.

No, of course not.

She had started dating his son's basketball coach.

Now, he would be forced to do something to discourage them both.

Jane had been bad again.

It was just like when they were married. She never did learn her lesson.

He shivered and coughed into the handkerchief he kept handy all the time now.

Looking down, he saw signs of blood on the brown cotton handkerchief.

He would need to have his routine check-up again.

Then he'd get back to doing what needed to be done so he could get his son back.

CHAPTER FIFTEEN

ane

THE NEXT EVENING, just after the dinner, Jane walked beside her sisters on their way to *Yarn Around the Cove.*

It was almost the last quilting meetup of the island crafters before the holidays.

Jules turned to Jane, teasing in her soft voice, "I've heard Ward has been spending a lot of time with you, Jane. Is romance in the air between the two of you?"

Heat warmed Jane's cheeks as she remembered the passionate kisses between them yesterday at the cove.

Jane spoke softly, "Ward has been helping me to find more answers about our parents' deaths. The truth is, we are getting to know each other a lot better. But we'll wait and see how much further our relationship goes."

Jules grinned. "In other words, there's romance between the two of you, but he hasn't asked you to marry him yet."

At her sister's words, Jane's cheeks heated a little more. It was frustrating sometimes how well her sisters knew her.

"A little romance, I suppose," Jane admitted.

She was relieved when Charlie changed the subject.

"Jane, do you have news about the search into our ongoing mystery?" Charlie asked as they walked up the sloping hill towards Main Street.

"I do have news." Jane explained that she and Ward met with the detective and their plan to add a hidden video to record the evidence locker.

"Is that legal?" Alex asked.

Jane shrugged. "Detective Sullivan admitted it might be borderline illegal, but he doesn't know what else to do to get the evidence we need."

"Ward and I also walked to the cove. We went inside that old shed," Jane added.

Lizzie's eyes widened.

"Even though it wasn't fun to be back in that old building, it was worth it because we found something." Jane explained about finding pieces of wood that had the names of their parents' boat and investigative reporter Sean O'Connor's boat.

Charlie released a breath. "Somebody must have hidden the broken wood from those boats in that old shed. The question is, why would they do that?"

"Good question." Alex turned to Jane.

Jane shrugged. "I don't know the answer. But Ward

and I are taking the wood shards to the police to be analyzed. The wood from those boats might be too old to find anything, but we'll at least give the police the chance to check it out."

"Good," Alex commented. "Maybe you should talk with Sarah O'Connor at the quilters meeting tonight. It's likely she'll want to know if you found pieces of her father's boat."

Jane nodded slowly. "You're right. I'll do that."

Having a talk with Sarah wasn't the only conversation she needed to have at tonight's quilters meeting.

With all the new clues they'd been uncovering, it was time to be bold to get more of the answers they needed.

MRS. O'CONNOR STOOD behind the podium in front of the large group of crafters at her shop, *Yarn Around the Cove*.

The older lady spoke with enthusiasm and love for her community, "I want to thank you all for all your hard work these past few weeks. Next week, you'll be able to work on stitching your square for the Christmas Craft Show."

"Remember, this square is about a memory you hold close to your heart. That way, when the quilt is finished, your square will tell your story and the big quilt will tell all our stories."

The community of women clapped with enthusiasm.

Mrs. O'Connor continued to share from her heart. "We're grateful this memory quilt is now completed, thanks to your dedication to finishing it. The quilt's unveiling and presentation to a member of one of our founding families will be held in ten days. I hope to see you all here."

The audience clapped in appreciation.

Soon, everyone stood their feet and began walking around, connecting with one another.

As soon as Jane saw Sarah O'Connor, she walked over to talk with her.

"Sarah, it's good to see you," Jane began.

The young woman grinned, "Since my grandmother is the host, I felt it was my duty to be here for her."

"That's good of you. I'm sure your grandmother appreciates it." Jane smiled warmly.

"She does. She's always been so good to me. It's the least I can do," Sarah spoke softly.

"Families are a blessing," Jane said. Looking at Sarah, she couldn't help but remember her dad, the late Sean O'Connor.

Jane looked around to double check that their conversation was private.

"You look like you have something serious to tell me," Sarah whispered. "Let's walk over to this corner where there aren't so many people."

Relief flooded Jane that the young woman could sense when they needed to talk in private.

Jane spoke in a low voice, "I wanted to let you know, Ward and I walked near the cove the other day. We discovered an old shed and were shocked by what we found inside."

"What did you find?" Sarah suddenly became fully alert and studied her intently.

Jane cleared her throat. "We found broken pieces of wood from my parents' boat and from your late father's boat. One of the wood pieces had the faded words, *Island Pearl.*"

"Oh my goodness." Sarah's eyes widened and she whispered, her voice hoarse, "That's the nickname my father gave me. When I was a little girl, he would call me his island pearl. I remember when he named the boat after me, I felt so special."

Jane was touched by Sarah's emotional response to their finding of her late father's boat.

"I wondered about that." Jane cleared her throat. "But here's the thing. Ward is helping me dig deeper into what happened. We found some old photos from Miss Hattie's collection that seem to show someone's been hiding something. I wanted to ask if you would publish my article in your newspaper once we have the evidence we need?"

Sarah nodded. "Of course I will, Jane. We'll blow this coverup wide open. My father would have done exactly the same thing. Lately, I've been reading my dad's journals. I've realized how passionate he was about finding the truth and uncovering secrets on this island."

"I believe that. Did you find anything interesting?"

Sarah sighed. "Not yet. I'll let you know if and when I do. You know, after reading through my dad's written notes, I realized something. I want to be as good a reporter as he was. I want to follow in his footsteps."

"You are, Sarah. Your dad would be proud of you." Jane smiled warmly.

Sarah grinned. "Thanks, Jane, your words mean a lot

to me. I see Violet Hayes coming our way. It's time for me to go. That woman is looking at you, Jane, and she doesn't look happy. Brace yourself."

Jane forced a smile as Violet walked her way.

The older woman's chilly tone cut through the silence, "I see my daughter-in-law didn't join us tonight."

"No, she didn't. Adele told me she was feeling a little under the weather, so she decided to stay home."

Violet scoffed. "Except Adele isn't at her home, is she? That's the sad part about it. My son, Roy, continues to ask Adele to return to live in their home, but it seems you've decided to hold my son's wife hostage."

"Adele is not a hostage, Violet," Jane replied. "If you talked with your son about the situation, you would soon learn that Adele has repeatedly asked Roy if he would attend marriage counseling with her. Sadly, he continues to say no."

The older woman huffed. "I'm not convinced that counseling would do any good. Adele should return home to live with my son, her husband, like a good wife should."

Violet pointed her index finger at Jane and demanded in a menacing tone, "And you need to stop meddling in their affairs."

With those words, the older woman spun on her heel and walked away.

Jane stood, motionless in shock, as she watched the woman leave. Glancing around the room, she saw several women staring at her.

At the moment, all she really wanted to do was go home.

But, as she began to walk through the crowd of people, without warning, someone else grabbed her arm.

"Jane Stafford, there you are. I want to talk to you." Mrs. Florrie Cantrell-Jones' tone was cool and disapproving.

The older woman wore a wide brimmed hat tonight, similar to her sister-in-law, Ida Cantrell.

The brim was pulled down so all Jane could see were her stern grey eyes.

Jane replied, with respect, just like her late grandmother had taught her, "Hello, Mrs. Cantrell-Jones. What did you need to talk to me about?"

Florrie sighed with exasperation. "As if you don't know."

Jane waited silently, waiting for the older widow to say her piece.

The older woman spoke in a low voice, "I've heard from someone that I trust, that you've been asking a lot of questions around the island about what happened to your parents."

Jane nodded. "That's true. Our late grandmother specifically wrote in her journal and asked my sisters and I if we would continue to search for answers to our parents' deaths."

"Well, if your late grandmother asked you girls to do that, then she wasn't right in the head before she passed," Florrie Cantrell-Jones insisted.

Jane bristled and her shoulders straightened. "I assure you, she was thinking clearly before she died, Mrs. Cantrell-Jones."

"Well, whatever your stubborn grandmother had in

mind, I don't know. But what I do know, is you and all your questions are causing problems for my son-in-law, Sheriff Hart. You are making the sheriff's job more difficult than it needs to be," the older woman insisted.

"That may be, but my sisters and I will need to do what we promised, to honor our late grandmother's last request," Jane replied.

The older widow's eyes were stony with anger. "You're as stubborn as your grandmother. I'm telling you that the sheriff's office determined, years ago, that the investigation into your parents' deaths was closed. You and your sisters need to stop asking all these questions."

Jane replied softly, "I'm sorry you feel that way. But we can't stop. We must continue our search, if for no other reason than to honor our late grandmother's last request."

A warning cloud settled on Florrie's features. "Then I'm afraid the recent newspaper article about you must have been correct. Some folks worry that you are turning into a nuisance in our peaceful island community. I believe that's true. We don't need your kind here. I think it would be best if you would take your son and leave."

In spite of the shiver of fear that crept up her spine, Jane met the older lady's cold eyes, boldly. "And I believe that my late grandmother, who was well respected on this island, would disagree with you. And I intend to honor her last wishes."

"You definitely have that Stafford stubbornness. But, be careful, Jane. That path might lead you into trouble you never expected. Don't say I didn't warn you." With that, the older widow woman walked away.

Jane was left standing, like her feet were in disbelief.

Her best friend, Kenna, walked towards Jane. "You look a little pale. Are you feeling alright?"

In a shaky voice, Jane explained what Mrs. Cantrell-Jones had said to her, "Kenna, her words sounded almost like a threat or a warning of some kind."

Kenna shook her head. "That woman. I never did like her. But even though she is an old lady who speaks her mind, I wouldn't worry about her. She's just trying to scare you, to stop you from asking questions."

Jane rubbed the back of her neck.

A deep crease of worry formed between her brows as she remembered the conversation.

"Maybe. I suppose there's not much I can do about what she does." Jane turned to her friend. "For myself, I can't stop searching for answers. She'll have to accept that."

"I doubt she will accept it. But I admire your tenacity, Jane." Kenna looked around at the thinning crowd. "Should we make our way outside where there's not so many people?"

Jane nodded.

They slowly made their way between the crowd of people.

As they were nearing the outside doors, Jane couldn't help overhearing a conversation.

A new woman to their community was speaking with Linda Hart.

"I heard you own a store. What products do you sell?" the stranger asked.

Linda replied, "Christmas supplies and children's toys. But I don't own the store any longer. I sold it a few months ago to a man who sells children's toys."

"Oh, that's exciting. Who bought your store?"

"A man who recently moved to the island. His name is Devon Hollingsworth. He has franchise stores across the country. You might have heard of Hollingsworth Children's Emporium? He owns that franchise."

"Hmm. I didn't realize that."

The voices faded as Jane continued to walk through the open door with her friend.

As they stood outside on the sidewalk, Jane whispered to her friend, "That's a shock. A couple of weeks ago Ward and I saw my ex-husband walk into Linda Hart's store. That was just after we had left the store. But I hadn't realized then, Linda had sold her store to Devon."

Kenna shook her head. "I can't help but wonder why?"

"If you ask me, I think my ex-husband bought Linda's store because he wanted to make it simpler for himself to continue his questionable activities. If he's involved in what Ryan and Miles are doing, it makes it easier to hide in his own store," Jane replied in a low voice, tense with anger.

Kenna's eyes grew wide. "I guess we'll need to wait until we see more evidence to know for sure if that's what he's doing."

"That's true. But there's a big part of me that's angry that my ex-husband has decided to move to the island to stay. He's invading my life and my son's life."

Kenna reached for her hand and squeezed it. "I totally get that, my friend. I'm sorry he's doing that to you."

A wave of apprehension swept through Jane. "Thanks,

Kenna. Yet, in spite of knowing the odds are against me, I can't back down now. The stakes have never been higher. I'm resolved to make a peaceful and happy life — for me and my son — without worrying about someone trying to harm us."

"I know, Jane. And that's as it should be." Kenna was silent for a minute before she spoke, "I wonder if Devon moved here to try to reconnect with his son?"

Jane shook her head. "If that was his reason, then he's going about it the wrong way. Sending us threats and trying to intimidate Noah and me is not the right way for my ex-husband to get closer to his son. "

"I hope he realizes that before this is all over." Her friend looked over at her.

Jane sighed wearily. "I really hope so too, Kenna. But, sadly, that doesn't seem to be Devon's way of doing things."

Later that evening, as Jane entered the house, her housekeeper Mrs. Morrison met her at the front entrance.

Anxiety filled the older woman's features. "Jane, you won't believe what happened today."

Jane was starting to take off her shoes, but stopped mid-way as worry flooded her. "Is my son alright?"

"Yes, Noah is fine."

She released a sigh of relief. "Okay, then start at the beginning, Mrs. Morrison. What happened today?"

Jane walked down the hallway and stopped at the small countertop to hang up her car keys.

Mrs. Morrison followed behind her and began to explain, "I picked up Noah from the school after basketball practice like usual. But today, there was a man who was at the gym who was talking to him. Later on, your son told me the man was telling Noah to come with him. But your son, he's smart, and he said no."

Anxious thoughts filled Jane's mind. "Was the man wearing an old-style Fedora hat?"

"Yes, the hat did look old-fashioned," Mrs. Morrison agreed.

"I thought so. That was most likely my ex-husband." Jane ran a shaky hand through her hair. "Noah is never to go anywhere with that man, Mrs. Morrison."

"I understand, Jane." Her housekeeper continued, "But that's not the only thing that went wrong today."

Jane stopped walking and turned to the older lady. "What? What else happened?"

Her stomach churned with anxiety and frustration. What else could go wrong?

"When we got home, I opened the mailbox to pick up the mail like I usually do. When I reached inside, I pulled out a small broken Christmas decoration. Then Noah also found a threatening note. I placed them over there." Mrs. Morrison pointed to the broken pieces on the countertop.

Jane picked up the pieces and saw that it was a Christmas ornament from the first year Noah had been born.

It was a photo of her holding baby Noah in her arms.

"This is from my ex-husband. Only he could've had this in his possession." A cold knot formed in her stomach.

With a shaky hand, she reached for the note.

Jane's voice trembled as she read it out loud. *Your actions are making this worse. For everyone. Stop searching for answers or next time someone will get hurt.*

The gray-haired widow gasped. "Why would your ex-husband do such an awful thing? Why would he threaten you?"

Jane spoke softly, "For a few reasons. He doesn't want me to keep asking questions of folks on the island about my parents' deaths because he's worried I'll learn about his questionable activities. The other reason Devon is threatening me, is because he really wants Noah back. But, with how harshly Noah's father treated him in the past, I don't believe my son would go anywhere with him willingly."

"Oh heavens." Mrs. Morrison shuddered and made the sign of the cross.

Jane was silent for a moment, deep in thought.

"I must keep my son safe, Mrs. Morrison. I think it's time we keep him at home and away from school." Jane's nerves tensed. "Don't worry, I'll explain everything to his teachers."

The older lady nodded. "That might be for the best. If Noah is at home, I'll be able to protect him."

Nervously, she bit her lip and a terrible tenseness flooded her body.

"Thanks for letting me know what happened today. You did well. I have a lot to think about. For now, however, I need to look in on my son. Goodnight, Mrs. Morrison." Jane gave the older lady a gentle hug before she walked down the hallway.

Reaching her son's bedroom, she stopped and quietly and opened the door.

Noah lay in his bed, sleeping so peacefully.

She released a sigh of relief and closed the door.

As she got ready for bed, she decided to text Ward.

Jane told him of what had happened at the crafter's meeting.

Ward replied. *I can't believe those old biddies. Don't listen to Violet or Florrie. They are just trying to scare you.*

Jane hesitated. *I know. But it makes me more protective of my son. When I got home, Mrs. Morrison showed me a broken Christmas ornament that had been left in my mailbox. And there was also a handwritten note left in Noah's jacket.*

Quickly, Ward texted back. *Do you think it was Devon?*

Pain squeezed her heart as a vivid memory from that last Christmas filtered through her mind.

Jane hurried to reply. *Yes. There's no question. Devon is the only person who would've had that Christmas ornament from when Noah was a baby.*

She hesitated before she sent another text. *I don't know how my ex-husband would have known which jacket was Noah's at school. Perhaps he's been watching my son. I decided to keep Noah home from school for the next few weeks to keep him safe.*

Ward quickly replied. *That's understandable. As far as your ex, more than likely, he has been watching you. Lately, it's easier to find you, Jane. You've gone public by getting your wedding planning business license in your own name. Also, you've taken Adele Hayes into your home. As you learned tonight, that has made some folks a little unhappy.*

Then Jane remembered her housekeeper's words and texted back. *But Mrs. Morrison said that there was a man with blond hair wearing an old-style Fedora hat talking with Noah after basketball practice today. My housekeeper told me the strange man offered to drive Noah home. My son said no. Does this man show up at Noah's basketball practices, Ward?*

Jane needed to know. All of these issues were causing even more worry.

Ward replied. *Hmm, good question. You say your ex-husband has blond hair and wears an old-fashioned Fedora hat?*

Yes.

Suddenly, the loud ringing of Jane's phone filled the silence.

It was Ward.

"Hi there," Jane answered.

Ward replied, "Hello, Jane. I needed to call and explain."

A flicker of apprehension coursed through her.

He hesitated. "Your description of your ex-husband sounds like a man who has been showing up to the basketball practices for a few weeks now. He offered to pay for new team uniforms. When we talked, he told me his name was D.J."

Jane sucked in a quick breath.

Fear and anger knotted within her.

"My ex goes by that nickname sometimes." Jane's voice flooded with anxiety. "I can't believe he was there this whole time."

"I'm sorry, Jane. I didn't recognize him," Ward explained in a soft voice.

Disbelief and anger flooded her. "So, all this time — for the past few weeks — you've seen my ex-husband at Noah's basketball games? And you didn't tell me?"

"I honestly didn't remember what the man looked like."

For Jane, the only thought running through her mind was to protect her son.

In her mind, Ward's words sounded like excuses.

Feelings of betrayal and abandonment flooded through Jane.

"I can't believe you didn't remember who Devon was. The whole point of me showing you my ex-husband's photo weeks ago was so that you would be able to identify him and protect my son from being near him," she replied in a tense, clipped voice that didn't allow for questions or responses.

"I'm sorry, Jane." Ward's heartfelt words faded into the background in her worry and fear for Noah.

The tension was so thick in the air, a person could cut it with a knife.

Jane's voice turned quiet, yet was laced with steel, "I'm sorry, Ward. I can't be in a relationship with a man who would abandon me and Noah at a time when I need support and help. This feels similar, like what happened between us in college when you abandoned me. I can't be with a man who won't protect my son. I'm sorry. Goodbye."

She hung up and turned her phone off.

As she lay in bed, she sobbed until she didn't have any tears left.

Once again, her heart was breaking from the pain of losing Ward.

Only this time, Jane didn't think she would recover.

CHAPTER SIXTEEN

ard

Ward rubbed his tired eyes.

Sleep had eluded him last night, after his talk with Jane.

He was still reeling from shock.

She had ended their relationship.

It was the truth. He hadn't proven that he could protect the one person who mattered most in the world to Jane — her son.

The longer Ward thought about it, the more he realized he should have known who that man was.

He should have had the ability to identify Jane's ex-husband from that photo she showed him weeks ago.

Sorrow hit him like a steel weight.

He'd failed her.

Now, he'd lost Jane.

What was even more heartbreaking, was that this was the second time he lost the woman he loved.

Was there anything he could do to win her back?

The only thing Ward knew he could do, was to be faithful in his efforts to find answers for Jane.

His thoughts swirled as he adjusted his repairman uniform.

Hopefully, this disguise would be enough to give him access to the evidence locker room.

As Ward walked into the police station, he realized there was one thing he could do to win back the woman he loved.

Ward followed his friend Officer Shelton into the evidence locker room.

He began to fix some lights that had gone out. He was good with figuring out wiring, so this job seemed perfect for him.

Of course, he wouldn't be able to do this without Neville. He was a police officer who could give him access to this high security room.

The day was just ending for many workers at the police station. Officers and other personnel were eager to get home.

Officer Shelton had a piece of evidence to add to the locker, so he was busy organizing that detail.

Meanwhile, Ward stood on the top step of the ladder in the corner of the room. He had just taken out the ceiling tile and removed the broken lights and replaced them with new ones.

Then came the tricky part.

He found the perfect spot to set in place the small panoramic video camera in the ceiling. It had a motion sensor, so he hoped the recording would capture anyone who walked into the room.

He had figured out how to make a small hole in a portion of the ceiling tile so the video camera could slip through without being seen.

As he climbed down the ladder, Ward said a quick prayer that the video recording would work well and the officers dealing illegal substances would be caught.

A DULL ACHE pierced Jane's heart as she remembered her talk with Ward last night.

Parking her car, she walked into the local flower shop on Main Street.

It was difficult to focus on organizing the flowers for Madison's wedding when her heart felt so heavy.

There was an ache inside as she faced the fact that she was no longer in a relationship with him.

She still loved him.

Fingering the soft petals of the roses, her blood soared as unbidden memories sprang to mind.

The welcome bell to the shop tinkled in the air as Jane continued to look through the vast array of flowers.

"Jane, how nice to see you." Kenna playfully bumped her shoulder.

Jane looked up into the kind eyes of her best friend. "Kenna, I'm happy to see you too. What brings you to the flower shop?"

"It's my mom's birthday. I wanted to surprise her by dropping off her favorite flowers." Her friend looked through the flowers and then turned back to Jane.

Kenna studied her closely with furrowed brows.

"What's going on with you? My friend, you have the same sadness on your face from when your beloved Grams died. Tell me what's going on?" The concern in Kenna's voice was her undoing.

Jane explained about the conversation she had with Ward last night. "I was so shocked that he didn't protect Noah from my ex. I can't take that lightly. It's one of those deal-breakers for me."

Kenna hesitated for a moment.

"I can tell you want to say something, Kenna. Just spit it out. I won't break. I promise." Jane curled one eyebrow upwards.

Her friend sighed. "Alright, I will tell you. When you mentioned that you showed Ward a photo of your ex-husband weeks ago, is it fair to say that Devon's appearance might have changed since that photo was taken?"

Jane ran a hand through her hair. "I suppose. It was taken years ago. Devon probably has changed. But he still always wears that silly Fedora hat."

"But do you see how it would be possible that Ward could see Devon in person and not recognize him?" Kenna's gentle prodding was annoying, but, as usual, she had made a good point.

"Yes, I suppose I do." Jane sighed. "But what about how I feel about it? It felt like a betrayal of my trust. It felt like Ward had abandoned me all over again."

Kenna reached over and squeezed her hand. "I'm sorry

it felt that way to you, Jane. But let's really look at what happened. If Ward honestly didn't recognize Devon when he showed up at basketball practice, then you must know Ward wasn't trying to deliberately betray your trust."

Jane shrugged. "I suppose. But it hurts all the same."

"I understand the terrible feelings of the past came back to haunt you. It sounds like you believe Ward not recognizing the photo of Devon was a deliberate action on his part not to protect your son. You believe he betrayed your trust," Kenna explained. "But you see, I don't believe that's what he meant by it."

"You think I've allowed my deep hurt from the past with Ward to cloud my judgement and I overreacted." There was a heavy feeling in her stomach.

"A little, yeah." Her friend studied her for a moment more. "I think, if you would give Ward another chance, you'd soon discover he's the most loyal, faithful, and trust-worthy man. Not only that, I believe he's head over heels in love with you. He's perfect for you, Jane."

Jane rubbed the back of her neck and released an exhausted sigh. "Maybe you're right. But I need to see for myself that he is a man I can rely on and trust."

"I think if you give him a second chance, Ward will prove that he's that kind of man." Her friend's words encouraged Jane.

Jane awkwardly cleared her throat. "I really hope you're right."

"I am." Kenna looked at her watch. "Well, I've loved talking with you, Jane, but I've got to get going."

Her friend reached over and enveloped Jane in a big hug.

A warmth flooded her. "Thanks, Kenna. Once again, you've managed to help me see things with a new perspective."

"I'm glad. See you soon." Her friend walked away, bought her flowers, and waved goodbye as she left the store.

After choosing flowers she wanted, Jane left the flower shop, still thinking of what Kenna had to say about Ward.

Perhaps she had overreacted.

As she drove towards the country club, her thoughts spun with questions. Could she take Kenna's advice?

Jane chewed on her lower lip as she parked her car.

Despite uncertainty, she decided to extend the olive branch to him.

With all her heart, she hoped she wasn't making a mistake.

❦

AN HOUR LATER, Jane stood in the large room at the country club, making last minute preparations for Madison's wedding.

The bride and groom chose to have the rehearsal dinner three days before the wedding day. It was a time that worked well for everyone involved.

She was sure this would be one of the most elaborate and expensive weddings of the year.

Grateful that it was the end of the day, Jane did her last-minute check on all the details.

Suddenly, her phone rang.

"Hi, Jane. Detective Sullivan here." There was an eager confidence in his voice.

"Hello, Detective Sullivan." Jane stopped what she was doing and waited. The detective wouldn't have called her unless it was important.

"I have good news. We've got the video evidence," Detective Sullivan told her.

Jane sighed in relief. "Oh, I'm so glad."

"Come to the station. Meet me at my office in thirty minutes and I'll show you what we've found."

"I'll be there," Jane replied and disconnected the call and hurried to finish her work for the day.

As she drove to the police station, Jane's thoughts were focused on getting that final piece of evidence on Ryan Hart and Miles Carter. Her only hope was that it would lead to proof that her ex-husband was somehow involved in their crimes too.

When she stepped into the detective's office, she stopped when she saw Ward sitting at a chair across from the office desk.

"Hi, Jane." Detective Sullivan waved a hand for her to sit next to Ward. "I called Ward to also meet here today. After all, it's because of his efforts that we have the video evidence today."

Her shoulders tensed as she sat on the chair next to Ward.

Turning, she stole a look at the man who continued to cause her sleepless nights, despite the ending of their relationship.

Jane sensed she saw a mixture of sadness, apology, and love that lingered in his dark eyes.

It took her breath away.

She nodded quickly and forced a small smile.

Turning back, she looked down at her clasped hands on her lap, her thoughts swirling.

Why does Ward continue to affect me this way? I had to end our relationship for a good reason. My head knows that, but my heart refuses to accept it. Why do I still feel love for this man?

"Jane, I want to explain what happened," Detective Sullivan's low voice interrupted her deep thoughts.

"Of course." Jane straightened her shoulders, forcing herself back to the present, so she could hear what he had to say.

The detective began to explain, "As you know, Ward managed to successfully plant the video camera in the evidence locker room. One evening, Ward and Officer Shelton managed to get a video recording of Officers Ryan Hart and Miles Carter. They were going in and out of that secure room."

Detective Sullivan continued, "The video clearly showed both officers switching a white powdered bag from a holder they carried under their vests. Then they replaced that fake powder with the real drugs that had been already tagged and processed in the evidence locker room."

Jane sucked in a breath. "In other words, they were stealing the real drugs from the police station and replacing them with fake ones."

"That's correct. Which is clearly an offense." The detective shook his head, disbelief written on his face.

"We could charge the two police officers already, but it would be helpful to have an eyewitness or two before we do. Recently, an undercover officer found evidence of cocaine in Ryan Hart's yacht. He only found that evidence because you suspected something illegal was going on."

A warmth crept up Jane's cheeks at his thanks. "I was happy to help."

"But we want to keep investigating to pull in bigger fish in this drug trafficking scheme. It would be helpful if we could find someone who has been buying these drugs."

"What do you need us to do, Detective?" Ward asked from where he sat next to Jane.

She turned to Ward, surprised that he still included her when discussing their search for answers.

"Just keep your eyes open and your ears to the ground as you talk with folks in the community. If something looks suspicious, let me know." Detective Sullivan spoke with confidence and it boosted her own.

Ward nodded. "We'll keep at it, Detective."

"There is one other thing we found that we wanted to show you." Jane reached into her tote bag and pulled out two pieces of wood she had wrapped in plastic. "We looked in that old shed that's along the cove. It's the same shed we saw from Miss Hattie's photo collection."

"Of course. And you found something?" Detective Sullivan took the piece of wood that Jane gave him.

Jane explained, "Yes. We found two broken wood pieces from the late Investigative Reporter Sean O'Connor's boat and from my parents' boat. The name of Sean's boat, *Island Pearl,* is written on the wood. Also, the name of my parents' boat, *Lady Anne,* is on the other piece of wood we found."

"There was also a nail with a piece of fabric on the

wood from Sean's boat and I wanted to bring it to you. It's very strange that somebody went to the trouble to hide the broken pieces in a shed years ago, when the police stated Sean died from a boating accident."

"You're right. That is very strange." Detective Sullivan looked at the broken wood piece.

Jane nodded. "Sheriff Jerry Hart was in charge of the investigation at the time. After a brief investigation, the sheriff determined that Sean's death was an accident and he closed the case."

"I will get the forensic team to look at both wood pieces. It's been years and the wood is old so they might not find anything. However, because the wood was kept inside a shed and didn't suffer the ravages of severe weather, the forensics team might find something," the detective said.

"That would be incredible if they found something. We need answers," Jane agreed.

Ward nodded. "We do. Thanks, Detective Sullivan, for your help today."

The detective stood to his feet and walked around his office desk.

Both of them shook Detective Sullivan's hands, and then he walked them to the door.

Jane turned and said, "Thanks for the update. I'll keep my ears open. I suspect my ex-husband plays a part in this illegal trafficking ring."

"I know you do. But remember, Jane, we need proof first before we can charge him." Detective Sullivan's voice was calm, his gaze steady.

Jane sighed. "I know. But I'm determined we'll find a way to get the evidence we need."

"Good girl." The detective opened the door. "We'll get to the bottom of this and get what we need, Jane. I promise you that."

Jane smiled. "Thanks."

She walked out the door beside Ward.

Just as she was about to get into her car, Ward spoke, "That was good news from the detective today."

"Yes, it was. I'm glad. Now we just need to find more evidence, so all the truth comes out." Jane turned to Ward, uncomfortable as he studied her.

"We'll find the proof we need, Jane. I promise you that." Ward offered her that warm smile, like before, and it caused an ache in Jane's heart.

Ward was still so faithful to help her, despite all the accusations she had flung his way.

As she drove away, her heart was heavy.

Her love for this man still consumed her every waking moment.

However, the biggest problem was, she couldn't seem to forgive his mistake of letting her son be in close proximity to his abusive father.

JANE SIGHED in relief that all had gone well with Madison Hayes' wedding rehearsal.

The wedding day would be in three days.

She was thankful most of the details had been organized.

The dinner was almost over and dancing had begun.

Jane was eager to get home, but she couldn't leave the rehearsal dinner quite yet.

Her faithful assistant Adele was talking in the corner of the room with her estranged husband, Roy.

Jane had been watching Roy Hayes all evening.

Since he was Madison's only brother, he was one of the groomsmen in the wedding party.

However, as the evening wore on, every once in a while, she would watch Roy escape to a different room or washroom and return a few minutes later.

Each time Roy returned to the party in the large room, it looked like he was sweating, his pupils were dilated, and his hands shook.

Was Roy drunk? Or was he ingesting something else?

One thing was for sure. Something was causing Roy to become more and more uncontrollable as the evening went on.

Jane couldn't help but overhear Roy's voice as he talked with his wife. "Adele, please come back home. I've gone without you long enough."

Adele replied with quiet, desperate firmness, "I can't come back home yet, Roy. I asked you to agree to marriage counseling, but you've refused. I've also asked you to get help for whatever is causing these mood swings. Again, you've refused to get help."

Roy's voice grew louder, "But I need you to come home. We need your income to help pay the bills. I need you to manage things like you used to."

Adele shook her head, her voice resolute, "I'm too afraid

to come home with these mood swings you've been having this past year. I'm convinced I'll get hurt again like last time. I won't come home until you agree to what I've asked, Roy."

Jane stood to her feet and started walking towards Adele. She wanted to be close to the younger woman in case she needed support.

But, when Violet Hayes walked over to her son and daughter-in-law, Jane simply waited a short distance away at the drink table.

Violet's steely voice came through loud and clear, "Roy and Adele, I won't have the two of you bickering back and forth at your sister's wedding rehearsal."

The older woman then turned and glared at Adele. "You need to go back to live with my son — your husband — where you belong. You're so stubborn. It's that woman's influence on you, isn't it? Jane Stafford has poisoned you against your own husband. When you are finally free of that woman, it'll be none too soon."

Jane's hand shook and some of the juice in her glass spilled onto the table.

She didn't appreciate being falsely accused of poisoning a young woman's mind.

If anything, the opposite was true.

Her true joy was to help women coming from abusive relationships to believe in themselves again and to find hope and happiness in their lives again.

Having Adele in her home had been a revelation. Jane realized that she truly loved to be a support and encouragement for women that needed help.

Maybe the past number of years working as a volunteer at different women's shelters across the nation had given her greater courage to help women in need.

That's why it hurt to hear Violet Hayes judge her and assume the worst, when all she was trying to do was help Adele.

Jane had to sheath her inner feelings when Violet walked past her. The older woman's fiery glare could have drilled holes in steel.

Straightening her shoulders, she shifted on her feet as Adele walked towards her.

"I'm ready to leave if you are, Jane," the younger woman whispered in a shaky voice.

Jane placed a comforting hand on her arm and nodded. "Sure. We can leave. We both need to try to get a good rest after this eventful day."

Adele muttered, "I just hope the wedding day won't be as stressful as tonight's rehearsal."

"I hope so too." They got in Jane's car and began to drive home. Her thoughts were puzzled over Roy's behavior.

"I'm sorry for the way Roy treats you, Adele," Jane said softly, wanting to put all the pieces together.

"I wonder if there is something Roy is taking that causes him to lose control? Is your husband addicted to alcohol or is it something else? Tonight, I noticed his hands were shaking and he was sweating more than usual."

Jane turned to her friend looking for answers.

Adele shrugged. "I don't know. When we first married, Roy only drank occasionally. But then he started drinking more. Then, last year, when Roy became friends with

Ryan Hart and Miles Carter, things went from bad to worse. He would have these terrible mood swings. Then, not only did Roy start to get nosebleeds more often, but his hands started to shake, and we began to have problems financially."

"I'm sorry, Adele." Jane parked the car in front of her home, her thoughts swirling with what Adele had told her.

"It's alright, Jane. But I won't go back to my husband until he has agreed to make some changes," Adele stated in a firm voice as she opened the car door.

"That's understandable." Jane hesitated, as an idea formed in her mind. "Adele, you go ahead inside the house. I'm going to go for a drive. I'll be back soon."

"Alright. Good night." Adele walked inside the house.

An idea had formed in Jane's mind as Adele had explained the situation between her and her husband.

However, she realized it wouldn't be wise if she went on her own. Could she ask the one man who had helped her find answers these past few weeks? Would he help her?

All she knew was she needed to try.

She texted Ward.

Would it work for you to meet me outside Roy Hayes' house tonight? I've got an idea.

Ward quickly replied. *Sure. I'll be there in a few minutes.*

JANE DROVE TO ROY HAYES' house and parked a little

farther down the street. She didn't want to alert Roy if he came home early.

Walking towards the house, she kept watch for Ward's car.

Soon, he arrived and began to walk towards her.

Gratefulness bubbled up inside her.

The fact that he'd agreed to help her, in spite of the way she'd treated him in that last phone call, spoke volumes for his character.

"I parked a short distance away," Ward explained when he reached her. "So, what's your idea?"

"First of all, thanks so much for coming to help me, Ward." The words rushed out of Jane's mouth. "I want to apologize for being so angry with you last time we spoke. You didn't deserve that."

Ward smiled warmly. "I forgive you, Jane. How could I be angry at you — a mother who is simply trying to protect her child? I understand why you were upset."

"You are very generous with me." Jane's cheeks grew warm.

He stepped closer. "Not generous enough, I think."

"Thanks, Ward," Jane spoke softly. But, at his nearness, she sensed her own uncertainty.

She stammered awkwardly, "But I still believe it would be best if the two of us remained friends instead of something more."

"I understand," Ward said in a dull, troubled voice. He shoved his hands into his pockets, his shoulders slightly hunched over.

Jane ached with an inner pain at the regret and disappointment etched across his face.

Swallowing, she didn't know what to say. Instead, she quickly changed the subject. "At the moment, I think we should focus on what we came here to do."

Ward curled an eyebrow upwards. "What was the idea you had for us to meet here? You didn't quite explain."

"No, I didn't. Sorry, I was in such a hurry to get here." Heat crawled up her neck to her cheeks as she explained, "Adele told me last year things with Roy went from bad to worse after he became friends with Ryan Hart and Miles Carter."

She paused. "That's when I had an idea. I thought we could try to search through Roy's garbage. I'm not sure if he's using drugs, but it wouldn't hurt to double check."

"That is a good idea." Ward looked around.

The street was quiet and dark, except for the street lights.

It looked like most of the neighbors were already sleeping at this time of night.

"I think we need to go to the backyard. That's likely where he keeps the garbage bin," Jane whispered as she walked.

Reaching into the tote bag at her side, she pulled out a flashlight.

Ward followed close behind.

They reached a small garage behind the house.

Ward whispered, "Hopefully, we'll find the bin around here somewhere."

Jane continued to walk to the other side of the garage.

"There it is." Jane pointed and grinned. They found a large, round trash bin. It was set out on the side of the road, ready to be picked up by the garbage truck.

Jane lifted the lid and discovered two large garbage bags inside.

Ward pulled out both bags and they set them on the ground.

"Is it legal for us to go through Roy's garbage?" Ward looked at her with somber curiosity.

"It is. Once a person has brought their garbage and set it by the curb for collection, it is considered abandoned property. That means we don't need a warrant to search." Jane pulled on gloves and handed a pair to Ward.

"That's good to know." Ward held the bags steady.

"I always keep two pairs of gloves in my tote bag as a wedding planner. I'm never sure what spills or problems I'm going to run into," Jane whispered as she began to open the first garbage bag.

She held the flashlight with one hand while both she and Ward began to take items out of the bag.

"This trash smells awful." Jane coughed at the terrible scent.

Ward nodded. "It does, but hopefully we'll come across something that will help us out."

They continued to dig through the stuff in the trash.

It wasn't until they were nearing the bottom of the bag that they found a couple of items that looked noteworthy.

Jane pulled out of the crunched up clear bag.

With her gloved fingers, she pulled out the tube.

"I think this small, white tube might give us evidence. It could be that Roy's DNA is on this tube and on this bag." Jane looked over at Ward with excitement in her eyes.

"That's really good. I've also found a bunch of tissues

which might have DNA on them. These might prove useful to the detective." Ward pulled them out.

After they searched the other garbage, they found more tissues from nosebleeds.

Together, they placed all that they found into Jane's tote bag.

"I'm going to text Detective Sullivan," Ward commented. "He did tell us to let him know when we found something."

"It's late, but you're right. He'd probably want to know right away," Jane whispered as she began to place all the trash back into the large, black bags.

Soon, both garbage bags were back in the trash bin, just like they'd found them.

Jane placed the wide straps from her tote bag over her shoulder as they walked back to their vehicles.

Ward walked beside her towards her vehicle. They had just reached her car when they heard the sound of an engine. The car's headlights were pointed in their direction.

"Let's get down. I think that might be Roy Hayes." As she heard Ward's low urgent whisper, Jane hurriedly crouched down low on the other side of her vehicle.

They watched as Roy stumbled out of his vehicle and finally made his way to his house.

"Good, he's gone." Jane sighed with relief. "Thanks, Ward, for helping me search tonight. I appreciate it."

Ward sent her a crooked smile. "I'm here for you, Jane. For whatever you need. I hope you know that."

Her pulse pounded at the heartrending tenderness of his gaze.

"I do and I'm grateful," she whispered and had to fight her own battle of personal restraint.

His eyes darkened and he stepped closer. His hand touched her shoulder in a soft caress.

"Jane…" Ward started to whisper, but was interrupted as, all of a sudden, his phone beeped.

Jane jerked and stepped back, surprised.

He looked at his phone. "It's a text from Detective Sullivan. He wants us to come to the police station right away."

Jane raised one eyebrow. "That was quick. Did he say why?"

"He said it was important, if we think we found new evidence, that it be processed right away," Ward replied with a shrug.

"Alright." Jane walked to her car door and said to him, "I'll meet you there."

As she started to drive to the police station, Jane's thoughts swirled as she remembered their near kiss.

It seemed, every time she saw Ward, it was more and more difficult to keep her distance from him.

She would need to forgive him. But, beyond that, was she ready to begin their relationship again?

Now, more than ever before, she didn't know what to do.

Her mind said no, but her heart screamed yes.

How could she choose between the two?

CHAPTER SEVENTEEN

Jane

Jane finished the last bite of the freshly made pancakes.

Noah's plate was empty and he was drinking the rest of his milk. "I'm going to get my baseball glove and ball. Coach told me a few days ago he would come here and play catch with me this morning."

Adele stood to her feet to help Mrs. Morrison wash the dishes.

Jane leaned over to her son and whispered, her heart heavy, "I'm sorry, Noah. Coach Hampton won't be stopping by to play with you. We had an argument the other day. He won't be coming by to visit us anymore."

Noah eyebrows lifted and his youthful eyes widened with disbelief. "Why not? Is Ward a bad guy?"

Jane shook her head. "No, son. Ward is a good guy, kind and generous."

It was true. That's exactly the kind of guy he was. Hadn't he proved it to her over and over again?

"I think Ward is one of the good guys too. Why did you make him go away, Mom?" Her son's voice broke miserably.

Guilt and regret flooded through her.

Her thoughts, jagged and painful, flitted through her mind, crushing her heart.

"I'm sorry, son. Something happened and I was scared Ward wasn't safe anymore." That was the simple truth, although it didn't explain everything.

Noah nodded, his features quiet and withdrawn.

Unexpectedly, her son spoke in a subdued voice, "You always tell me I don't have to be afraid, Mom. But you look scared all the time."

Terrible regret formed a fist in her belly.

She could not escape the words of wisdom coming from her young son.

What was it that her beloved Grandmother used to say? *And a little child shall lead them.*

How true those words were in her own life today.

"You're right, Noah. I haven't been a good example to you at all." Her voice came out raw, aching with defeat.

Noah reached over to hold her hand. "It's okay, Mom. I love you. I just want you to be happy. And I guess I thought you were happy with Coach Hampton."

Jane turned to Noah, her lips wobbly with a teary smile. "I was happy."

"Then why don't you forgive him for whatever he did

wrong and be his friend again? If I loved someone, I'd forgive them and tell them the truth." Noah spoke of such weighty matters in very simple terms.

Unsuspecting, she'd been trapped in her own hypocrisy by her young son.

A stab of remorse and regret lay buried in her breast.

Her fears trapped her from being vulnerable to give and receive love.

She saw that clearly now.

"You're right, Noah. If I love someone, I should forgive them and tell them I love them." Jane reached an arm around her son's shoulders and kissed the top of his blond head. "You are wise beyond your years. Thanks, son."

"Aww, Mom. You're kissing me again. It's alright as long as none of my friends are around." Noah grimaced.

Jane giggled. "Duly noted. Now why don't you and I play some ball together?"

"Really, Mom? Alright. Let me get my stuff." Noah slipped on his red baseball hat and grinned as he hurried away.

Soon, they were outside in the yard, throwing the ball back and forth. As they played, Jane's thoughts were focused on Ward.

Was she brave enough to fully trust him with her heart? Did she have the courage to tell him she loved him?

NOAH and she had been playing ball for a long time when, suddenly, Jane's phone rang loudly.

"Noah, I need to take this phone call." Her son nodded and she quickly answered the call.

"Hello, Jane, this is Detective Sullivan."

"Hello, Detective." Jane said as she hurried inside the house towards her home office.

"I've got news," the detective continued. "The team started checking those samples you and Ward dropped off last night. It is Roy's DNA on those white tubes used for snorting cocaine. The plastic bags also had Roy's finger-prints, along with traces of cocaine."

Jane nodded. "I wondered if he was taking drugs. Now we know. But I guess we don't know who sold Roy those drugs."

"Actually, we do." Detective Sullivan explained in his take charge voice, "We brought Roy Hayes in for ques-tioning and he took the deal we offered. We said the police would go easier on him if he told us who sold him the drugs. He agreed to the deal and named Officers Ryan Hart and Miles Carter in his statement."

Jane gasped in surprise. "Roy did the right thing to confess. But I'm still shocked that it's all true. It's difficult to believe that trusted police officers like Ryan and Miles have been trafficking drugs."

Detective Sullivan replied, "It's not only hard to believe, it's an embarrassment to the police force. And I can't help but wonder how many other people were involved with Ryan and Miles' drug trafficking ring?"

"Good question." Jane looked out her office window that faced the cove. "Will you be charging Ryan and Miles for their crimes soon?"

"Soon we will bring them both into the police station

for questioning," the detective replied. "I pulled some strings with some important people I know and managed to set an appointment with the judge tomorrow. The judge will decide, at that time, if the evidence we have against these officers is enough for an arrest warrant. It will be a relief to have this over and done."

"I can't help but agree. I'm relieved these crimes are being solved. However, I won't be completely settled until we find evidence that proves my ex-husband is involved somehow in that drug trafficking ring." Jane sighed in frustration. "I don't want him getting away with his crimes if he's involved."

"I understand. Keep your eyes and ears open and I'll do the same."

"I will." Jane couldn't help but ask, "Were you able to get those old wood pieces to the forensics lab for analysis?"

"Yes, I sent them to the lab. But I haven't heard back yet." The detective sighed. "I'll let you know when I do."

A wave of disappointment swept over Jane. "Alright. I appreciate you letting me know."

Detective Sullivan continued, "Thanks for all you and Ward have already done to search and get to the truth." Detective Sullivan's kind words made Jane smile.

"I'm happy to help." Jane sighed as she hung up the phone.

Jane paced the floor in her home office, pondering all the facts the detective told her.

If Detective Sullivan would be making his case to the judge tomorrow, then she needed to talk with one more person.

Jane gathered all the information she needed, she slipped the bulky envelope into her tote bag, and hurried out the door.

"SOMEONE TO SEE YOU, SARAH." Jane waited while the secretary at the newspaper *The Vineyard Tales* knocked on the editor's door.

"Come in," a woman's voice called out.

Jane walked into the editor's spacious office.

"You came to see me." Sarah walked over to give her a hug. "I'm glad you stopped by. I hope that means you have something to tell me."

Jane smiled and sat on a soft chair in front of the stacks of papers and documents that were on Sarah's desk.

"I do have a lot of new information." Jane shared what she and Ward had discovered about Roy Hayes and all the evidence they had on the illegal activities of the two police officers.

Sarah was scribbling with her pencil as fast as she could on a notepad as Jane told her the story.

"So, do you have photos of all that you've found?" Sarah asked.

Jane reached into her tote bag and pulled out the envelope.

"Yes. Everything I have is in here." Jane handed it to Sarah, who opened it up.

She moved things around on her desk and spread out the photos to see them easily.

"Walk me through what each photo represents." Sarah turned to Jane.

"Sure." Jane went through the photos one by one, explaining the importance of each one. "The fact that we have Miss Hattie's photo from six years ago, showing Ryan and Miles transferring crates and boxes from one unidentified boat to Ryan's boat, is important."

"What do you mean?"

Jane shared what she had learned. "Seven years ago, I learned Ryan Hart was transferred. He was put in charge of the narcotics division in the police department. Ryan bought his yacht six years ago. The question is, how was he able to purchase an expensive yacht on a police officer's salary unless he was involved in something questionable?"

"Do you know who owns the unidentified boat?" Sarah asked.

"Not yet, but, unless I miss my guess, I think it belongs to my ex-husband. Somehow, I'll find out." Jane continued to explain what she learned, "Also, the detective said Roy Hayes confessed that he buys his drugs from Ryan and Miles. So now we also have eyewitness testimony."

Jane explained the details of the photos that remained. "Now we wait until Detective Sullivan talks with the judge. After he tells the judge the facts of his case, then the judge will decide if there's enough evidence to issue an arrest warrant for those two police officers."

"Well, I hope that judge does the right thing." Sarah turned to Jane. "Ever since my father died years ago in what the police said was an 'accident' I've had a passion for true justice."

"Speaking of your dad," Jane added, "I gave that old piece of wood, with the name of your father's boat on it, to the detective. He sent it to forensics. He said not to get my hopes up, but I thought we might as well try and see if they find anything."

Sarah smiled. "My goodness. I hope they do find something. I'm grateful you did all the difficult work to gather this evidence, Jane."

Jane shrugged. "Like you said, when somebody close to you dies and you don't believe they got the justice they deserved, it changes you. I have a passion to see justice done too."

Sarah grinned. "That we do."

"So, will you be willing to rework the article I wrote so it sounds more professional?" Jane asked. "You're better at writing articles than I am."

Sarah nodded. "I will be happy to do that. I'll add the photos to complete the story. We'll blow this coverup wide open. My father would have done exactly the same thing. I'm happy to follow in his footsteps."

Jane stood to her feet. "It might be a good idea to wait to publish until after I hear from Detective Sullivan that he has arrested those two officers."

"I hear you. I'll wait for your call." Sarah walked her to the door.

Jane turned. "I know I'm getting myself deeper into this mess by having my name in print on this article and spilling the beans on the coverups from men we've respected in this community. I'll likely get backlash from folks for writing this article, but I feel like I'm doing the right thing."

"You are doing the right thing, Jane. Don't worry, the publicity will fade in a day or two after the article is published, it usually does," Sarah replied. "Thanks for stopping by, Jane. We'll talk soon."

Jane said her goodbyes and walked back to her car.

A sliver of fear shot up her spine.

Was Sarah right that the publicity will fade in a day or two? Or would there be an angry outburst against her and her son, or worse?

❧

When Madison's wedding day arrived, Jane arrived two hours early.

As she hurried to double check last minute details, her thoughts returned to the news Detective Sullivan gave her yesterday.

He let her know the judge had been satisfied that there was enough evidence for the police to arrest Police Officers Ryan Hart and Miles Carter.

The two men had been arrested yesterday.

Today, her article appeared in this morning's newspaper.

She worried that some folks at the wedding would be very upset about it.

But, getting the truth out there was one of the ways she had chosen to be brave.

Yet, even though Jane had decided to go public with who she was and what she knew, she was all the more careful to protect her son.

She was grateful Noah was safe at home with Mrs. Morrison.

Walking down the church aisles, she double checked the roses and baby's breath that hung along the pews.

The Christmas-themed wedding was appropriate since it was only a few days until the holiday.

Only a few weeks ago, Jane would have hated any mention of the holiday filled with laughter and cheer.

But, since coming to the island, she had come to terms with the Christmas holiday. Perhaps it was because she'd enjoyed making that Christmas memory quilt with the ladies in Sweet Beach Cove. Or perhaps it was because Ward had held her close at the Christmas Country Dance.

Whatever the reason, Jane was aware that the walls around her heart had shifted when it came to the festive holiday.

Soon the church began to become crowded with wedding guests until most of the pews were filled.

Jane spoke into the headset microphone to Adele, "The bride and bridesmaids are waiting. Are the groomsmen ready to go?"

Her assistant spoke softly, "They're ready, Jane."

"Let them know it's time to walk to the front of the church." Jane was used to synchronizing all the wedding details.

Everything was timed to perfection.

Jane walked out to see the happy bride walk down the church aisle on the arm of her father.

It didn't take long before the bride and groom were in front of the pastor.

Jane was grateful she could observe the wedding, hidden behind a large pillar on one side of the church.

When the pastor asked the bride and groom to say vows to each other, Jane looked around at the guests.

Unexpectedly, she saw Ward only two pews away from where she stood.

He peered over at her, his eyes filled with an intense longing.

Her heart lurched madly.

He was so very good looking in his navy-blue suit, and she reacted so strongly to him.

The bride and groom began to speak their vows.

Jane's heart beat faster at the intensity of Ward's dark eyes.

She tried to throttle the dizzying current that ran through her.

All of a sudden, a vivid image popped into her mind of her standing at the front of the church with Ward, speaking vows to each other.

Her heart became aware of the deep significance to their visual exchange.

A deep longing burned inside her to push past barriers of fear and distrust so she could be with Ward for the rest of her life.

The problem was, she didn't know how.

Ceaseless, inward questions haunted her.

Was it possible she had suffered far too many years of fear and abuse with her ex-husband that she was unable to give herself to any man ever again?

As that thought swirled round and round in her mind, a painful ache grew heavy in her heart.

To live a life of quiet desperation and to live alone because she chose fear instead of love was not what she wanted.

Noah told her to be brave.

That meant she would need to be courageous from now on.

৯০

THE MASTER of ceremonies was toasting the bride and groom.

The guests joined in the toast at the lovely wedding reception at the country club.

Soon the band began to play and guests started dancing.

Jane stood in the background watching the wedding guests.

Don and Violet Hayes were enjoying the wedding of their only daughter. Roy Hayes was seated with his parents, continually asking the waiter for a refill on his drink glass.

Adele sat together with them, but she looked nervous.

Jane noticed Ted and Lola Cantrell at a table with Bobby and Susan Sutton and Sheriff Jerry Hart and his wife, Linda.

As she glanced between the faces of Roy Hayes and Bobby Sutton, Jane released a soft gasp.

Jane didn't understand why she hadn't noticed before the similarities in the facial features between Roy and Bobby? And the more concerning question was, what did it mean? She would need to ask her sisters about that.

As she looked back at the other table, suddenly Sheriff Hart turned towards her, sending her a hostile glare.

She pushed back the anxious thoughts that flooded her mind.

Jane was sure he must have read the newspaper article she wrote.

Turning her head, she spotted her sisters, thankful to have family support when she needed it. They were seated at a table next to Miss Sadie and her sister, Miss Hattie.

Warmth flooded her at seeing a few friendly faces among the guests.

Continuing her perusal, she noticed Ward seated next to his father. He was busy helping serve his older father's needs. He was every inch the gentleman.

Every once in a while, Ward glanced over at her, sending her his handsome smile.

And every time a tiny shiver of delight would spread throughout her body.

She pushed those thoughts back as her sisters began to walk towards her.

Jane had called them and given her sisters an update yesterday on what was going on. They seemed worried about her, but she did her best to soothe their fears.

"You doing alright back here, Jane?" Lizzie asked, as her other sisters walked towards them.

Jane nodded. "I'm fine. At most weddings, I'm somewhere hiding out of the way, as the wedding planner. Don't worry about me."

Alex shook her head. "Looks like Sheriff Hart is none too happy with you for writing that article."

"I know, but it needed to be said. Sarah's newspaper was the perfect place for that article." Jane shrugged.

Charlie looked between Jane and Alex and asked, "What newspaper article?"

"I've got it in my purse. I'll read it to you," Lizzie replied.

"In the past few weeks, since I've returned to our beautiful island community, I've come across some hidden mysteries that have troubled me.

As many of you know, my childhood was spent on this island, first, with my parents and six sisters. Then, when my parents died in what the police said was a boating accident, my sisters and I went to live with my grandparents, William and Elizabeth Stafford.

However, my beloved grandmother, who passed away not long ago, was so disturbed by the fact the police labeled her son and daughter-in-law's deaths as an accident, that she asked all seven of her granddaughters to promise to search for the truth of what happened years ago.

We've been faithful to her dying request.

But our search has led down some unexpectedly thorny paths.

For instance, in the past few weeks, a friend and I discovered evidence that there's been a drug trafficking ring that has lasted for years, right under our noses, here in Sweet Beach Cove.

A local detective, after reviewing the evidence before a judge, finally arrested two men who were charged with not only possession of drugs but selling and trafficking drugs. The biggest shock to me was the identity of these men. Police Officers Ryan Hart and Miles Carter.

Our own police force has been involved in crime? I'm

stunned by what's happened to our beautiful and peaceful island community.

There have also been hints that others have been involved in this terrible drug trafficking ring. We won't stop until the drug trafficking is exposed and stopped here in our family-friendly island community.

There are other mysteries my sisters and I have discovered during our search for truth, but I won't mention them... at least not yet.

For my sisters and I, one of the biggest shocks we've had as we've searched into what truly happened that night our parents died, has been the hostility of some folks in our community.

It's terrible how folks you've known all your life, whom you viewed as trusted friends and safe to be around, can suddenly turn on you.

I've asked myself, have these folks turned against me because they have the most to lose if the truth is exposed for everybody to see? Is there something they are hiding?

These are some of the questions that worry me and keep me up until the wee hours of the morning.

I hope these are questions that concern you too if you've made your home in Sweet Beach Cove. I hope that together we can make our island community a pleasant, family-friendly place for everyone again."

Lizzie sighed. "That's where Jane's article ends. I think you simply wrote the truth, Jane."

Charlie added, "Not everyone we know appreciates the truth as we've started to learn. Especially not when some folks have gone to a lot of effort to keep their secrets hidden for years."

"Very true." Alex's face clouded with uneasiness. "I

hope you'll be careful, Jane. This article could turn some folks around here into enemies."

"I know." Jane paused to catch her breath as fear caused a tight knot in her belly. "But I can't let it go, especially if my ex-husband is somehow tied to this drug trafficking ring. I need to expose the truth so our community will be safe again. I know what it's like to live in fear for years. I don't want our children to have to live in worry for their safety."

All her sisters nodded in agreement.

"That's something we all agree on, Jane. I want you to remember we're here for you, for whatever you need," Lizzie whispered and gave her a quick hug.

Soon Jane was embraced by everyone in her family.

"Thank you all so much." Unshed tears filled her eyes and a warmth rippled through her veins. "I needed to hear that today."

"Love you, sis," Charlie whispered, just before all the sisters walked back to their tables.

The wedding reception continued and soon dancing began.

The bride and groom danced together to a slow love song sung by the band.

Before long, the guests joined in the dance.

Jane realized her job as wedding planner was officially over for this wedding.

She was just starting to clean some things up, when someone spoke from behind her, "Thank you for planning a beautiful wedding for us."

The bride and groom walked towards her, just as Jane completed her tasks.

Walking beside them was Madison's friend Brandi.

Jane had also been busy planning the details for Brandi and her fiancé's wedding, which was coming very soon.

"Madison and Troy, you are very welcome. I was happy to plan your happy day." Jane hugged the two of them. "Has it been a fun day for the two of you?"

"Yes. There've been no big problems, so that's good. We're grateful to you." Madison laughed lightly and her new husband nodded.

The bride turned to look at her friend. "Brandi wanted to talk to you too. Troy and I will mosey along and chat with more wedding guests. Thanks again, Jane."

Madison and Troy slowly walked away and were soon talking with more friends.

Brandi turned to her with a broad smile on her lips. "Jane, I want to say thanks for the amazing work you've already done to plan my wedding."

"You're welcome, Brandi. I am happy to do it." The bride had her wedding dress, the bridesmaids' dresses were on their way, and the flowers were ordered.

She was pleased at how quickly the details had come together.

Brandi glanced over both shoulders, as if looking for someone. She released a frustrated sigh. "I wanted you to meet my fiancé. But now he disappeared again."

"I'm sorry. Hopefully I'll get another chance to meet him." Jane smiled.

Brandi's brows formed a deep crease of worry. "My fiancé has been acting so strange today. One minute he's reading an article in the newspaper and the next minute he's talking in riddles. I don't understand what's going on."

A heavy thud hit the bottom of her belly.

Jane instantly became wide awake. "You say your fiancé read the newspaper and then began to talk in riddles?"

"Yes," Brandi huffed in irritation. "He started saying weird things, like, *Brandi, it looks like I'm needed elsewhere. I've got to go. I have a dog and a boy to take care of. It's time I take back that which is rightfully mine.* He was acting strange. I didn't understand, because we don't have a dog and we definitely don't have a boy."

Shock flew through Jane.

Fear shot up her spine.

Jane forced herself to speak calmly, "That is strange. I don't think I caught the name of your fiancé, Brandi?"

The bride-to-be grinned at Jane. "Oh, silly me, I forgot to tell you. My fiancé's name is Devon Hollingsworth."

Shock flew through her.

It was as she feared.

Her ex-husband was Brandi's fiancé.

These past few weeks, she had been planning the wedding of her ex-husband and his new bride.

Ice spread through her stomach.

A sharp pain of foreboding pierced her brain.

She hurtled back to earth as reality struck.

"I have to go. We'll talk later, Brandi, alright?" The words rushed out of Jane's mouth, her thoughts going ninety miles an hour.

Brandi's eyes widened in surprise. "Okay, I suppose."

Jane left the woman standing there and hurried to pick

up her tote back which she'd left in the corner of the room.

She hurried, half walking, half running, out of the country club, her only thoughts to protect her son.

All of a sudden, footsteps echoed behind her.

"Jane, wait." Ward's voice echoed behind her. "Where are you going in such a hurry? Something's wrong, I can tell."

Jane glanced behind but kept walking. "I have to get home. Fast. Noah might be in trouble," Jane sputtered. "I don't have time to talk, Ward."

"Alright, I won't ask any more questions. I'm going to take my dad home. Then, I'll meet you at your place." Ward watched her get inside her car. He yelled after her, "Don't do anything rash! Wait for me. I'll be there as fast as I can."

Jane simply waved.

Hurriedly, she drove out of the country club.

She could barely hear Ward's words.

Her thoughts were so focused on her son.

Brandi's words continued to run round and round in her mind. What did her ex-husband mean when he told Brandi, *I've got to go and take care of a dog and a boy?*

What evil plan did Devon have in mind for Noah's dog, Buddy, and, more importantly, for Noah?

She pressed on the accelerator, urging her car forward.

Jane knew she wouldn't be able to forgive herself if any harm came to her son at the hands of his abusive father.

STARING out the window from the bedroom on the second floor of his house, he smiled.

Finally, he arrived at the safe house he had specially built for his son to live here with him.

Noah had fought him, so he'd had to give his son some of that special potion to help calm the boy's nerves.

He reassured himself that he'd done everything to make his son's journey to his new home as easy as possible. Now Noah was finally resting upstairs in the bedroom he had built specially for him.

It was to keep him safe.

No longer would the boy's mother be able to control his boy or keep him away from his father.

His son was his to control. Nobody would be able to take away what was his any longer.

He'd made sure of that.

His son's dog wouldn't last much longer, and neither would the old woman.

Since he'd read the article, and learned that two of his business friends were arrested, he had to rearrange the timing of his plan.

But that was alright. He was used to making necessary changes.

It was all going just like he had planned.

He was good at planning.

Turning, he looked at the photo on his nightstand.

Hadn't he planned the peaceful departure of his stepmother?

As he ran one finger along the face in the photo, memories returned.

When his stepmother first married his dad, he was six years old.

She was a good person at that time. She was nice to him back then.

But then, a year later, his dad died.

Without warning, his stepmother turned mean.

Just for not saying the right words, or looking at her the wrong way, his stepmother locked him in the cellar, sometimes for a few days.

She would give him only water for those hard days. Almost every day he would hear her say what a wicked son he was.

But then he got older, and the day finally came when he was bigger and stronger.

One night, just before she went to bed, he had told her that he had a special drink to help her sleep better.

He had mixed her favorite wine with the digitalis medicine, digoxin. Not long after she drank the mixture, his stepmother died from heart failure.

Now, she was at peace. Now, his stepmother was made good again. Now, she was good, just like that first year after she married his father.

If Jane tried to find Noah and discovered that he had hid his son in this house, then his ex-wife was being bad.

That meant he would need to make Jane good, like she used to be.

He would be forced again to do what he'd done to his stepmother in order to make Jane good again.

He would need to do it quickly.

No longer would he let Noah's mother have any more control or influence over his son.

CHAPTER EIGHTEEN

Jane

Jane parked her car in front of her house and ran inside.

Before she'd taken two steps, she spotted her son's dog, Buddy.

The dog lay motionless under a table in the corner.

His large eyes were barely open and he was having trouble breathing.

She breathed in a quick, sharp breath at the sight of vomit all over the floor.

Panic caused her chest to tighten.

Immediately she yelled out, "Noah? Mrs. Morrison?"

If her ex had done something terrible to the dog, then what about her son and her housekeeper?

Frantically, Jane ran down the hallway, opening doors,

searching the rooms. She stopped only long enough to call the veterinarian's office.

After talking with his assistant, Jane hurried to do what she could to help the dog.

Mixing together some salt and water, she brought the cup over to the dog. Forcing his mouth open, she gently dribbled the mixture down his throat.

It wasn't long before Noah's dog began to heave. Buddy threw up whatever he had swallowed. Jane hoped he got rid of most of whatever had been bothering his stomach.

After she cleaned up the mess again, she hurried to fill his drinking bowel with water.

Immediately afterwards, she rushed to the kitchen, yelling the names of her housekeeper and son.

Jane ran until she reached the other side of the kitchen counter.

She stopped, shocked.

On the floor, lay her housekeeper.

Her legs were stretched wide apart, her arms at different angles.

A small amount of blood pooled by her head.

"Oh heavens, Mrs. Morrison." Jane went down on her hands and knees and checked the older lady's pulse.

She sighed in relief when she felt a pulse and continued to speak to the older lady.

The loud ringing from Jane's phone pierced the silence.

Hurriedly, she answered, her voice raw full of shock.

"Hello."

"Jane, this is Adele. I wanted to let you know I'm on my

way back to your place." Her faithful assistant's calm voice soothed her.

"Adele, I'm so glad. I just came home and my son's dog was sick and now I've found Mrs. Morrison lying on the floor. There's blood on her head. I think somebody struck her."

"I'll be there to help as soon as I can."

The housekeeper began to moan and turned her head slightly.

"Mrs. Morrison, are you awake? Can you tell me what happened to you?" Jane whispered, desperate to know what was going on.

She stood to her feet and, after pouring water on a clean cloth, kneeled down to wipe off the blood from her face and neck and on the floor.

"That man. The man with the Fedora hat barged into the house. He must have given the dog something to make him sick. When he saw me, he asked where Noah was and then he hit me on the head with something." The older lady reached up and rubbed the side of her head.

"Where's my son?" Jane asked, her chest feeling as if it would burst.

"I thought Noah was in his room," the older lady said softly.

"I need to find him." Jane stood to her feet. "I'll call the ambulance to get the help you need, Mrs. Morrison. Adele will be back home soon to help."

Jane hurried away down the hallway and, after speaking with the emergency number, she knocked and opened her son's bedroom door.

Her body stiffened in shock at the empty room.

Stepping further inside the room, she searched everywhere.

"Noah, are you here, sweetheart? Are you hiding in your closet?" Jane opened the closet doors, hoping he was playing a game of hide and seek.

After searching in all the rooms, she realized her son was gone.

Her breath caught in her lungs.

Sheer, black fright swept through her.

Did her ex-husband steal her son from her own home?

The thought tore at her insides.

She had tried so hard to make a real home that was safe here with Noah. Perhaps her hope had only been an illusion.

Somehow, the people close to her had been hurt anyway.

Turning, she hurried back to the kitchen.

Jane called the police to let them know her son was missing, giving them the information they needed.

As she reached the kitchen, she hung up the phone, just as she noticed Adele walking into the house.

"Jane, what happened?" Adele hurried towards them, her eyes bright with concern.

"Mrs. Morrison said a man barged into the house, fed Noah's dog something, then asked where Noah was, and then hit our housekeeper on the head and she fell down on the kitchen floor."

"Where's Noah?"

Jane swallowed and a crease of worry formed between her brows. "He's not here. I have to go find him."

"Of course you do, Jane. But there's blood on your

dress. Do you want me to grab you a pair of jeans and a sweatshirt?" Adele asked, seeing Jane's confused look.

"I need to hurry." Jane didn't even have time to notice. She wasn't thinking. She couldn't go searching outside for her son in high-heeled shoes and a formal dress for the wedding.

Adele hurried back. "Here's a change of clothes. I found your fanny pack too."

"Thanks, Adele. You're a big help." Jane sent her a wobbly smile and hurried to the washroom to change.

Quickly, she changed into jeans and a sweatshirt. Tightening the fanny pack around her waist, she placed it under her sweatshirt.

Jane hurried out towards the kitchen, just in time to see Adele helping Mrs. Morrison drink some water.

"I need to run. I must find my son." Jane's voice sounded hoarse to her own ears.

Slipping on her jacket and gloves and boats, she opened the door.

"Of course, you go, Jane. I'll be here to help Mrs. Morrison. Find Noah. We have faith you'll find him and he'll be home soon." Adele's words faded as Jane hurried out the back door.

As soon as she walked to the front yard, she stopped and looked around.

"Noah, where are you?" She called her son's name a few times. She wasn't sure where to start. Should she walk towards the cove first or to their back yard, which led to a grove of trees?

Since Noah often played in the back yard, she decided to start there.

There was no sign of him as she walked the length of the backyard.

Jane stopped in her tracks and glanced around, wondering which way to walk to find her son.

Suddenly, she spotted a small trail leading into the pine and poplar trees that lined her backyard.

A few weeks ago, she remembered looking out the window, watching Noah walking his dog along this trail.

She decided to follow it and see where it led.

At this point, she was desperate to try any path that might lead to finding her son.

Jane started walking along the narrow trail.

Sticks, leaves, and pine cones were mixed together with the dirt and packed snow. They had a light snowfall a few days ago, and there were still traces of the white powder in between the trees.

Hurrying along the path, Jane looked down at the path so she wouldn't trip over roots or branches in her way.

Unexpectedly, she looked further down on the path ahead and spotted something pink.

Crouching down, she picked it up, and stared at the oval-shaped pink pill in her hand.

She gasped in surprise.

This is Noah's medicine for his skin problems. Did he accidentally drop it when he was playing with Buddy?

She stuffed the medicine pill in her pocket and continued walking the trail.

However, during the next hundred feet or so, she spotted two more pink pills.

Awareness hit her like a bullet train.

Her son had, somehow, purposefully dropped his pink

medicine pills on the trail. Even when his terrible father dragged him away, her son figured out a way for someone to find him.

A flicker of hope relieved some of the heaviness that lingered in her chest.

She hoped it wouldn't take long to find her son.

JANE CONTINUED to follow the trail until, unexpectedly, it led to a clearing.

Acres of green lawn surrounded her. A large, white, historical house stood in the distance.

She was aware this must be her neighbor's property.

Why would Noah's trail lead her to this place?

Jane continued to walk across the green lawn. Every so often, she found another pink, oval-shaped pill.

As she got close to the house, she noticed metal bars on the front door and on the windows.

Relying on gut instinct, she decided to walk around the house first, instead of knocking on the front door.

An eerie feeling suddenly overcame her. There was something strange about this place.

She reached the back of the house and looked around. Walking in between tall trees that were close to the house, she looked upwards.

Jane sucked in a quick breath in shock.

On the window, at the very top of the house, was a red handkerchief hanging from the window.

It was the same red handkerchief, with white stitching,

that her late grandmother had given to her son on his ninth birthday.

She was sure of it.

Noah must be inside.

That meant, most likely, this was her ex-husband's home on the island.

With that thought, another shock flew through her.

How long had Devon been her neighbor?

Had he been stalking her, watching her every move?

Jane remembered all the threatening notes, Noah's stuffed animal, and the crushed Christmas ornament.

Alarm and anger rippled along her spine.

How dare this man invade and try to ruin her life and steal her son?

A fresh resolve settled like hardened cement at the bottom of her belly.

I am going to save my son. I will figure out how to free him from the clutches of his cruel father.

Jane looked up, towards the window where Noah's handkerchief swung in the chilly wind.

Turning her head, she studied the tall trees next to the house. There was one that seemed stronger, with a thicker trunk than the others.

Could she climb it?

Determined, she grimly placed one foot on the lowest branch and gripped the tree trunk with both hands.

It took a long time, but, finally, she reached the level of the window.

Leaning, she slowly swung her body forward and knocked softly on the window.

Jane wanted to be as quiet as possible in case Devon was nearby.

She didn't see anybody, so she knocked again, a little louder this time.

Suddenly, Noah's face appeared at the window.

His blue eyes widened at the sight of her.

Tears pricked the back of her eyelids and she blinked them back. She was so happy to see her son.

Jane motioned for him to open the window.

After struggling for a few minutes, her son managed to open the window.

"Mom, grab my hand," Noah urged.

Jane reached for his hand and, with her other hand, grabbed the windowsill. She pulled herself through the window, with her son's help, and landed with a thud on the floor of the bedroom.

Standing to her feet, she wrapped her arms around her son.

"Noah, I'm so glad I found you," Jane whispered in a wobbly voice.

"Me too, Mom. Don't worry, I'm okay." Noah's arms wrapped around her, holding her tight. "I'm so happy you found me."

As much as she wanted to hold her son in her arms, she forced herself to step back.

Hurriedly, she looked him over. "Did he hurt you in any way?"

"No, Mom. I'm good."

Jane released a sigh of relief. "I'm glad."

"Listen, we don't have much time. The two of us need

to get out of the place as fast as we can." Jane picked up Noah's jacket and tossed it to him. Quickly, he put it on.

Jane asked, "Did your father say anything about what he planned to do with you?"

Noah shrugged. "He said something about wanting the two of us to get off this island. Then he told me he had big plans for me. When I argued with him, and told him I wanted to stay with you, Dad told me you were a liar. He said you weren't to be trusted. Dad told me he was the only person I could trust. But I don't trust him, Mom."

Jane's eyes grew wide.

She shook her head in disbelief. "Good, I'm glad you don't. Remember, your dad tries to control by whatever means necessary. Whether it's by mental manipulation or by physical force. He'll do anything to get his way."

Without warning, the bedroom door opened wide.

Devon's low voice was loud and threatening.

His lips thinned in anger. "I'm glad you remembered, Jane. And I'm here to make sure you don't forget it!"

Her ex stood in the open doorway.

His voice was cold and lashing.

His hand shook, with a gun pointed directly at her heart.

Panic rioted within her at the sight of her ex.

Somehow, Devon must have heard the two of them talking in Noah's bedroom.

Her heart hammered, her breathing ragged at the sight of the one man that had terrorized her life for years.

Devon's face was pale, and his body thin.

Bald spots were visible on his head, and his hair was beginning to turn gray.

Even though she'd just seen him, she was still shocked at the way the past few years had altered his appearance.

Her ex looked worse than she had ever seen him.

Devon glanced sharply between the two of them.

"Now. Jane, walk away from Noah," his voice had grown cold and menacing.

With a swift movement, he pointed the gun in the direction he wanted her to go.

Jane swallowed and stepped away from her son.

Panic welled in her throat.

His voice was cold, "Say goodbye to your son, Jane. I'm going to take you far away from Noah. I have big plans for you."

His mouth took on an unpleasant twist.

Her nerves tensed immediately. What did this cruel man have in mind?

As her thoughts were going full throttle, her son spoke up, "Dad, what are you going to do to my mom? Where are you taking her?" Noah asked in a wobbly voice.

Jane turned to her son, and saw the color drain from his face.

Overwhelming remorse and heartbreak flooded her that she hadn't saved her son in time.

"Noah, you ask too many questions. I will do what must be done." Devon's face turned cold as he looked over at his son. "Your mother has controlled you and poisoned your mind for too many years. Don't you see? Now, it's my turn. You are going to come with me now. You don't need your mother."

Noah gasped and interrupted, "But..."

"Quiet, Noah. Or it'll go worse for your mother." His harsh words had their intended effect.

Her son stayed silent.

With a cold low voice, he continued, "Jane, you are coming with me. Walk towards the door and keep walking. I have the perfect place planned for your stay. Now move!"

Jane stepped forward. With one last glance at her son, she mouthed the words, *I love you.*

Tears pricked her son's eyes and Jane thought her heart would break.

The cold end of the gun barrel pressed against her back. "Move faster. Down the stairs."

As she stepped down the stairs, she heard her ex-husband click the lock on Noah's bedroom door.

Jane reached the main level of the house.

Devon opened the door to another set of stairs that went down to the basement.

"Now, go down these stairs." Devon waved the gun in his hand once more.

When they finally reached the basement, her ex-husband walked to a small room in the farthest corner.

It was a very small room.

Drafty, cold, and dark.

The only light was from a small window near the ceiling.

Cold cement ran the length and width of the area.

The space looked enough like a prison cell to be one.

Jane shivered, both from fear and from the cold.

"You had to get in my way, didn't you? You had to get my friends arrested. We were doing so well with our little side business too." Devon's voice was absolutely emotionless and it chilled her. "There are consequences for getting in my way. I thought you learned that years ago, but I guess I was wrong."

"This time you'll learn. When you wrote that article, you sealed your doom. You were very reckless, Jane. I think you're beginning to realize that whoever tries to uncover the secrets hidden on the cove, dies."

He erupted in a brittle laugh. "Anybody who digs deeper, trying to find answers to your great-grandfather's shipwreck, the pink diamond, or the cause of death of Sean O'Connor, or the deaths of your parents, dies. Anybody who tries to uncover my secrets will pay the highest price."

Her ex-husband's stone-cold eyes glittered as he stared at her.

"You got too close. Now, you must pay the penalty. You will be locked inside this cellar until you die, alone." His rough laughter mocked her. "You, Jane, have always been a mistake. You were never good enough for me. You're a stupid blonde. And you're not fit to be Noah's mother. You're not worthy to be loved. Now, you'll never see your friends, your family, and, most importantly, you'll never see your son, Noah, again. Goodbye, Jane."

"No, wait!" Jane called out, wanting Devon to see reason.

It was too late.

Her ex-husband slammed the door and turned the key to lock her inside.

Jane choked back a frightened cry.

At this moment, she was forced to face her two biggest fears.

The first fear was being trapped in a small, enclosed space with no way out. And the second fear was that her son would be separated from her by his cruel father.

Fear, stark and vivid, spread through her body.

Tension crawled up her spine, bunching her shoulders.

Devon's words continued to circle round and round in her mind like a stuck record always circling back.

You'll be locked inside this cellar until you die, alone. You, Jane, were always a mistake. You're not good enough for me. You're a stupid blonde. And you're not fit to be Noah's mother. You'll never see your friends, your family, and, most importantly, you'll never see your son, Noah, again.

Jane lifted both hands against her ears to try to stop the constant barrage of mocking words.

Pacing back and forth across the small room, the memory of Uncle Tony's words echoed similar insults.

Jane remembered the day like it was yesterday.

It had been Christmas Eve and she'd been a small, eight-year-old girl at the time. She had accidentally dropped a custom-made glass sculpture.

The gift her grandparents had given to her parents for their anniversary, had shattered into tiny pieces on the floor.

Tears filled her eyes and she'd sobbed because she had completely ruined her parents' special anniversary gift.

Even to this day, remorse flooded her as she remembered.

However, Uncle Tony's cruel words had cut deep inside her like a knife wound.

He'd made her feel small.

He'd made her feel like the fact that she had been born was a mistake. He'd made her feel like she was unworthy to be loved.

Why do you always ruin things? Can't you do anything right? All you ever do is make big mistakes. You're a stupid little girl who makes a mess wherever she goes. Face it. No one will ever want you. No one will ever love you.

Tears blinded her eyes.

The nauseating sinking of despair flooded her body.

Her knees went weak and she lowered herself onto the cold cement floor.

Pressing her hands over her face, a raw, primitive grief overwhelmed her.

Dread flooded her heart. It felt like, once again, she was reliving the childhood trauma from when she was eight years old.

The pain in her heart became a sick and fiery gnawing.

A bitter cold despair crushed her soul with its weight.

Her heart squeezed in anguish as she realized that, after all these years of trying to look, act, and be perfect, it was never going to happen.

Years ago, had Uncle Tony been right all along? Was she just a stupid girl who just makes mistakes wherever she goes?

Worse still, had her ex-husband been correct? Was she not fit to be Noah's mother? Was she not good enough to be loved?

She gulped hard, hot tears slipping down her cheeks as she rocked back and forth on the cold cement floor.

Horrible thoughts flooded her mind.

Jane's thoughts darkened at the recent turn of events. Her son had been kidnapped from their home. She had failed Noah.

Her thoughts shifted to Ward.

Ward had done everything he could to help her solve these mysteries. He had been incredibly helpful and kind to her.

Yet, out of fear, she had ended their close relationship.

She didn't deserve him.

He'd been good to her, but she'd assumed the worst of him.

It was when he had danced with her at the Christmas country dance that Jane fell in love with him, even more than when they dated in college.

Not only had Ward been the one to bring the joy and warmth of Christmas back to her, but he'd also brought love back to her heart.

But, just when she realized that she loved him, he made a mistake in not recognizing her ex, and she let her fears consume her.

Regret weighed her down, leaving her with an inexplicable feeling of emptiness.

Her sorrow was a huge, painful knot, deep inside.

All those words of shame came back to haunt her.

Maybe it's true all I do is ruin things. Maybe it's true all I do is make big mistakes. Maybe it's true that no one will ever love me.

A flash of wild grief ripped through her.

Tears blinded her eyes.

Jane cried for all that she'd lost, until she had no tears left.

Wiping her eyes, she noticed a tiny bit of light shining on the floor.

Looking up, she saw the small window, near the top of the ceiling.

The sun's rays caught the reflection of the pearl on her necklace. It shone brilliantly against the wall.

Her fingers squeezed the pearl necklace her late grandmother had given her as a little girl. The gift had been given not long after her parents died.

Precious memories of that moment with her beloved grandmother returned.

Remember what Grams said about the pearl and about who you are. She said you are valuable, beautiful, and precious.

Jane recalled her grandmother's words. She had committed them to her memory.

Remember, Jane dear, whenever you're scared, think of this small pearl. A pearl is the only gem produced by a living organism. The pearl goes through an ordeal — because the pearl layer protects the oyster until it's out of harm's way. But, after all the trouble it goes through, a beautiful stone is formed.

The pearl emerges from the conflict, victorious and beautiful. Perhaps that's one of the reasons the Good Book tells us that a woman is more precious than jewels and her value is far above rubies or pearls.

That's who you are, Jane.

My darling granddaughter, you have just emerged from a fiery trial with the deaths of your mom and dad. You are like this pearl — emerging even more beautiful and stronger from all the hardships you've suffered.

I want you to always remember to hold onto faith, no matter what conflicts or trials you suffer in life. I'm giving you this pearl necklace to help you remember that, much like the precious stone of the pearl, you are valuable, beautiful, and precious. During difficult times, hold onto faith, hope, and love. Promise me you'll try to remember."

The promise she'd made to her beloved Grams weighed heavy on her heart.

She would keep her promise.

She would do her best to see herself as valuable and precious.

Jane decided she would hold onto faith, hope, and love like never before.

Looking around, Jane studied the confined basement room where she was trapped.

The walls were thick cement blocks on all sides.

The wood door was thick, and it was locked tight.

The only way out was through the upper window.

But the window was too far up for her to reach.

Jane turned her head to look around the room.

There was nothing here, except some old, wooden cradles and rocking reindeer.

Were these ruined products of his that her ex-husband didn't want?

Discouraged, she couldn't think of any way to crawl up to that window.

Remember to have faith.

She reminded herself as she thought of what to do.

Nothing came to mind at the moment.

So, she walked over to look at one of the wooden cradles. There must have been at least fifty of them stacked all over the room.

Her fingers ran along the side of one of the cradles.

The products were made sturdy and strong.

The bottom was wide enough for a baby, with room to grow.

Deciding to look underneath the cradle, she noticed there were strong crosspieces across the bottom to hold everything in place.

She ran one hand along the bottom, when, suddenly, her hand caught on a lever.

Pulling it, she noticed that it opened up a secret compartment along the bottom of the cradle.

Leaning closer, she saw many bags of white stuff inside. Pulling one of the bags out, Jane's eyes widened.

Was this bag full of drugs? To her, it looked like it might be cocaine.

Looking further into the open compartment, it looked like there might be at least twenty bags inside. Each was filled with drugs.

Setting the cradle down, she looked around the room.

Her thoughts were hurried.

If each of these cradles has a secret compartment, that's a lot of drugs my ex-husband is smuggling. Is he trafficking these drugs to other dealers?

If that's the kind of illegal stuff Devon was doing, he was in a lot of trouble.

Jane smiled, feeling hopeful.

Now, she had the proof she needed.

She could only show the proof of his crimes to Detective Sullivan if she could somehow escape this room.

Jane glanced around again.

There wasn't much in this room except the wood

cradles, the wood reindeer-style rocking chairs, and a large pile of two by four lengths of wood.

Unexpectedly, an idea came to her.

What if she made a pile of all that wood in front of the window?

Eagerly, she cleared all the cradles that were in front of the window.

Then, she began to stack the wood in their place.

When she finally set down the last piece of wood, it reached about halfway up the brick wall.

Maybe the stacked wood would be high enough so that she could reach the window.

Quickly, she arranged the wood cradles so they would be a sturdy support for the wood planks she lined up against the wall.

Next, she climbed onto the stacked wood.

Jane was pleasantly surprised that now she could see out the window.

As she studied the window, she noticed it was an awning type of window with the hinge on the top.

Jane pushed with all her might against the bottom and, finally, the hinges squeaked.

She tried to push it again but realized there was a latch she needed to unlock.

After she did, this time, when she pushed the window, it opened wide.

Shimmying her body, she twisted and turned until, finally, she was free, falling onto the grass below.

Jane looked back at the small window opening, shocked that she had managed to free herself.

Now, it was time to get help.

She had to save her son.

Without warning, loud voices came from the direction of the front of the house.

Jane took a quick, sharp breath.

Hurriedly, she leaned her back against the side of the house so she wouldn't be seen.

Her heart nearly stopped as she heard her son's voice in the distance.

Noah's voice was worried and shaking, "Dad, why do I have to go away from my mom? I don't want to leave her here all by herself."

Devon's voice was like steel. "Noah, you will be better off without your mother. She's a scheming, stubborn, she-wolf. You don't need your mom, son. You'll stay with me from here on out."

"But what about my dog and my friends?" Her son's voice broke miserably.

His father's voice replied firmly, "I'll get you a new dog and you'll have new friends."

"I don't want to leave everybody." Her son's words carried a tumult of pain.

Jane quickly covered her mouth as a sob erupted.

Her anguish for her son peaked to shatter the last shreds of her control.

From a distance, she heard the last part of their conversation.

"That's too bad. It's time you came to live with me. Your mother has had you for far too long, poisoning your mind against me." Devon's curt voice lashed out at her son. "Now, we'll go down to the cove and take my boat. We'll begin a new life together at a place I have in mind. And I don't want to hear any more complaining, Noah."

Jane was numb with increasing anger and shock.

Their voices disappeared into the distance.

There was no way she would let her ex-husband take her son away.

Slowly, Jane began to walk along the side of the house until she reached the front porch.

Seeing no one, she released a sigh of relief.

Jane ran towards her home. She needed to get help.

The sun was starting to go down, and time was running out.

She needed to hurry and retrieve Noah out of the cruel hands of his father.

ard

WARD DROVE his car up to Jane's house, just as she came running through the trees in the backyard.

Quickly, he stepped out of the car at the sight of her.

His heart beat fast at the sight of her.

"Jane, where have you been? I couldn't find you or Noah." Ward grabbed her in his arms and held her for a moment. "I've been so worried."

Tears shimmered in her eyes.

She hurried to explain all that had happened. "Even though Devon locked me inside that dungeon-like room, finally, I made my escape."

Ward set his jaw in determination. "He must be a madman. Where's Noah?"

"Just as I managed to escape, I overheard Devon talking to Noah. He is taking my son to the cove. He plans to take Noah away by boat," Jane's voice cracked. A single tear ran down one cheek. "We need to hurry."

Compassion flooded him at the sight of the stark fear in her eyes.

Ward reached over and, with his thumb, he caught the tear that trailed down her cheek.

"It'll be alright, Jane. I will do everything I can to bring Noah back to you." Ward pulled out his phone and dialed a number. "Let's go. I'm calling Detective Sullivan to meet us at the cove."

Ward grabbed her hand.

He talked with the detective and asked him to meet them at the cove.

Then, together, they ran across the acres of grass until they reached the cove.

He was determined to do whatever it took to help Jane bring her son back home.

The woman he loved needed him.

THE SUNSET WAS across the horizon line as they reached the edge of the property that connected to the beach area and the cove.

Jane glanced downwards towards the cove. "I see a flash of red over there. That might be Noah's baseball hat."

There were quite a few motorboats along the cove this evening, which was unusual.

"Good. Let's make our way down to the beach." Ward grabbed her hand and they made their way between the trees towards the beach.

They came to a cluster of trees that wasn't far from where Devon and Noah were standing on the beach.

Devon was busy loading some boxes and barrels onto his boat.

"I have an idea," Jane whispered. "When Devon's not looking, I'll walk quietly through the water, until I reach the other side of that stranger's boat. That way, hopefully, I won't be seen. Then, when I see Noah by himself, I'll grab him and we'll get away."

"I don't know, Jane. It's too risky." Ward ran a hand through his hair. "Maybe you would be safer if you had someone to stand watch. I'd be happy to go with you."

"Alright." Jane watched and, soon, Devon turned his back and began to dig inside one crate, looking for something.

"Let's go." Jane hurried across the sand and ran into the water on the other side of the stranger's boat.

Ward followed close behind.

She peered behind the stranger's boat, watching for a moment when her ex-husband wasn't looking.

"Let's go." Jane saw her chance and swam under the water until she reached Devon's boat.

Earlier, Jane saw a ladder on the side of Devon's boat. She just needed to reach it.

Out of breath, Ward whispered, "I'll watch out for you from here, Jane. But, if something goes south, I'm coming to get you."

She grinned. "Thanks, Ward."

Jane began to climb the ladder. When she reached the top, she looked over and saw Devon looking the other way.

Seeing her chance, she hurried onto the boat.

Since her ex's smaller yacht had a tall bridge where the helm was located, she hid in front of it to catch her breath.

Her heart raced and she forced herself to breathe evenly.

As she began to make a plan on how to get Noah away from Devon, she suddenly spotted a motorboat coming her way.

It looked like Detective Sullivan and Officer Shelton.

Behind her, she heard Devon's voice telling Noah to sit still while he went to steer the boat.

Her ex-husband began to move his yacht forward.

But, by that time, the police boat was in front of him, blocking his way.

Detective Sullivan spoke using a loud speaker, "Devon Hollingsworth, turn off the engine. You're under arrest for kidnapping a minor. We will be coming aboard your boat."

Devon yelled, "The boy with me is my son! You can't arrest me for taking my own flesh and blood."

Jane shuddered at the curses coming from the location of the helm.

The detective spoke into the microphone, "The boy is under the guardianship of his mother. You are being arrested for kidnapping him."

"We'll see about that!" Devon's loud voice boomed in the background.

Jane heard footsteps coming closer.

Without warning, Devon appeared from around the corner of the boat's bridge. Somehow, he must have spotted her there.

"Jane, you managed to escape, did you? Now that I have you again, you won't get away. It's time to use you as a ransom."

The gun in her ex-husband's hand was pointed directly at her.

Quickly, Devon grabbed Jane and held the gun to her head.

With an angry, threatening voice he said, "If you try to board this boat, I'll shoot. Don't think I won't."

Jane shivered in fear. Panic filled her lungs.

How was she going to escape this time? Maybe she really was about to die.

"Don't shoot," Detective Sullivan said over the loud speaker. "We'll drop our weapons, then you can drop yours too."

Devon said angrily, "No. Here's what will happen. You'll drop your weapons and get your boat out of the way. Then, I'll drop my weapon, and you'll let me and my son leave."

The detective nodded and began to put the boat in reverse.

Jane was stunned. Were the police going to let Devon get away with stealing her son?

All of a sudden, a commotion came from behind her.

Devon turned, pointed his gun, and fired a shot, grazing Ward's arm.

Ward rushed forward, knocking the gun out of Devon's hand.

Her ex began to fight against him, but Ward was stronger.

Soon, Ward held Devon down on the floor of the boat deck, in a tight hold.

Jane spotted the gun at a distance and saw her chance.

Hurrying over, she grabbed the gun.

As Jane pointed the gun at Devon, she firmly stated, "Now, you won't be able to escape with my son, Devon."

Fury almost choked Jane at the fact that her ex-husband tried to kidnap her son and take him away from her forever.

It was only a matter of minutes before Detective Sullivan and Officer Shelton came on board the boat.

Officer Shelton placed handcuffs on Devon and led him off the boat.

Jane hurried over to check on Ward. "We need to get you to the hospital. Your arm is bleeding."

Ward looked at his arm. "It's just a graze, I think. I didn't break any bones."

"Still, we need to get you patched up." Jane looked at his arm, not liking the amount of blood still oozing out of the wound.

Reaching into her pocket, she pulled out a large, white handkerchief.

"Hold this handkerchief over your wound until we can get to the hospital, alright?" Jane asked, as she placed the white cotton over his wound.

"Sure." Ward grinned as she took care of him.

The detective started to leave, but quickly turned back.

"Good job, you two, on catching Devon Hollingsworth. One more thing. If you two could come to my office tomorrow morning, I have a few questions." Detective Sullivan spoke to both Ward and Jane. "You make a good team. And, Jane, I'm glad you got your son back."

"Thanks, Detective. We'll be there tomorrow," Jane said in a wobbly voice. "I am very grateful that Noah's safe and sound."

As soon as the detective walked away, Noah ran to her. "Mom, are you alright?"

She opened her arms wide, grabbing her son in a big hug. "I'm alright, kiddo. I have to admit to being scared when your dad took you away."

"Me too. But, Mom, I can't believe you risked your life to help me." There was a catch in her son's voice and he squeezed her tighter.

Jane kissed the top of his blond head. "Oh, Noah, I love you so much. There isn't anything I wouldn't do to help keep you safe."

"I love you too, Mom. Let's go home, okay?" Noah whispered.

"Yeah. Let's go home." Jane smiled. "But, first, we need to take Ward to the hospital."

Her brows creased in worry as she looked at Ward.

He grimaced. "Let's get this over with."

When they finally made it to the hospital, the doctor in the emergency room was able to see him right away.

After looking him over, the doctor said Ward was

lucky the bullet had only grazed his arm. After cleaning the wound and stitching him up, the doctor placed a gauze pad on the wound, gave him pain medication, and sent him home.

"Do you want to go home now?" Jane asked as they left.

Ward shook his head. "I'd rather talk with you. I'll go home later."

Jane smiled warmly. "Alright, if you're sure."

It was time for them to have a serious talk.

During the trauma of the last hours, she'd had time to think about all that she wanted to say.

Jane only hoped Ward would be willing to hear what she had to say.

&

"I'm so thankful you're back home safe and sound." Jane tousled Noah's blond hair. "Buddy's happy to see you too."

Buddy, Noah's dog, had his big paws on his chest. Every once in a while, he would lick his cheek.

Her son hugged his dog and blinked back tears. "I'm glad I'm safe and that Buddy is doing alright now too, Mom. I can't believe Dad hurt my dog and tried to kidnap me away from you. Then he locked you up. Dad never stops trying to hurt us does he?"

"You're right. He doesn't stop." She shook her head. "However, from now on he'll be forced to stop. Your dad will be going to jail for a long time."

"It sounds terrible to say it, but I'm glad. Now we can

live peaceful lives again. No more running, right?" Her son asked, a question lingering in his big, blue eyes.

Jane nodded. "No more running."

Noah reached up and hugged her close. "I love you, Mom."

"I love you, Noah," Jane whispered, and held him for a long time. "Have a good sleep, son."

Noah smiled as she tucked in his blankets around him.

Jane was still smiling as she walked back to the kitchen.

Ward sat at her kitchen table, waiting for her.

"Do you want a cup of coffee?" she asked. A cup of java was just what she needed to give her courage for the talk ahead.

"Sure, thanks," Ward replied, eyeing her with concern.

Jane walked to the kitchen to start the coffee.

Looking around, she saw a note on the counter from Adele.

Hurriedly she read what she wrote.

"Adele wrote to let me know Mrs. Morrison is doing well, but the doctor would like her to stay for a few more days at the hospital. I'll visit her tomorrow to see if she needs anything." Jane set the note down on the counter.

The kitchen was open to the dining area so it was easy to talk to each other.

"Good idea. I'm glad she's doing alright." Ward shook his head. "I still can't believe Devon beat up your house-keeper. I hope he goes to jail for a really long time."

Jane nodded. "I can't help but agree. Anyway, I'm thankful we don't have to worry about him any longer. We can let the police deal with him now."

She was so weary of thinking about Devon. She had spent far too many years doing that.

"Noah's doing alright?" A crease formed between his brows.

Jane nodded. "Yeah, for the most part anyway."

Carrying two mugs of coffee, she set them on the table between them.

"I think the rough treatment from his dad caused trauma." Jane's voice shook as she remembered all her son had been through. "Oh, Ward, I have so many regrets because I placed my son in harm's way."

He reached over and lightly squeezed her hand. "It wasn't your fault, Jane. It's your ex-husband's fault for thinking he could simply steal your son away from you. Not to mention the other abuse he forced on you."

A tiny glow cheered her at his defense of her.

"Thank you, Ward. I can't believe you're still faithful to support and encourage me, even after I treated you badly." Jane flushed miserably, regret flooding her at how angry and cold she'd been towards him.

His eyes darkened and he stared at her with a look that was as soft as a caress.

Her heart hammered in her ears.

Ward said, "That's because you mean the world to me, Jane."

His words and compelling eyes riveted her to the spot.

A realization came over her that it was time to tell him all that was on her heart.

She caressed his hand, studying him intently. "Thanks, Ward. And you mean a lot to me too. In fact, that's what I wanted to tell you."

He leaned closer.

She tried to throttle the dizzying current racing through her.

"I'm listening." His intense focus let her know that she had his undivided attention.

The words rushed out of Jane's mouth. "First of all, I wanted to tell you I'm sorry for putting up walls between us. And I'm sorry for assuming you had abandoned me and Noah. Today, when I saw how much my ex-husband has aged, it made me realize how different he looks than he did in that photo from years ago. I was wrong to assume you would be able to recognize him."

Ward smiled gently. "It's alright. Do you forgive me, Jane?"

She cleared her throat. "There's nothing to forgive. I was the one at fault for judging you wrongly. Do you forgive me, Ward?"

"You know I do. Somehow, forgiving you has always been easy for me, Jane." He caressed the top of her hand with his thumb.

A rush of pink stained her cheeks. "You're too good to me, Ward. Noah told me the same thing a few days ago."

He grinned. "What did he say?"

Jane smiled warmly. "Noah said, 'I think Ward is one of the good guys.' My son told me that I needed to stop being scared. He said, 'Mom, if I loved someone, I'd forgive them and tell them the truth.' Noah is wise beyond his years."

"He is." Ward waited quietly as she continued to share her thoughts.

Jane swallowed back emotion and continued, "When I

was trapped in that prison-like cell at Devon's house, I had a revelation."

"Oh, what's that?" He raised one eyebrow, curiosity written on his face.

Jane sighed. "I realized, ever since my childhood, I've tried to somehow be this perfect woman. I was desperate for acceptance, approval, and love."

She added, "Ever since we've known each other, I've assumed you wanted this perfect woman. It wasn't anything you said, it was simply my own poor self-image and misguided beliefs. I assumed, if you knew the real me, you'd walk away or abandon me, like everyone else."

"For the record, I don't want you to be perfect, Jane. I just want you to feel like you can be the real you. The real you is wonderful." The warmth of Ward's words were a healing balm to her wounded heart.

"Thanks, Ward." Jane sighed. "While I was locked up in that room, I realized that my thoughts and beliefs about myself had been locked up for so many years. I realized that the only person still locking the door behind me and keeping me trapped from being who I really am, is me. I want you to know I've decided to be brave and show you, and the world, the real me. The woman I was meant to be."

Ward's smile widened as he listened.

"What I mean to say, is that I'm finally ready to be vulnerable with you." Jane stood to her feet and walked over to the mantle in the living room, picking up something she brought back to where Ward waited.

His eyes widened as he looked at the two small, broken pieces of glass in her hand.

"I want to give you this." Jane reached over to give him what she held in her hand. "Here are two broken pieces of that glass sculpture I broke on my parent's anniversary that Christmas years ago. I wanted to give these pieces to you, to show you that I have decided it's time to stop being closed off from the people around me."

"I don't want to hide anymore because of shame, insecurity, or fear. I want you to know I am choosing to be vulnerable. I am choosing to show you the broken pieces of who I really am."

Her voice shook as she continued, "I don't know what happens next between us, but I want you to know the real me. And I want to tell you that if you still want to be in this relationship, I do too."

"I'm in." Ward's words overflowed with confidence and love. He pushed his chair back, and motioned for her to come sit with him. "Come here, Jane."

Her legs felt weak as she moved towards him.

Ward gathered her into his arms, so she sat on his lap. He held her snugly against his chest.

"I love you, Ward." She buried her face against his throat, as his arms wrapped around her.

"Do you know how long I've waited to hear those words from your lips?" he whispered into her ear. "It feels like a lifetime."

With one hand, he moved her head back so he could see her eyes.

"I love you, my sweet Jane." Ward lowered his head and his mouth covered hers hungrily.

She wrapped her arms around his neck and gave herself freely to the passion of his kisses.

His lips parted hers in a soul-reaching massage, and gave her a series of slow, shivery kisses.

Her senses reeled and she leaned closer to him.

For the first time, in what felt like forever, Jane felt like she was where she belonged.

In Ward's arms, she believed she had come home to safe harbor.

CHAPTER TWENTY

THE LAST WEEKEND BEFORE CHRISTMAS, Mrs. O'Connor's quilt shop, *Yarn Around the Cove,* was decorated with all sorts of eye-catching garlands and mini-lights for the annual Christmas Craft Show.

Arriving early, Jane busied herself stitching the two last meaningful designs for her personal quilting square.

Just as her sisters walked through the shop door, Jane finished the last stitch.

Jonathan walked in the door with Lizzie by his side. Her sister's three adult children Will, Jake, and Annie followed close behind.

Christopher stayed close to Annie.

It looked like things were getting serious between them.

Alex arrived with her husband, Sam, and their young daughter, Zoe.

As soon as Charlie arrived, she made a beeline to talk with Zach Whetstone. He was newly retired from many years serving in the Coast Guard.

Jane smiled softly. She couldn't help but wonder if those two would get married someday.

She noticed Jules walk into the craft show with Chesmu Sagamore at her side. His stepsister, Dr. Mika Sagamore, and her daughter, Choluna, were with them.

Katie and Torrie, her younger twin sisters, had arrived alone. Would those two get their second chance at love?

Jane's thoughts turned towards Ward. Heat rose from her neck to her cheeks as she remembered his kisses.

She was pleased he planned to come to the Christmas Craft Show today.

"Jane, are you doing some last-minute stitching?" Charlie teased.

She looked up, her eyes widening in surprise to see Charlie standing next to her.

"Yep. I just finished. It's good to see you." Jane stood to her feet, holding her quilting square in her hand. "Charlie, I saw you talking with Zach Whetstone. Is there something going on between the two of you?

A rush of pink stained her sister's cheeks. "No. We're just friends. Goodness, Jane. We've been friends all our lives, not to mention Zach and his dad are our neighbors."

Jane smiled. "Stranger things have happened than falling in love with a childhood friend, sis."

Charlie simply shook her head. "Well, that's not happening for me."

"I guess time will tell." Jane grinned teasingly.

Her sister's lips puckered in annoyance.

Jane simply smiled.

Her friend Kenna and her five other sisters walked towards them. "What are you two up to?"

Jane held up the quilted square. "I finally figured out what my last two designs should be for my personal quilt. I finished it just in time."

"Can you tell us about them?" Alex asked, ever the curious sister.

Jane grinned. "You'll just need to wait like everyone else. Mrs. O'Connor asked if those of us who stitched personal quilts would share the meaning behind our design."

"I look forward to it," Alex replied. "There are so many folks from our community who showed up tonight."

"I agree," Lizzie commented. "It's nice to see everyone enjoying the craft show."

Alex replied, "Well, I wouldn't say everyone is enjoying the craft show. I see those three older ladies, Ida Cantrell, Florrie Cantrell-Jones, and Linda Hart, on the other side of the room talking together. Sometimes those women look over in our direction with a frown on their faces."

Jane's friend Kenna chimed in, "There's a reason for that. All three women are very angry with Jane. The fact that she kept pushing for answers, and was instrumental in finding evidence for drug trafficking connected to Ryan Hart and Miles Carter, is one of the big reasons for their anger. Not to mention that article she wrote."

"I suppose." Alex looked around. "But, from what I can see, Violet Hayes is another woman who is angry with you, Jane."

Jane sighed heavily. "She has been that way ever since her daughter-in-law, Adele, left her son, Roy, to live at my home. Recently, her son decided to go to rehabilitation for his drug addiction. He's also agreed to marriage counseling. So Violet should be happy at how things have turned out."

Charlie nodded. "That's true. She should be thrilled."

Jane shrugged to hide her confusion. "I don't understand, why she would still be angry. It's what Violet wanted all along."

"Violet will get over her anger soon enough, Jane. Anyway, it's good that you have helped Adele through this rough patch," Alex added.

"It's something I wanted to do. I remember what it was like to live with an abusive husband. I needed to do what I could to support her." Jane squeezed her pearl necklace.

"And now you also have Ward by your side." Charlie grinned. "Is he coming tonight?"

Jane nodded. "I called Ward and asked him to come tonight. I wanted him to have a chance to see for himself what I've been up to."

Jane's friend Kenna added, "Sounds like the two of you are back together."

"We're together again." Jane swallowed back emotion. "After Devon kidnapped Noah, and locked me in that basement prison, I had a lot of time to think. I realized Ward had been so good to me, but still I rejected his love."

Jane sighed. "The truth was, I allowed my own fears to

hold me back from accepting his love. I decided I would stop hiding and show him and the world who I really am. We had a good long talk about everything. Now, we're back together."

Her friend Kenna grinned. "I'm so happy for you, Jane. This is the best news I've heard all day."

Jane's sisters who stood beside Kenna were all smiles as they heard her announcement.

"Tell us, what has happened with our unsolved mysteries since you returned safely to your home, Jane?" Lizzie asked.

Jane replied, "Well, as you might have heard, my ex-husband, Devon, has been charged with kidnapping, as well as drug trafficking."

"After I told Detective Sullivan about the drugs I found in a secret compartment in one of Devon's children's toys in the basement, the police raided his house. Turns out, they found a lot of drugs, both in the house and on Devon's boat. He'll be in jail for a very long time."

Lizzie shook her head. "I'm not surprised. I always wondered if Devon was involved in something illegal. Not to mention the fact that he locked both you and Noah in his house. It's terrible how he treated you. I'm glad he's in jail."

"I agree." Alex turned to Jane. "You also mentioned that Ryan Hart and Miles Carter were arrested for drug trafficking."

Jane nodded. "Yes. The police found evidence of drugs on Ryan's boat. The two of them were also taking drugs from the police station's evidence locker room. Also, Roy Hayes confessed to buying drugs from Ryan Hart. So, they've been charged. But I think Sheriff Hart plans to fight it in court."

Charlie asked, "I am curious if Sheriff Hart is going to be found guilty as well?"

"Maybe, but it might be for a different reason," Jane said.

"Oh boy, that sounds dire. What do you mean?" Charlie asked.

Jane bit her lip and looked around the room hurriedly. She wanted to double check their conversation was private.

Leaning close, she whispered, "You remember those pieces of wood we found at the shed near the cove?"

"Yes." All her sisters remembered.

Jane cleared her throat and spoke softly, "I had a call from Detective Sullivan yesterday. He said the forensics team looked at the two wood pieces. They couldn't find anything on that piece of wood from our parents' boat."

"However, on the wood taken from Sean O'Connor's boat, they found a nail sticking out of the wood. Attached to the nail was a piece of fabric. When the forensics team looked closely, they found traces of blood on the fabric. The detective told me it's an exact match to Sheriff Jerry Hart."

"That's unbelievable," Charlie whispered. "So does that mean he's responsible for the death of Sean O'Connor?"

Jane shrugged. "Maybe. The police will need a lot more proof than blood on fabric, from an old nail, to charge him with murder. And I still haven't found the reason why old Sheriff Elias Hart sold his property to the Petersons years ago. We'll find answers somehow, someway."

"We will." Lizzie shook her head in shock. "I'm surprised. Grams was right when she wrote in her journal that there are more secrets that folks on the island have hidden that need to come to light, so the truth can be exposed."

"True. That's all I've learned for now," Jane said. "However, we'll need to keep our eyes and ears open to see if we can find more evidence that the sheriff had a part in Sean O'Connor's death."

Charlie chewed on her lower lip, a sign of worry. "Why? Do you think there's a connection between Sean's boating accident and our parents' deaths?"

Jane nodded. "I'm beginning to think that might be true. But, right now, I couldn't tell you what the connection is. And I don't have any proof. At least, not yet. Anyway, for now, let's keep this information to ourselves."

"Agreed." Lizzie sighed heavily. "All this talk of murder makes me shudder."

The sisters all nodded in agreement.

Alex added, "And there are still more mysteries to solve. Matty's journal let us know that, as boys, Ted, Jerry, and Bobby were always eager to do almost anything to make money. It does make me question how far those boys were willing to go to get their hands on a big pile of money. Did any one of them have something to do with Matty's death?"

Jane gasped. "I sure hope not. Our dad was friends with all four of those boys. He grew up with them. He trusted them."

"All I know is, sometimes, it is the people closest to us

that we trust who sometimes cause the most trouble. Detective Sullivan told me that," Alex replied.

Charlie said, "Well, right now we don't know all the answers. Hopefully we'll be able to dig deeper into that and figure out what actually happened the day Matty died."

A crease of worry formed between Jane's brows. "I hope so too."

"Anyway, we won't worry about that tonight." Charlie smiled.

Just then, Mrs. O'Connor walked to the podium and began to welcome everybody to the Christmas Craft Show.

"I guess we should take our seats. We'll talk later," Jane whispered.

She spotted Ward, who waved her over. He had saved her a seat next to Noah and Mrs. Morrison.

Jane was grateful her housekeeper had finally come back to live with them. She had come to see the older widow as part of their family. Noah looked on her as a second grandmother, a fact which she loved.

As she sat beside Ward, she reached over and held his hand.

Jane loved having this man near her.

Ward turned to her, with that special look in his eyes that he reserved just for her.

Happiness filled her as she sat beside him. Her feelings for him were intensifying every day. She couldn't help but wonder if he felt the same?

"Next, we'll have our Memory Quilt giveaway." Mrs. O'Connor spoke from where she stood on the platform in front of the large crowd.

The matronly widow, who started the shop and the annual Christmas Craft Show, spent the first hour giving the microphone to quilters to share the inspiration behind their personal quilted square.

However, now, she shifted topics to focus on the big giveaway.

"As many of you know, with every craft show at *Yarn Around the Cove*, we have chosen to make a special quilt and give it away to one of the founding families who were the first to come here to Sweet Beach Cove decades ago." Mrs. O'Connor's smile broadened as her gaze swept the large crowd.

The crowd clapped and, as everybody became quiet, Mrs. O'Connor continued, "Many quilters from our community came together weekly to stitch the squares that formed this lovely quilt."

"This past week we finally added the middle square to complete the project. The winners of this memory quilt are Miss Sadie Franklin and Miss Hattie Franklin, in memory of your great-grandparents Amos and Harriet Franklin. Please, ladies, come to the front for your gift."

The quilt hung to the side with a beautiful mixture of blue, green, and yellow. The quilt looked like it was bursting with spring colors.

The two lovely African-American women grinned as they walked to the platform.

Miss Sadie spoke first. "My goodness, what a surprise. Thank you, Mrs. O'Connor for this quilt. And thank you to all the hard-working quilters who crafted this beautiful quilt. This is a very meaningful memory for us of our great-grandparents."

Miss Hattie scooted her sister over and grabbed the microphone. "Before my sister talks on and on, I have something to say too."

She grinned at her sister. "Like Sadie said, this quilt is a lovely memory and keepsake of our great-grandparents. They came to this island, newly married, with only the clothes on their backs and hard-working hands."

Miss Hattie added, "Our parents would often tell us stories of how Amos and Harriet helped many folks, giving a helping hand where they could. So, Sadie and I want to tell all of you we are so grateful for this reminder of our ancestors, whom we honor and love today. Thank you."

The crowd clapped as the two sisters walked off the platform, holding the memory quilt between them.

Mrs. O'Connor walked to the microphone. "Now, we have a few other crafters who created their own personal quilting square. The next person I want to ask to come to the front to share the story behind her design is Jane Stafford."

Her legs felt weak as she stood to her feet and began to walk towards the platform.

She was nervous and a little scared to tell her story in public.

However, she was done with hiding and running away in fear.

When she first moved back to the island, she would

have never had the courage to speak in public to share her story.

Instead, she had continued to hide in fear and shame. Afraid to be seen as who she really was.

But today, she was stepping forward with courage.

Picking up her quilted square from the side table, she walked onto the platform.

"Hello, everyone." Jane's voice wobbled slightly as she smiled at the crowd. Her legs shook, but she continued to speak. "I wanted to tell you about this square I designed and let you know the inspiration behind the symbols I added."

She held out the blue, square, quilt piece for everybody to see.

"You can see on the top corner I stitched two pieces of broken glass. There's a story behind this. When I was a young girl at my parents' anniversary party, I was carrying out the very special crystal sculpture my grandparents had made to give as a gift, when I fell and broke the sculpture."

"Afterwards, a mean uncle told me all the awful thoughts that I rehearsed in my head about myself. His words confirmed they were true. I was a girl that always messed up and made mistakes. That I wasn't good enough. That I wasn't worthy to be loved. Those were some of the flawed beliefs, held onto as a child."

Taking a deep breath, Jane went on, pointing to the design stitched in white and gold of the pearl necklace. "Then, after my parents died, my beloved grandmother gave me a lovely pearl necklace. I remember vividly, Grams telling me that a pearl has to go through a lot of conflict to become a beautiful gem."

"She told me that the Good Book says that a woman's worth is more precious than jewels and her value is far above rubies or pearls. Then Grams asked me to hold on to faith, hope, and love."

Jane swallowed back emotion. "The memory of Grams' words was what got me through when my son was recently kidnapped. That's why stitching the outline of my pearl necklace onto my quilt was important to me."

There were tears in the eyes of many folks as they listened.

"Then there were three other details I added to this quilt. The red handkerchief that my Grams embroidered for my son, Noah, before she passed away. The handkerchief helped me find Noah when he was kidnapped," Jane explained.

"The next item on my quilt is the pink diamond. As many of you know, this diamond has been an unsolved mystery for my family. This gem reminds me of what it means to be faithful and to never give up on your family."

Jane shifted on her feet. "Finally, the last detail I added to the center of my quilted square is a red, broken heart."

Pointing to the heart, she explained, "I chose to stitch the broken heart together with white thread as a symbol of what happened to me. I came to this community with a broken heart and living in fear, but with help from the kind folks in this community, friends, and those that love me, my heart has healed."

As Jane spoke, her gaze found Noah's smiling face, and then lingered on Ward's handsome features.

He looked at her with a smoldering love that shone brightly.

Tears of thankfulness found their way to her eyes.

"Lastly, I wanted to read the words to you all that I stitched in white inside the mended heart. This says it all for me: *Not broken. Healed by Love.*" She smiled and looked over at the crowd. "Thank you."

As Jane walked back to her seat, the guests clapped, cheering loudly.

She smiled warmly at Mrs. Morrison, at her son, and finally she turned to Ward.

The look of approval in his tender gaze was just the encouragement she needed.

"After listening to your story, and the symbols of your journey on your quilt, I'm in awe. You are an amazing woman and an inspiration to us all, sweetheart," he whispered and reached over to squeeze her hand.

"Thank you, Ward." A warm glow flooded her body at his wards.

A happy smile remained on her lips until the Christmas Craft Show was over.

Jane said goodbye to her sisters and walked with Mrs. Morrison, Noah, and Ward to the door.

Jane asked, "Mrs. Morrison, would you take my car and drive Noah home? Ward will drive me home a little later. I'd be happy to do that. The holidays are here and we still have some Christmas cookies to bake, don't we, Noah? Maybe we'll make a treat for Buddy too." The lovely widow's smile widened.

Noah's eyes brightened at her suggestion. "That's a great idea. Mom, I'll see you later."

"Alright, Noah. And thanks, Mrs. Morrison." Jane hardly had time to get the words out before they hurried together down the sidewalk towards the older woman's car.

"They left in a hurry." She turned back to look at Ward.

He slipped an arm around her shoulders, and they walked out the doors, down the sidewalk towards his car. "Noah's excited about those Christmas cookies."

"I know. My son definitely has a sweet tooth." She turned to him and grinned. "I think he gets that from me. Christmas is the time when all the sweet desserts come out."

"True enough." Ward opened his car door.

Jane asked, "By the way, how is your arm feeling?"

"Good. The doctor double-checked my arm and said the wound is healing well." Ward shrugged. "Don't worry about me."

"I do worry." She bit her lip. "I still feel guilty you were wounded trying to save my life."

"Don't. I'm happy you weren't hurt, that's enough for me." He leaned over and kissed the top of her head.

Smiling, she got in the car.

As soon as he was seated next to her, he whispered, "We were talking about Christmas holidays earlier. I was hoping we could spend some time together. What are your plans, Jane?"

She turned to him with a big smile. "Well, I was talking with Lizzie, and she invited Noah, Mrs. Morrison, and I to join their family at the inn for Christmas Eve dinner and later to open a few gifts. My sister asked me to invite you and your father to join us."

"That's really great," Ward whispered in a low voice. "My father and I would be happy to join you on

Christmas Eve. I have a special gift I've been waiting to give you."

"Really?" Jane's heart beat faster. "I look forward to it."

"Me too." He drove back to her place and walked her to the front door.

Snowflakes fell gently from the sky and landed on Jane's nose.

"Oh my goodness." Holding out her hand, she captured a few of the tiny, white snowflakes. "It's Christmas. I love it."

Ward regarded her with somber curiosity. "Are you saying you look forward to Christmas, Jane?"

A soft smile rested on her lips as she looked into his eyes. "I do. I know you're surprised, because I used to hate Christmas. But that was because my heart was hardened from all the painful memories that I endured for years during Christmas time. However, the truth is, that in the past few months, my heart has been healed."

"My heart is free and I'm happy." Jane broke away from Ward and did a little dance under the blanket of falling snow.

Turning back to Ward she caught both of his hands in hers.

Jane whispered, "Grams was right when she said, *Christmas is a time of hope, miracles, and love.* Being with the man I love tonight is the best way to begin this holiday."

"I agree." A slow smile spread over his lips, and he swung her into the circle of his arms. He kissed her like a man starving for his last meal.

Jane felt her knees weaken from the intensity of his kiss.

Finally, he pulled back a little, still holding her in his arms and whispered, "I look forward to seeing you on Christmas Eve, sweetheart. Be prepared for a big surprise."

With those words, he walked back to his car.

Jane waved goodbye with a shaky hand as he drove away.

She knew the next couple nights until Christmas, she would hardly sleep in anticipation.

hristmas Eve...

JANE CARRIED two mugs of hot apple cider to Ward and his father.

They sat together on the large sofa in the great room at Lizzie's beach house.

Old, familiar Christmas carols played softly in the background, adding to the festive atmosphere.

"Thank you, my dear," Ward whispered as he took both mugs, handing one to his father. "The apple cider smells like cinnamon and reminds me of Christmas."

She nodded as she picked up her own hot cup. "It does. This was the hot drink Grams loved to serve during the holidays. I'm glad you and your dad joined us tonight."

His gaze was as soft as a caress as he looked at her. "I

wouldn't have missed another chance to spend time with you, Jane."

She looked up, and her heart lurched madly at the adoring look in his eyes. "Thank you, Ward. I feel the same way."

It was true.

Ever since they declared their love for one another, every day her love for him deepened and intensified.

Her sister Lizzie began to speak, "I know you are all eager to open gifts. Our tradition is that we open a few presents on Christmas Eve and the rest of them on Christmas morning."

She cleared her throat. "However, before we do that, I wanted to tell you all that I'm amazed and very thankful all of us could gather together at our late grandmother's old house this Christmas."

Lizzie placed a hand on her heart and a slow smile turned up the corners of her lips as her gaze swept the great room at the beach house. "Thank you all for joining us."

"Of course, sis," Charlie was quick to respond. "It's special for all of us."

Jane nodded as she looked around the room at all her sisters, their husbands, and their children.

Noah was with Charlie's twin sons, Waylon and Dutton.

They were playing a new board game.

Her son was thrilled to have cousins with whom he could play games.

"Let's begin with the gifts." Lizzie grinned and walked to the tree and picked up a gift for Jonathan and three other gifts – one for each of her young adult children.

They went around the circle of people, everybody taking turns giving and receiving a gift.

There was so much chatter and laughter in the room. Everyone was excited to receive a present.

Charlie held up her gift of a small boat, a keepsake replica of her great-grandfather's ship.

"Thanks, Lizzie. It's so similar to the ship Gramps kept above the mantle in the den. It reminds me of my love of boating, my love of the island, and my love of family."

"Does that mean you and your boys will be moving back to the island soon?" Jane teased.

"I have taken some time to look over Gramps' old boat and the cabin that I inherited." Charlie stirred uneasily as she spoke. "That old cabin needs fixing up. But I'm not sure yet about moving back to the island."

Alex grinned. "There's still lots of time, Charlie. However, just so you know, it would be wonderful to have you join us here."

Charlie smiled. "That's my weak spot. I would love to be closer to my family too. I'll think about it, I promise."

Jane wondered if Charlie's love of family would tip the scales in favor of moving to the island.

She hoped so.

"Jane, we're thankful you made it out unharmed from that scare with your ex-husband."

Alex grimaced. "I can't believe he did that to you and Noah."

Lizzie turned to Jane. "We're glad you're alright. What are your plans now?"

Jane glanced at Ward, and then over at her sisters. "About that, it looks like my plans took a little twist. Yesterday, Mrs. Peterson called. She told me that she and her husband have decided to sell the waterfront property. She offered me the first opportunity to buy it, since I'm living there. I told them I would like to buy their place. I gave them an offer and they accepted it."

Lizzie's jaw dropped in surprise. "Jane, that's so exciting. We'll be neighbors."

"I'm excited too." Jane turned to her sisters. "And, since I'm buying that acreage with the large house, I came up with another idea. I would like to renovate the bedrooms in the main house so it could be used as a women's shelter."

"Ever since Adele lived at my home for a few weeks, I realized my deepest desire is to make a difference in women's lives that have suffered through abuse. Mrs. Morrison, Noah, and I will live in the guest house while the main house is being renovated. Anyway, those are my latest plans."

Charlie grinned. "What a wonderful idea, Jane. It's good that you're turning around your own suffering and using it for good, to help other women. You're making a difference, Jane."

"Thanks, sis. I hope so." Jane turned to Ward and realized she hadn't given his gift. "Since it's my turn to pick a present, I want to give a gift to Ward."

She walked over to the Christmas tree and pulled out a long, circular present.

Ward stood to his feet and walked over to where Jane stood by the Christmas tree.

She handed the gift to Ward.

A puzzled look crossed his features and he began to unwrap the gift.

His eyes widened in surprise as he quickly unwrapped the present.

"Jane, you gave me your special quilt."

Jane swallowed back emotion. "Like I told everyone at the Christmas Craft Show, this quilt is about my personal journey. I wanted to give you a gift to show you I'm finished hiding in shame and fear. I've decided to live a life filled with hope, miracles, and love instead. A life that my beloved Grams would've wanted for me. I love you, Ward."

His eyes filled with tears and he replied, with a husky voice, "Jane, thanks doesn't seem enough, but I do thank you. This quilt will always hold a special place in my heart. I love you too, sweetheart."

"Aww... the two of you are making us all cry." Lizzie wiped a tear from one cheek.

Ward stood to his feet and grinned as he glanced at everyone in the room.

His voice broke with huskiness, "We're not done yet. I have a gift I want to give Jane. A present which I think will be unexpected."

She watched as Ward reached for a small gift box under the tree.

"I want to do this right," he murmured as he handed her the beautifully wrapped gift.

"What is this?" Jane peered up at him.

Ward had his rogue smile firmly in place. "You'll need to open it and see."

He waited as she tore off the wrapping.

Carefully, she opened the box and gasped.

A beautiful, oval-shaped, diamond ring lay in a black, velvet, jeweler's box.

Her hand flew to her mouth as she looked over at Ward.

The man she loved crouched down in front of her.

He was kneeling.

Her wildly beating heart was the only sound she could hear.

Reaching for her hand, Ward whispered in a low voice, "Jane, ever since you returned to the island, I began to hope that you would somehow find a way to give me a second chance."

Awkwardly, the man she loved cleared his throat before continuing, "You forgave me for foolish mistakes and you did give me that second chance. I still feel like I need to pinch myself, ever since you told me you loved me."

Ward's voice sounded vulnerable and raw. "Jane, you are the only woman I ever loved. I've waited many years to tell you I love you with all my heart, sweetheart. Will you make me the happiest man alive and agree to become my wife?"

His eyes darkened, and he looked into her eyes with an intensity that was overpowering.

For a long moment, Jane felt as if she were floating as she stared at him wide-eyed.

Her heart lurched with excitement.

The next moment, Jane threw her arms around his

neck and said excitedly, "Yes. I would be honored to be your wife, Ward. I love you."

The sounds of clapping and cheering from family and friends were heard in the room.

Charlie called out, "Look, Jane, you and Ward are standing near the Christmas tree, under the mistletoe. That's the same mistletoe where our parents kissed on the last wedding anniversary celebration we had with them. Ward, you must kiss your wife-to-be. It's tradition."

"In that case, I see no reason to break tradition." Her husband-to-be repositioned her body so that she faced him.

Heat stained her cheeks. She placed her arms around Ward's neck, pulling him closer.

Without hesitation, his lips came coaxingly down on hers.

She drank in the sweetness of his kiss.

Jane's heart flooded with love for this man. Impatience stirred inside her. She couldn't wait to be married to Ward. She was eager for the three of them to be a family.

At long last, Christmas had become a happy holiday that would have a very special place in her heart.

Someday, Jane would tell her children and grandchildren that her fresh start began under the mistletoe, during Christmas, at her grandparents' old beach house.

For Noah, herself, and Ward, this December holiday had become what her beloved grandmother had intended all along for their family.

After all she had suffered, her heart finally echoed Grams' words: *Christmas was a time of hope, miracles, and love.*

Jane stole a look at the handsome face of her husband-to-be.

Finally, her and her son's dreams would come true.

Noah would have a dad who loved him, and she would enjoy marriage with this kind and compassionate man, a love that would last forever.

THE THANK YOU FOR READING JANE'S STORY!

Watch for Charlie's love story coming next, in *The Vineyard Beach Wedding!*

Charlotte (Charlie) Stafford, is a busy Marine Biologist and mother trying to juggle both work and home life in the city.

Since her husband died seven years ago, Charlie has done her best to be a good mother to her boys. But, she can't help but feel like she's failing.

When her teenage sons start getting into the bad crowd at school, it's a wake up call. Her mothering instincts tell her it's time to rethink how she wants her young teenagers to grow into adulthood.

Maybe it's time for a move.

After much debating, Charlie decides to move back to her childhood home on Martha's Vineyard. From her late grandmother, she inherited her grandfather's two boats and that ten acres of waterfront property.

She has taken a sabbatical to try to rest and figure out what she wants to do next with her life.

As she is beginning to explore the island again, once again she runs into a childhood friend, Zach Whetstone.

Zach is recently retired from the Coast Guard. He lives with and is a big support to his aging father.

They begin to go boating and diving again together like they used to as teenagers. But, what they find under the water shocks them. And it forces them to search further into the mystery of the deaths of Charlie's parents years ago.

As they work together to try to find answers, their attraction begins to grow into a romance that puts fear into Charlie's heart.

She already lost a husband she loved. She doesn't think she can let down her guard again to love another man.

However, Zach won't let Charlie go. He woos and does his best to prove to her that he is the one man who will never let her go.

Will Zach win Charlie's tender heart? And will Charlie allow herself to be vulnerable enough to fall in love again?

ABOUT THE AUTHOR

Melody Archer lives in Alberta with her husband and their four young adults.

Recently, her oldest son married his new wife from Brazil. Their family has been enjoying getting to know their new daughter-in-love.

She loves new and classic romantic movies, green smoothies and going on adventures with her family.

Melody would love to connect with you :)

ACKNOWLEDGMENTS

Thank you to all the wonderful people who helped me
with this book.

To my cover designer, Wilette from Red Leaf Book
Design, thank you for designing this gorgeous book cover.

Thank you also, to my two very helpful proofreaders
Michaela and Bernadette who patiently read through each
chapter, helping me make this story so much better.

A big thanks to all my wonderful Advanced Readers (my
ARC reading team), who faithfully read this book.

Lastly, a huge thanks to two of my young adult children
who read through the manuscript, giving me all kinds of
great suggestions on how to make this a better story.

Thank you everyone. I really appreciate you!:)